PRAISE FOR

Talk To Me

"A widely respected network TV anchor falls from grace when a vicious tirade is caught on camera, leaving him to revive his professional reputation—and sense of purpose." —*Entertainment Weekly*

"With a publicly decimated career and a neglected family in his wake, ex-TV anchor Ted Grayson finds himself taking a hard look at the life he's led and the ways in which he can build a better life in this perceptive new book by John Kenney." —*Southern Living*

"Kenney's dark humor evokes understanding. . . . A surprise twist reveals that hope and empathy can prevail." —*Shelf Awareness*

"Timely, darkly humorous . . . A smart, very 21st-century story."

—AARP

"With depth and sympathy . . . [Kenney] saves a sweetly ironic twist for a redemptive ending. [*Talk to Me* is] a powerful and moving rendition of a story we've been waiting to hear: what it's like to be that bad guy in this ripped-from-the-headlines situation." —*Kirkus Reviews* (starred review)

"A blunt, hilariously nuanced but devastatingly emotional tale of the age of internet and instant news . . . And yet, you'll laugh because Kenney is profane, with a biting, spit-out-your-coffee kind of wit that underscores the pathos and irony of it all. . . . *Talk to Me* will make you think, and you won't want to put it down." —*Marco Eagle* (Florida)

"Kenney's timely satire succeeds with significant nuance. . . . Most winning, though, are Kenny's incisive considerations of parenthood, familial love, and what actually matters when all is seemingly lost." —*Booklist*

"For all the fast-paced and knowing entertainment it provides, *Talk to Me* may also serve as a useful antidote to rushed judgment when the next celebrity scandal erupts." —*BookPage*

"A superbly crafted story of a swaggering news anchor who disgraces himself, facing shame and regret in an era when being human in public is a blood sport. *Talk to Me* is moving, full of punch and sorrow—and told at the velocity of a man plummeting to earth."

—Tom Rachman, author of
The Italian Teacher and *The Imperfectionists*

"This high-voltage tale about a one-percenter learning to navigate a vastly changed America will move you to reconsider what you're ready to forgive. Timely, keenly observed, and my favorite kind of funny, John Kenney's latest hits (superbly) home."

—Courtney Maum, author of
Touch and *I Am Having So Much Fun Without You*

"A poignant, and often hilarious, portrait of a man in the midst of an extremely public downfall. Kenney, with humor and tenderness, gives us Ted Grayson, TV anchor of a bygone era as he fumbles through a changing media landscape and one terrible mistake and its fallout. This is a very human, very timely story." —Vanessa Manko, *author of The Invention of Exile*

"This book is a tender father-daughter story, a cautionary tale about forgetting what's important, and an indictment of our toxic instant overreaction culture. Wrap it all together and what do you get? A very funny and unexpectedly touching novel." —Eddie Joyce, author of *Small Mercies*

Previous Praise for John Kenney and *Truth in Advertising*

"The protagonist, Finbar Dolan, is Don Draper stripped of all his glamour, success and pomade. What Fin, a midlevel copywriter, does have on Don is a sense of humor. . . . Framed around a surprisingly sweet romance, as well as Fin's eventual confrontation with his painful family history, this debut offers a pleasing lightness-to-heart ratio." —*The New York Times*

"Peppered with colorful impressions of New York City life, *Truth in Advertising* is a quick-witted, wry sendup of the advertising industry and corporate culture. . . . Delivers a clear-eyed, sympathetic story about complex family ties and the possibility of healing." —*The Washington Post*

"[Kenney's] insights are dead-on. . . . [His] plot is perfectly balanced between the insanity of both work and family, and the ending is satisfying without being saccharine. . . . Engaging and entertaining . . . The joy is in the journey, of spending time with a character that is, at times, annoying and thoughtful, arrogant and scared, childish and mature—in other words, someone like the rest of us." —*Dallas Morning News*

"You'd expect that a man who writes humor pieces for the *New Yorker* would be funny—and he is. John Kenney, who also worked as an advertising copywriter, knows that world and skewers it mercilessly and hilariously in his debut novel. . . . It would also be safe to say that amazing things will most likely be happening in John Kenney's literary career right now. Truthfully." —*Cleveland Plain Dealer*

"*Truth in Advertising* has a cinematic sense of motion. . . . [Kenney is] a naturally comic author who has created a likeable narrator in Fin Dolan. . . . Humor springs from a deep well of family-induced anguish, and soon enough comedy and tragedy are braided throughout the narrative." —*Chicago Tribune*

"This debut novel reads at times like a laugh-out-loud standup routine. What sustains it, though, is much more substantial: an engaging, believable plot, a fascinating if jaundiced view inside the contemporary world of New York advertising, and most of all, a lead character you're glad you get to know. . . . It's a measure of Kenney's writing talent that the regular gusts of delicious, smart-alecky ad agency banter among Dolan and his witty comrades and the painful-to-read scenes depicting the toxic relations among siblings feel equally real in this novel. . . . [A] smart, cinematic story." —Associated Press

"We're sold on Kenney's trenchant, quick-witted debut." —*Entertainment Weekly*

"Kenney, who's worked as a copywriter for 17 years, mines this rich territory for satire. . . . Fin's struggle to understand his dad brings a layer of emotional complexity to the tale. . . . Kenney's novel wrestles with deep questions: What makes a good man? What makes a good life? What should one's contribution to the world be?" —*Bloomberg Businessweek*

"Here's a smart one . . . Lovers of the city will find much to love in this relatable, redemptive, and sometimes very funny story."

—*The Denver Post*

"The comedy sparkles [with] mordant one-liners, snappy banter, and hilarious workplace scenarios."

—*The Boston Globe*

"It's the stuff of Jonathan Tropper novels and Judd Apatow films and every Zooey Deschanel fantasy."

—*USA Today*

"The rare novel that's truly cinematic. It is sexy, the plot twists in just the right places; simply put, it's untamable. You will laugh almost as much as you will relate to the plight of the protagonist . . . .This book might just rouse the creative genius in you, too."

—*Interview*

"It will make you laugh out loud at times and it will also touch you deeply. . . . This is the sort of book where you really care about the characters. . . . You will not be disappointed in *Truth in Advertising*. The plot is highly entertaining, but it is the joy of getting to know such a realistic, likeable, believable character as Finbar Dolan that makes this novel such a treat. Fin is the sort of guy you will enjoy spending time with."

—*Seattle Post-Intelligencer*

"A snortingly funny debut . . . Although Nick Hornby is the obvious reference—humor and heartbreak of ordinary life—this wonderful book is more J. Alfred Prufrock."

—*The Phoenix* (Boston)

"With wry wit, excellent pacing, and pitch-perfect, often hilarious, dialogue, Kenney has created something remarkable: a surprisingly funny novel about an adult American male finally becoming a man. Highly recommended."

—*Library Journal* (starred review)

"No one makes me laugh like John Kenney. So I expected *Truth in Advertising* to be very funny, and it is. But I was unprepared for how deeply felt and richly observed it would be. This is a beautiful novel and a dazzling debut."

—Andy Borowitz, The Borowitz Report

... Talk to Me ...

JOHN KENNEY

G. P. PUTNAM'S SONS | NEW YORK

PUTNAM
— EST. 1838 —

G. P. PUTNAM'S SONS
Publishers Since 1838
An imprint of Penguin Random House LLC
penguinrandomhouse.com

The Library of Congress has catalogued the G. P. Putnam's Sons hardcover edition as follows:

Names: Kenney, John, author.
Title: Talk to me / John Kenney.
Description: New York : G. P. Putnam's Sons, [2019]
Identifiers: LCCN 2018005887 (print) | LCCN 2018013811 (ebook) |
ISBN 9780735214385 (ePub) | ISBN 9780735214378 (hardcover)
Subjects: LCSH: Domestic fiction.
Classification: LCC PS3611.E6665 (ebook) | LCC PS3611.E6665 T35 2019 (print) |
DDC 813/.6—dc23
LC record available at https://lccn.loc.gov/2018005887

First G. P. Putnam's Sons hardcover edition / January 2019
First G. P. Putnam's Sons trade paperback edition / January 2020
G. P. Putnam's Sons trade paperback edition ISBN: 9780735214392

Printed in the United States of America
1   3   5   7   9   10   8   6   4   2

Book design by Gretchen Achilles

For Lulu and Hewitt

We share our lives with the people we have failed to be.

ADAM PHILLIPS

Talk to Me

Ted has been pushed out of an airplane.

Ted Grayson had been pushed out of an airplane.

He had been pushed because at the last moment he was frozen with fear and unable to jump. Now he was falling at 120 miles per hour and the feeling was an odd combination of terror and relief. The speed of the fall when he exited the plane took his breath away. His goggles sucked to his face; his eyes felt as if they were being pulled back into his head, the pressure tremendous. Ted fell and he fell and he fell and he felt that he would never stop falling. It had been exactly two point five seconds so far.

It was a Thursday. He knew that. A Thursday in mid-April. Or was it late April? He wasn't sure. Strange to not know the date. It was late morning. He was fairly sure of that. The small plane had climbed from the airfield on eastern Long Island into clear blue skies. As the plane banked left, Ted could see the ocean below. He sat in his jumpsuit, in the cramped quarters of the plane, Raymond next to him.

It had been cold on the plane. Colder still when Raymond slid the door open. The sound of the wind. The momentary panic-fear of what he was about to do. So Raymond had given him a little nudge. Fine. He'd pushed him, full on. He'd had to do that a fair amount in this job. People got excited and brave on the ground. Quite another thing to stare down from ten thousand feet with nothing between you and God's green earth but the thin silk on your back.

Ted fell.

He thought he might throw up. He thought he might pass out. He thought he might already be dead. It was happening so fast. He lay flat on his belly, just as they had practiced, Ted and Raymond, arms out, staring straight down. How he'd arrived in this position he wasn't sure. He raised his head and saw Raymond, smiling, two fat thumbs up, just another day at the office, as if they were sitting across from each other at a Starbucks enjoying Pumpkin Spice Lattes. Raymond tapped his oversized outdoorsman watch. It was time. Indeed, it was, thought Ted.

Raymond, the former army sergeant, who said he hadn't been planning on going up today. Raymond, who at first didn't recognize Ted. Raymond, who had to call in his pilot, Alvin, from out in Greenport. Raymond wore a GoPro camera on his helmet. Filmed the whole thing. "Hell, we even send you a little movie of it," he told Ted. "Email it to you before you're back in Manhattan."

The three of them had boarded the small plane, a 1982 Cessna T303 Crusader, according to Raymond. Miracle it still flew, he said, cackling, as Alvin pulled the stick back and launched them up over the airstrip, banked left, out over the ocean, the empty beaches of the Hamptons, climbing, higher, the noise of the engine drowning out Raymond's incessant talking, Ted seeing the ocean, a distant boat, and remembering Franny's words from the story.

. . .

Raymond held up three beefy fingers and pointed to them with his other hand, the agreed-upon sign. He folded one down. Two fingers now. Time slowed down for Ted. It was taking an eternity. Raymond folded another down. One finger. They'd gone over this on the ground, again and again. "I like repeat customers," Raymond had said. "That's why we wear two chutes. Both chutes fail, well, the good Lord has other plans for you . . ."

Here's what else went through Ted's mind.

Screw Ted Grayson. This speck of a man falling from the sky. The world had handed him a microphone and asked him to tell them a story. Engage me, they'd said. Inform me. Thrill me. Enlighten me. And what had he done? Bore them.

The memory of the time he tailgated a person because of a bad mood, because he was in a rush. Honking, flashing his lights, jumping out of his car at the stoplight and pulling from the backseat a wood-handled Bancroft tennis racket, waving it like John McEnroe, only to find an eighty-year-old handicapped woman at the wheel.

Also the time a diminutive homeless man reached out to touch him as he stepped out of a limousine, Ted surprised and frightened by the man, a contorted face shouting, "Fuck off, bum!"

And the time—fine, times—he'd been unfaithful to Claire. The years of distance, of ignoring her, of assuming she'd always be there.

And the time, recently, after the incident, he'd ignored the pleas of the network's lawyers and PR department and left the house, only to find a photo of himself on the cover of the following day's *New York Post*, disheveled, unshaven, having forgotten to zip his fly all the way up yet again, making what appeared to be a Nazi salute, when, in fact, it was simply a harmless attempt to hail a cab and escape the paparazzi.

Mostly, he thought of Franny. And the words she had used in the story. The world would see that she was lost to him. He couldn't reach her. His own daughter. He couldn't protect her now. And if you can't protect your child, what's the point of protecting yourself?

He went back to the hundreds of other images. Tiny, searing film clips that ran through his mind as he watched himself fall to Earth. The amount of callous, unthinking, uncaring asininity he'd committed in his life. The waste. A few years ago, a friend of Claire's died. A good man, a family man, a volunteer and coach. Overflowing church. Unfair, people said. But for Ted, who would show? No one would utter the word "unfair." The few who showed would wonder if they'd hit traffic after the service and what to make for dinner.

The decision was not spontaneous, he realized. It had been there all day. It had been there for weeks, in fact, during the whole nightmare. Now, falling, the image of it all so clear. Here was the answer to all that had happened. Ted had no intention of opening his chute.

He was tired of the shame. Tired of the deep sadness for the loss of his life. Of everything that had once seemed to make sense and now didn't. He was tired of being afraid of what would happen next, of what other public embarrassment would come his way. He had lost something vital to the living process that he was unable to name.

He heard the lead-in in his head. *Ted Grayson, the longtime anchor of the evening news, died today in an embarrassing skydiving accident on eastern Long Island. Sources say the disgraced former newsman may have taken his own life. He was fifty-nine. (brief pause) When we come back: pea-nuts. Are they the new superfood?*

No fingers now. Raymond made the motion to pull the chute. Raymond nodded. Ted nodded. Except then Ted did the one thing Raymond told him never to do. He pulled his arms in, aimed his head down, and suddenly he was Superman, heading toward the surface of the earth so fast he couldn't take it in. He had no control over his body so he began to roll. "Roll" is the wrong word. It was, instead, what Raymond had called a "death spin."

He was falling, in thin air. This line echoed in a distant place in his mind.

He could no longer move his arms and legs. He was going to pass out in a matter of seconds. He did not feel at all well. The fear and regret, a primal scream inside that he needed to give voice to. But nothing came out. How perfect. How fitting, he thought. America's anchorman, in his dying moments, unable to make a sound.

It's all there, on the GoPro. Ted's life, on video. Looking into the camera, asking, what happens next? What's the story?

Just keep watching.

We go live now to Ted Grayson in New York.

Three weeks earlier and Ted is in a mood.

Ninety seconds, Ted."

It was Lou, in Ted's earpiece. Ted's executive producer, Lou Arno.

They were in the middle of a two-and-a-half-minute commercial break, twenty-one minutes into the broadcast. One story left.

"The Triangle package," Lou said. "Your lead-in, the prerecorded piece. You'll have eight seconds after the story. You'll have copy. Not that you need it. It's almost like a real job."

Something about this last bit annoyed Ted. It was something Lou had said before, in his harmless Lou voice. But there was an edge to it. Or was Ted's bad mood filter adding the edge? He wasn't sure. Either way, it further unsettled his already stormy insides.

Ted glared in the direction of the control room, then reached for his cell phone under the desk. He checked emails, texts. There was one from Claire.

In Bedford. Please stay in city. Might be best to speak through lawyers at this point. Also, happy birthday.

If that didn't say love, what did? Ted thought. Almost thirty years of marriage.

There was a text from Polly, Ted's agent and attorney, asking if they were still on for dinner. Polly Klein (née Paulette, a name she loathed) would meet him at Cafe Luxembourg at eight.

"Roger that?" Lou asked.

Lou could see Ted from the control room, through the glass, as well as on the live feeds from the two cameras on set. He could also look up at a wall of ten monitors showing live feeds from some of the affiliates on the East Coast.

"Swell," Ted said. He was supposed to say "Roger Mudd." It was a thing he and Lou said. Roger Mudd was a newscaster years ago who did a famous interview with Senator Ted Kennedy, who had announced that he was running for president. Mudd asked Kennedy why he wanted to be president. Kennedy looked flummoxed, fumbled around for words. Some say it cost him the nomination against then president Jimmy Carter in 1980.

Now, for some reason, Ted didn't feel like saying it. The whole thing, the saying of it, annoyed and embarrassed him.

"What's wrong, Teddy?" Lou pushed.

Ted turned to raise his middle finger to Lou but instead knocked over his water, soaking his script and a goodly portion of his pants. He heard Lou laughing, which only pissed him off more. A production assistant ran over with a roll of paper towels, dabbing the desk and then, awkwardly, Ted's wet lap. A sweet young kid name Greg. Or Larry. He wasn't sure. Overeager.

"Okay, okay," Ted barked, regretting his tone immediately.

The poor kid reacted like a scolded dog. "Sorry. And, um, happy birthday, Mister Grayson," he managed with a smile as he scampered off.

"Oh, that's right," Lou said, fully aware that it was Ted's birthday. "Happy seventieth," he added, chuckling.

Lou was a difficult-to-determine fifty-nine, rail thin, an early-morning runner, poor sleeper, bald since the age of twenty-four, crew cut on the sides and back. Khakis, a polo shirt tucked in, and running shoes every day. In the winter, a fleece vest. A fast blinker, eyes darting. He had a hard time relaxing. But then, that was his job. Grace under pressure. A constant state of ready for the unexpected. The late feed. The botched feed. The live report gone bad. The show that was running short and needed to be lengthened. The show that was running long and needed to be cut. The breaking news story halfway through a broadcast. The raw rush of live TV. Lou loved it. He had been with the broadcast three years, having replaced Ted's longtime producer Roy Wilson, who retired after his third heart attack. Lou had hoped that he and Ted might become close. To date it hadn't happened.

Lou looked at his own phone, which seemed to beep nonstop. Links and feeds and reporters in the field, updates, weather, police scanner, fire scanner, White House, State House, London Bureau, Jerusalem Bureau, Jo-Burg, Moscow, Hong Kong, Beijing. Lou checked his phone and then looked back up, watching Ted, who—Lou could feel it—was in a mood. Lou would remember this, weeks later, months later. And not just because Lou had a bizarre memory for details, numbers, chronology. In the endless retelling to the initially small internal review board, then later to the larger investigative committee (the goddamned East German Stasi, if Lou were honest about it), to friends, to colleagues, to a reporter for the *New*

York Post, in a moment of candor he regretted and was partially mis-
quoted on (to his eternal regret and shame), and mostly to Phyllis,
his wife, who listened as Lou held a large scotch and stared off into
the backyard, when it still seemed so unreal.

Ted would remember it, too, of course. Though he would remember it differently and always with the makeup woman. The replacement. Natalia.

"The king is in a foul temper," Murray said to no one in particular. He
sniffed his fingertips, a thing he did that annoyed his two colleagues, one of his many tics. Scratching his head aggressively. Pok-
ing at his inner ears. Sniffing his fingers. The traits of a man who
lived alone.

Grace ignored him and continued typing. Jagdish looked up,
smiled the kindly smile one might offer a child who'd just said,
"Look, Dad! I put on my underpants all by myself." He then looked
back at his computer.

Ted's newswriting staff. Or what was left of it. They were in a
small room a floor above the studio, a window overlooking Midtown. It was dark and the lights of the buildings dotted the skyline.
Murray loved the view.

Where once, twenty years ago, there were eight or nine of them,
now it was this little band of brothers and one sister. And rumor had
it that there were further redundancies planned. A bank of flat-
screens sat above one wall, each showing the major networks, along
with CNN and Fox, all in commercial break before their final story.
A smaller closed-circuit monitor showed a live feed from the newsroom and Ted's $11 million hair being tended to.

Grace said, "I'm making a change to the story."

"Too late," Murray said, suddenly excited, in part because he loved when Grace did this, her last-minute changes that made a difference only to Grace, and also because she was speaking to him.

"Tell Lou. I'm sending now."

Grace looked up at Murray and Murray picked up the phone. If Grace had said, "Hang from the outside ledge of the window naked," he would have done it.

Lou picked up mid-ring.

"Little change coming through. Sending to prompter now."

He hung up.

Jagdish got up. "May I?" he asked Grace.

Grace smiled and Murray felt sick. Why couldn't she smile like that at him?

Jagdish read over Grace's shoulder.

"Soulful."

Jagdish had been born to a well-to-do family in Bombay and studied in London. He'd done graduate work (philosophy and religion) at NYU. He was planning his escape from newswriting, taking night classes in massage therapy with a focus on the fascia. Jagdish was convinced the fascia held the mysteries of life.

Murray got up and came over, read over Grace's other shoulder. The story was about the anniversary of the Triangle Shirtwaist Factory fire. Grace had rewritten the intro, the body of the story, and Ted's closing a dozen times over the past three days.

Murray wore T-shirts with ironic sayings. "Serial Chiller." "King of Nothing." "Stay Sassy." He looked a bit like someone who hung around Washington Square Park waiting for a chess game. Dirty fingernails, which he often bit and stared at, protruding belly, ring of unkempt hair around a bald pate, skin a bizarre color of yellow. He knew every capital in the world and had yet to be stumped. He could name all of the countries in Africa alphabetically. He secretly worshipped Ted and sometimes wondered what it would be like to be him. He'd gone to Harvard, Harvard Medical, quit halfway through, though he was on track to graduate at the top of his class. Then decided upon Columbia Law, where he was head of the law review, even though he had no intention of ever practicing law. His parents were scions of the Merck fortune. He lived alone on the Upper West Side in a rent-stabilized apartment. He wrote science-fiction novels, which he refused to send out to publishers. He felt the system was rigged, that Congress was enslaved to corporate interests, that mortgages were a scam, that banks were fundamentally illegal, that government was corrupt, and that culture had died. He was in charge of the newswriting staff.

Grace, for her part, wanted nothing to do with Murray. Grace was already in love but that love was unrequited because its focus—her therapist referred to it as a "neurotic obsession"—was Eddie Vedder, lead singer of Pearl Jam.

Grace had been on staff three years. "What connects the Persian Gulf to the Gulf of Oman?" Murray had blurted out as they were still shaking hands on the day he interviewed her for the job. None of the previous three candidates he had interviewed had gotten the correct answer.

"Oh, ahh, okay," Grace stammered. "We're starting. The Strait of Hormuz. Iran to the east, Dubai, the UAE, and Muscat to the west."

Murray was instantly drawn to Grace's oversized eyeglasses as well as the acne that dotted her forehead and chin.

"What story would you lead tonight's newscast with?"

"Climate change," she had said. "I'd lead with it every night for a week. Maybe a month. Then I'd do the same with the lack of women in Congress and in leadership positions in corporate America. Then food additives that are causing cancer."

Murray had nodded slowly the whole time, smiling without realizing he was smiling. And that's how you fall in love.

Later, after he'd hired her, during his occasional failed attempts to flirt, he asked her questions he remembered from high school dating.

"What kind of music do you like?"

"Pearl Jam," she'd said.

Murray nodded, not a fan. "What else?" he'd asked.

"Nothing else. I don't listen to anything else."

And Murray realized she was kidding. He fell deeper.

"Have you ever seen them in concert?" Murray asked. "I heard they're good." He'd not heard that but wanted a connection with her. In fact, he realized that he was imagining Radiohead while thinking about Pearl Jam and had no idea who Pearl Jam was.

"I have," Grace said.

"Where?"

"A lot of places. I've seen them a hundred thirty-six times."

Murray laughed. Grace didn't.

"Wait. Are you serious?"

Grace nodded. "I met Eddie once. In an airport. He was with his wife. Well, she was his girlfriend at the time. Jill McCormick. This was a few years after he and Beth Liebling split up. That killed me because I loved Beth and thought she was great for Eddie but I've been super happy with Jill because now they have the kids.

Anyway. It was Denver International and I saw him and it wasn't even the Admirals Club or anything. You wouldn't know it was him except of course you would because it's Eddie and he's a god. Like, a literal god. So, it's the time of CD cases and I've got a little carry-on one and I go over to him and I can tell he's not in the mood for this so I just say, 'I've been to a hundred nineteen of your concerts'—this was a few years ago obviously—'and in this case, I have room for twenty CDs and nineteen of them are Pearl Jam.' And he fights this little smile and says, 'What's the twentieth?' And I say, 'It's empty.' Then he said this is Jill and then I left and it was amazing."

Murray had been with Ted from the start. The youngest writer on his staff. The head writer couldn't stand Murray, so he tried to make him quit. Gave him the dullest assignments. The problem was, Murray found everything interesting.

Cheese contamination? Murray came back with a piece that traced the history of cheese production, how almost nothing has changed in five thousand years, how contamination is rampant.

Fall foliage? Murray came back with a two-minute piece on the life of a leaf, from spring to fall, photosynthesis and respiration, to its ultimate end as it aged, changed color, and died. They received dozens of letters about the piece.

An alarming increase in gum disease? Murray came back with a story so potent that it was said to move the market on dental floss, which in turn resulted in Johnson & Johnson deciding to invest heavily in media on Ted's broadcast.

And, of course, Cassini.

Murray had been assigned the story and delivered this copy to Ted just two months into his taking over the anchor chair.

"Two weeks ago, on October 15, 1997, a seemingly routine event happened at Cape Canaveral, Florida. A probe was launched. Probes are often launched. Satellites, too. We no longer stand in awe of space flight, no longer stop what we're doing, turn the TV on for classrooms of students, stand together at the plate-glass window of a department store watching a bank of color sets as rockets leave Earth's atmosphere. That world bores us today. But attention should be paid to Cassini-Huygens. That's the name of this probe. Named for the Italian astronomer who first discovered Saturn's rings, this twenty-two-foot-high marvel of engineering and ingenuity will not merely leave Earth's orbit. It will travel nearly five billion miles into deepest, darkest space. It will reach Saturn, will orbit it for years, and send back images no human being has ever seen, revealing the unknown. What a thing. What a hopeful thing, to reveal the light in the darkness. We will follow it, of course. We will make our own journey. Earthbound. From this chair. Each evening. For all of us here, I'm Ted Grayson. Good night."

When Ted first read the copy, he asked who had written it. He went to the newsroom and introduced himself to Murray.

"What's a guy who can write like this doing in news?" Ted had asked with his half smile.

"Well," Murray said, the other, older writers watching and listening. "I don't think this is for me. Thought I wanted to be a doctor. Then a lawyer. I don't know. I like to try things."

"Maybe try sticking around," Ted said, smiling.

Murray was in love. A big-brother love. An I-wish-we-were-best-friends love. A would-you-like-to-go-camping-this-weekend love.

That was almost twenty years ago.

These are some of the stories that are trending.

It was Jagdish's job to compile the top-trending stories on the major websites and then rewrite them for the network's site. Once, the news was what the networks told people it was. Now it was what people clicked on. People told the networks what was news, what they wanted to hear about.

During the last break, the big two-and-a-half-minute one, a graphic flashed the top five trending stories on the network's website. This was accompanied by a sponsor's logo. This week it was Dairy Queen. It rotated on a semiweekly basis.

A wildfire in the Los Angeles hills.

Mass shooting in Bangor, Maine, kills 12.

Terrorist attack in Baghdad.

Pixar movie tops weekend box office list.

Cheese causes cancer.

Trending. Sponsored by Dairy Queen. Is there a Royal Oreo Blizzard Treat trending in your future?

Ted was still looking at his phone, not really seeing the messages, when she started touching up his hair. He looked up and saw it wasn't Marie. Had he not noticed this before the broadcast? Ted looked at her and she smiled shyly. He'd seen the look a thousand times, the look that said *I can't believe I'm this close to Ted Grayson.* Something about this made him angry.

"Where's Marie?" Ted asked.

"Out."

"Who are you?"

"Natalia."

Ted hated having his hair touched. Marie knew this and did it in a way that she'd worked out with Ted over the years. She feathered it with her fingers, never a comb or brush, never hair spray. She would blow it in little puffs, the way one did with a baby's hair. Ted had fine, thin hair, the color of winter wheat. But he had, on the top of his unusually large head (a head made for television), an expanding bald spot that the eight million viewers of *World Nightly News* would never see.

What they did see was Ted's rugged good looks (the exact phrase used by the network in a recent promo to offset the new twenty-nine-year-old anchor at a competing network, a former Calvin Klein underwear model who was stealing shares at an alarming rate). Square of jaw, ruddy complexion that looked like he'd spent the afternoon sailing, marvelous white teeth.

Natalia pulled out a can of hair spray and doused his head, putting a comb to his naked crown with all the subtlety of someone operating heavy machinery. Ted pulled away as if she'd just sneezed on him. Lou was watching this from the control room. Indeed, Lou had given Natalia the advice to use the spray and lots of it. Lou thought this was funny. Lou liked to mess with Ted on his birthday. The control room watched Ted prepare for a "Ted" moment. The girl seemed oblivious. Ted felt the adrenaline rush come, like a three-year-old out of the gate at Churchill Downs.

"Sorry, I thought you liked . . ." the girl said.

Something about her voice stopped him. She had an accent. He hadn't heard it earlier. Strange. Ted felt he was good with accents, that he could place them. He'd traveled everywhere.

Ted took a deep breath, put his phone back under the desk.

"Russian?" Ted said confidently, hoping for a tone of false humility.

"Sorry?" Natalia said.

"You're Russian," Ted said, forcing a smile.

"Polish," she said, as if Ted had just asked whether she'd ever been in prison.

"Oh . . . yes. Of course. Marvelous country," Ted said.

They stared at each other, a too-long moment. Ted briefly toyed with giving a disquisition on the changes to Warsaw and Łódź, post–World War II, as well as the annual grain harvest estimates, to flaunt his intelligence (learned from a two-page briefing from the interns as well as the in-flight magazine that time he flew to Poland for the anniversary of the dockworker uprising).

Natalia appeared to be in her mid- or possibly late twenties. Pretty in a bland sort of way. Ted briefly wondered what she looked like naked. (Natalia, at almost the same moment, was thinking that Ted looked far older in person than on television and felt sad for him.) Though the reality was that she could have been a part-time yoga instructor wearing formfitting Lululemon pants and Ted wouldn't have looked twice. His celibacy—initially a gift from Claire and, for a time, a partially enlarged prostate gland—was a subject he rarely gave voice to. It wasn't merely his inability to maintain a marginal erection (a firmness Ted gauged as somewhere between a croissant and a stale brioche); the embarrassing truth was he'd lost interest in sex.

It didn't help that his right testicle hurt. It had hurt for some time, beginning as a dull pain in his lower abdomen and continuing in a straight line down to the testicle itself. The more concerning symptom was a fierce pain on the rare occasions when he ejaculated. The first time it happened, as he built toward a climax, the pain increased until, at the point where the train left the station, he howled out loud, a sharp, sustained pain emanating from the ball itself. A quick Google search suggested cancer. But then, most Googled health searches seemed to suggest cancer. How would one even begin to broach this subject with another human being?

"Hey, Glen. See the game last night? Also, does your nut ever have a really sharp pain as you're ejaculating?"

"Sixty seconds to air." It was Sean, the first assistant director.

Natalia continued to try to touch up Ted's hair. She wore a baggy sweater and scarf, perhaps because the studio was so cold, the way Ted liked it. Her lips were dry and cracked. She kept pulling them into her mouth, like a child concentrating. She didn't know she was being watched. Ted thought of his daughter. The memory so sharp and fast it was physical, sending a flood of sadness mixing with his low simmering anger. The result made him sigh audibly.

"How's the hair spray working out?" Lou said in Ted's ear. He heard Larry and Phil, director and control room lead engineer, chuckle through Lou's still-open mic.

"You're a shithead," Ted said.

Natalia looked up, wide-eyed.

"Not you," Ted said to the girl, in a kinder voice. He pointed to his ear. "The voice . . . in my head . . ."

She forced a smile and nodded slowly, the way one does to an insane person or a relative one doesn't really care for at the holidays. She had a job to do. She reached to comb his hair again. He pulled away again.

"Okay, that's enough," Ted said to Natalia. His tone. That Ted tone. Brusque, dismissive.

The girl was startled and apologized, which made Ted angrier, as he was the one at fault and he should be the one to apologize but he couldn't quite seem to do it. She grabbed her bag of brushes and combs and hair spray and scurried off to a dark corner of the set.

He looked at the hard copy in front of him. It was largely decorative, as the teleprompter rarely went down anymore and if it did there was Lou, in his ear, and a team of people at the ready to feed him information. In the new world, by the time the sixty-plus-year-old audience tuned in, the twenty-two minutes and thirty seconds that Ted shared—the remainder being commercials—was ancient news. Who gave a flying fuck about the evening news? Bored travelers waiting on a delayed flight out of Denver International? People leafing through an old *Sports Illustrated* at a barbershop in Brooklyn? The elderly watching after an early supper in the common room in a palliative care facility?

All of these people had one thing in common. They trusted Ted. And that's what made him valuable. They trusted his face and his voice and the words he said. You couldn't manufacture it, though God knows the networks tried.

The network wanted a "show," not a news broadcast. How else, the network marketers asked, can we compete against cable and digital, against the mindless-but-heavily-trafficked public bathroom of news-like pornography of the Huffington Post, BuzzFeed, Vox,

TMZ, Perez Hilton, and a thousand others, of Suzanne Somers opening up about Barry Manilow's gay wedding or an angry gorilla scaring the hell out of visitors at a Beijing zoo or the latest viral video of someone screaming at a police officer after a routine traffic stop, only to regret it too late, the shaming and bravery-through-anonymity comments crushing any social or valuable discourse? Photos of the latest twenty-one-year-old singer-actress-model in a bathing suit/her underwear/getting out of a limo in a too-short skirt. Tens of thousands of hits an hour, tweeted, forwarded, Face-booked, trending. An unstoppable cavalcade of digital shit flowing through America's computers and iPhones and tablets and TVs every second of every day. How can we get more of that on the evening news? They wanted to know.

Now they urged Ted (he was actually contractually obligated, as long as his ratings remained sufficiently strong) to speak to advertisers at the up-fronts, in the spring, when the network announced its fall lineup. *Two Guys and a Girl . . . Plus Another Girl . . . and Another Guy . . . Who's Gay.* This was an actual show. *Proctologists of Beverly Hills.* A reality show. *Back in the U.S.A.* A reality show about former long-term POWs adjusting to life in the States again. It was billed as a comedy.

Ted felt he understood his audience. They were the people he'd grown up with in Woonsocket. Working people. Ted had always worked. Started caddying at a local country club at ten. Busboy later. He'd worked construction during summers in college. He felt protective of these people, people for whom Hallmark cards were not ironic. For whom the sentiments in those birthday wishes and graduation hopes and Mother's Day greetings were a genuine expression of how they felt but were unable to find the words for.

In the large and powerful coastal cities, in the hipster, craft brew cities that dotted the Great Plains, people made fun of these things. Ted understood people who bought Hallmark cards. These were his people, his audience. He spoke to them without irony. Irony was the purview of the late-night talk show hosts who felt their worldview wasn't simply different but superior to others. They enjoyed making fun of people. Mean-spirited but with a smile. Ted believed this was part of the reason the country was so divided. Basic rules of civility were dead. The new nightly news—the late-night talk shows—continued to try to shock, pushing us further and further adrift.

But deep down in places he rarely allowed himself to go, Ted knew he was a lie. A handsome, large-headed, reasonably intelligent lie. They had made him this thing, this . . . character, this cartoon, really, where once, long ago, Ted had been a reporter. A writer. Ted used to write much of the news. Well, certainly some of the lead-ins. He'd been a good writer. He cared about the words, enjoyed going over the copy with the news writers. But that was so long ago. Now he barely glanced at it pre-broadcast.

And each year it seemed to get worse, more insipid. Two years ago, there was a mandate from the new owners that "the stories should grab us like the final scene of a blockbuster film. Hope. Joy. Tears. Also, kittens where possible." This had come when a large cable company had bought the network and it was only reinforced when an even larger entertainment company bought the cable company. They'd flown Ted and Lou to Los Angeles and had them meet with film producers and screenwriters for a week. "Creating better news." Ted and Lou thought it was a joke. Until they learned from colleagues that the other major networks had done exactly the same thing.

And yet Ted was convinced they could run repeats and no one would be the wiser. Two nights ago, they had done a story where Ted led in with this line: *Thousands of Iraq's Sunni population are fleeing from fighting with ISIS while that country's Shiite population remains oddly silent.* A reporter's voice was heard over the footage they cut to. "We have nothing," a mother of three said. "We have nowhere to go. I have a family. Who will help?" But instead of footage showing refugees on jam-packed roads from the Agence France-Presse Middle East arm, they accidentally ran footage of celebrities at the Cannes Film Festival. Eight million viewers and the network had received exactly zero calls about this.

For some time now, Ted had felt less of a grip, once so firm (look at the old Nielsens if you don't believe him), on the world and his place in it. He was surprised to learn that the world had passed him by. He'd assumed he was still important. But he wasn't. What was Tinder? Bumble? Grindr? Swipe right. Swipe left. Hookups. App world. Respond instantly. Send instantly. React instantly. Why reflect? The speed at which it all moved stunned him. But it wasn't merely that. It was the new vocabulary of the world. The crassness, the rudeness, the shock value, the push all boundaries. The new comedians who were hailed as geniuses. *Pussy. Twat. Cock.* Was this funny? People laughed. Ted winced. Was he a prude? Had he fallen that far behind? Was he that old? Everything seemed meaner to him now. Crueler. Where was Carson and a good interview with Jonathan Winters or Raquel Welch? Where once people marched, now they tweeted. They commented, instantly, often angrily, viciously, sometimes anonymously. They trolled. They said the vilest things, the cruelest things. Depressed? Thinking of killing yourself? Do it. Do it, faggot. We'll watch.

Ted had interviewed Google cofounder Eric Schmidt a while back. One line from the piece stood out for Ted. "The internet is ... the largest experiment in anarchy that we have ever had."

Ted looked up now and saw his image, in profile, on a monitor. Mouth slightly open, eyes wide and a bit glassy. Who is that old man, he thought. Who is that tired-looking old man?

"Thirty seconds," Sean said, too loud, startling Ted. Ted touched the top of his head reflexively, feeling the bald spot. Something about it, about the naked, vulnerable skin seemed to symbolize his whole life. How do you explain to people that after a while the money ($11 million a year) doesn't matter, that the houses don't matter, the fame doesn't matter? How do you explain to a nation that prizes those very things above almost all else? How do you say to your eight million viewers each evening, viewers who think you have a dream life, a dream wife, a perfect daughter, that you are a vapid, empty shell of a person with almost no real relationships and little to no integrity, that you'd given up long ago on being a journalist?

Ted looked up, took a deep breath, and made a mental note of camera one's exact position, because when they returned live he would look up into the camera as if he'd just been reading something important instead of a what he was actually looking at, which was a live feed of the Knicks game on his phone. And it was when he made his quick check that he saw the poor makeup woman. She was tapping the top of her own head and Ted was sure that she was mocking his bald spot, when, in fact, she was trying mightily to signal him to tamp down a few heavily starched hairs that were now standing up straight.

The history of the world is the history of miscommunication. War, divorce, comedy. She was the embodiment of Ted's expanding nude crown, and he was pissed because she was in his eye line. Which, everyone on this set knew, was a no-no. Indeed, it looked like she was holding up a cell phone and taking a picture of Ted.

In fact, Natalia was taking a video of Ted. She'd begun feeling a bit better and was excited about being on the set of the nightly news. She wanted to record Ted and show it to her sister. This was strictly forbidden by Ted. Everyone knew that. But despite his spiraling mood, Ted decided to roll with it. He was too uptight. Everyone told him this. Well, perhaps intimated it, as they were too afraid of him. He'd roll with it. Look at Ted rolling. What a chill guy.

And why the hell hadn't Franny at least texted her father a happy birthday? Ted wondered, a cocktail of anxiety and anger building in him. The communications department at the network maintained Ted's Facebook page. Well-wishers had posted birthday greetings on Ted's wall by the score. Not a word from his own daughter.

Sean started the countdown. "Quiet, please. In five, four . . ."

But he was also Ted Grayson and this was the set of the nightly news and this was serious business, as his acting in a few seconds would soon warrant and why was this total stranger in his god-damned eye line? Why didn't people take Ted more seriously and show him some respect? Just because he wasn't a firefighter or a cop or a soldier? He'd lived these events. He'd been there. He'd been in war zones. (And had the promos to prove it.) Granted he was a mile back from any front line, in a pressed shirt and air-conditioned tent, but still. He was at Ground Zero, covered in that dust, that plastic-death smell that haunted New York for months while the pile smol-dered. Okay? He was in Oklahoma City. In Sandy Hook. At the

Madrid bombings. At the riots in Ferguson. In Cairo for the Arab Spring.

Ted couldn't find his water. They hadn't refilled it after he spilled it. He felt a dry patch at the back of his throat. He wondered if he was coming down with something. No water. No time. Ted coughed to clear his throat and get some saliva going. His breathing was way off and he pulled his head up the same way he did every time, assuming his character, his best Ted expression, and there, just to the left of camera one, in his eye line, was the makeup woman, still there, only now she was laughing at something with one of the crew and Ted was sure she was laughing at him, though, in fact, she had just said to the crew member, with giddy delight, "This is so cool."

Ted suddenly hated her. He watched the crew member walk away and saw Natalia stare at him with a big smile, a smile Ted took as ridicule. How dare she, here, in his studio. But he would roll with it, showing his professionalism and magnanimity.

Or not.

"*Eye line*, you Russian whore!" Ted screamed, his voice exploding through the studio, all ten monitors in the control room showing his rage-filled face.

The moment he said it Ted remembered she was Polish and also didn't know why he'd used "whore," a word he hated.

Her eyes went wide.

Sean missed three. He didn't say "three." It's on the tape. He'd been so shocked by Ted's voice, by the word "whore" and the volume at which Ted said it, that, standing next to the camera, arm up, in control, about to tell the crew they were going live, he missed three. To his great credit, he managed to get out "two" and to point to Ted. He never said one, a thing his boss, his predecessor, had advised him, on the off chance the feed came in a beat early. Sean also hadn't realized that, with his other arm, he had gently moved Natalia back, as if to protect her.

Sean pointed to Ted, the red light on camera one illuminated, and Ted Grayson appeared in living rooms all over America.

"Our final story tonight took place one hundred and five years ago today, about two miles south of where I'm sitting now, at what was once the Triangle Shirtwaist Factory. One hundred and forty-six garment workers, almost all of them poor immigrant women, burned to death. Cary Simmons has our story."

If you go back and look at the clip—and you can, on YouTube— if you go back and look you can see that Ted wasn't himself that evening. Notice the sweat at the hairline. It's minor but it's there. Notice how hard he's gripping his pen, the pen he always held during the newscast, during any speaking engagement or interview. How his voice sounded a bit labored. Small things you probably wouldn't notice during the actual broadcast but that, when it became what it did, when the tape of what would happen next was released . . . well . . . you noticed.

They cut away to the prerecorded story as Ted tried to gather his breath. He pulled at the collar of his shirt, as he found he was sweating, which was surprising, considering how cold the set was. He could hear the story, see the video of the Triangle Shirtwaist Factory fire. A rag caught fire in a sweatshop on the eighth floor. The doors were locked and many of the women hurled themselves from the windows as horrified spectators watched from the streets below.

Natalia was still reeling from Ted's words. She stared hard at her feet and had difficulty breathing. She wanted to run and hide. She was afraid. She lacked her younger sister's confidence, her father's strength. For her, this kind of confrontation was a series of emotional dominoes, trip wires hit in rapid succession; shame/fear/embarrassment/self-loathing/sadness/anger. It took about seven seconds, at which time, without realizing she was going to do it, she somehow managed to force up her own personal flag at Iwo Jima by raising her middle finger and glaring at the king of nightly news. She also managed to mouth, "Fuck you."

Ted shared Natalia's shock. Who was this person? How dare she? This was Ted's set. Ted's home. It was his goddamned birthday. The feeling that came over him. Like the feeling of having the wind knocked out of you, or hitting your head so hard, as a child, and you knew you were about to cry, to scream and cry, the terrible pain of it on the way, but still a small moment before it came, the inhalation before the scream.

They were suspended for a moment, Ted and Natalia, and neither seemed to know what to do. It all lasted only a few seconds but time seemed to slow for both of them, to hang in the cold air of the studio, her thin, nail-bitten middle finger standing tall, Ted staring back, mouth open, confused look on his face.

For Natalia, he was every asshole she'd had to deal with since coming to this cruel city where people were so rude, so not European, so obsessed with money, so clueless and ungrateful for the extraordinary privilege of being a citizen of this country where taps had clean water, the streets were safe, the government wasn't entirely corrupt, where the courts meted out justice. English was hard and poverty was harder and the noise of the city was grating and she couldn't breathe. She worked every day she could. She tried. And this rich man calls her a whore?

For Ted, she was Claire. She was Franny. She was Ted's brittle and insecure psyche. She was Ted's bald spot. She was Ted's dreaded, depressing birthday. She was youth and possibility and hope, where he was the failed old guard. She was lost time and the place Ted rarely went but seemed to go more and more these days. Regret. Where had life gone?

And then a loud voice could be heard. Ted initially wondered where it was coming from but soon realized it was from him. Lou, Sean, and the two cameramen all pulled their headsets off, the sound was so loud.

"Who the *fuck* do you think you are?!! Show some goddamned respect!" Ted was out of his chair, pointing, leaning over the cheaply made anchor desk. "How fucking . . . Do you know who I am? I am somebody! I am somebody! I am Ted Grayson! You fucking Russian whore! You're a Russian whore! Get off my set!"

Lou ran in from the control booth. He'd not seen Ted like this in his three years. The temper, yes. Anger. But not this kind of volcanic eruption. Lou grabbed a production assistant on the set and told him to get the girl out of there. Lou started to make his way to Ted's desk but Ted held up his hand. "Not now, Lou!"

Lou scurried back to the control room.

Ted's tongue ran hard against the back of his lower teeth.

Sean, cool as Elvis, said, "Back in five, four, three . . ."

Ted looked at Sean, then looked to camera. He was rattled. He was blinking too quickly. Two seconds of dead air. Three . . .

For a second Lou thought the battery in his headset had died. Others thought someone had hit the mute button. They talked about it later, after it all happened, after it got bad. Ted was going out live to eight million viewers and 238 affiliates in all fifty states and Lou actually snuck a peek at the "on-air" indicator because this couldn't be happening.

Later, people would think—focus groups bore this out—they would think that Ted had been so moved by the Triangle Fire story that he was unsettled. They thought he was being sensitive.

Four, five . . .

"Ted," Lou said quietly into his mic on his headset. Mild panic. No. A bit more. Would he have to shut it down? Go to credits?

Six, seven, eight . . . Jesus Christ.

"Get ready to go to . . ." Lou started.

And then Ted spoke.

"March 25, 1911. May God have mercy on their souls. For all of us here, I'm Ted Grayson in New York. Good night."

Claire has breaking news.

What man isn't interested in sex?

For a time, dating roughly to the middle of Ted's stint as anchor, during which the marriage had fallen into a Cold War–like détente, Claire had focused single-mindedly on Franny, squash, and the Bedford house, with Ted coming in a distant fourth. He worked late hours, traveled often. They went weeks without a meaningful conversation. Yups and nopes. The occasional Franny updates. Passing in the kitchen. True, they were still seen in public at major functions—the Goya exhibit at the Met, the Memorial Sloan Kettering annual fund-raising gala. But it was a farce, neither talking to the other the entire evening, silence on the car ride home, off to their respective corners of the too-big house.

Later, when he would see their picture in the *New York Times* Sunday Style Section or in the pages of *Town & Country*, he wondered who they were, those good-looking, happy-seeming people.

He had never loved anyone other than Claire. Not really. College infatuations and summer flings. But with Claire it had been complete and all-consuming. He felt different around her, more himself. They'd gone to the beach one Saturday that first summer after they met. A day trip to Crane Beach on Boston's north shore. On the drive back, she had fallen asleep for a time. Ted looked over and felt like this was exactly where he wanted to be. This moment, this person. Nothing could come close. He was home. It was the start of everything.

And now, somehow, gone. How? he wondered. Yes, he had changed, as she liked to point out. Yes, he had become colder and more callous, less involved in the world, living in his "Ted bubble," as Claire called it. A world of privilege and fame and numbness to the real world. Also, she was sure he had the occasional affair.

Of course, he saw it differently. He attributed it to aging and the daily onslaught of horror he witnessed and reported on each evening. War, famine, torture, poverty, disease, natural disaster, murder, corporate malfeasance, faulty airbags that companies knew full well didn't work and yet, somehow, these people slept at night. It boggled the mind. Took one's breath away. Depressed the fuck out of you. Until it didn't. Until you read the words, waited out the commercial break, and looked forward to dinner at your table in the corner at Cafe Luxembourg.

Now, to the question of infidelity. Had Ted cheated? Define "cheat." Was cheating thinking obsessively about someone else? Gifts? Thoughts of divorce? Afternoons in hotel rooms? Then no, he hadn't cheated, except for the last two things. Fine, he had cheated. But it was only two or possibly as many as five times. He'd forgotten because it had meant nothing to him and, he'd wager, to the other person. The work of reporters in the field is not unlike that of people shooting a movie or engaging in a political campaign. Close quarters. Long hours. All meals together. An intensity of purpose. Also alcohol, God's punch line for life. He did it because it was there.

The sex. The women. Because he could. Because he was bored. It had nothing to do with love or affection. It was speechless, late-night, awkward fumbling in the dark, 5:00 a.m.–regretful, booze-soaked breath, where-are-my-pants sex.

For many years now, he'd simply lost interest in sex. And it's not that he didn't find Claire—find many women—attractive. But something had been lost. Even as recently as a few years ago, he used to sneak a peek at her while she dressed, after a shower, the towel dropping as she slipped underwear on, a bra and T-shirt. Now he no longer cared to see her in even the remotest stages of undress. Their distance—not just physical but emotional, the tones of voice they used with each other that they wouldn't use with anyone else, the resentment and anger and sadness—was complete.

A few nights before Ted's birthday, Claire had called, a thing she rarely did anymore. "We need to talk, Ted."

Ted knew everything he needed to know from Claire's tone, the strained calm a private school principal might use to parents of a child who kept lighting fires in class. He knew. Despite the distance of the past several years, he still knew her intimately. Noticed as she dressed differently, stayed overnight in the city. He'd catch her staring out the window, a smile on her lovely face. She'd met someone.

And so, he had driven to the Bedford house. He walked in and was greeted immediately and warmly by their dog, Bismarck, an aging German shepherd. Claire made Ted get a dog when they'd bought the Bedford house. She insisted on a big dog for those nights Ted was away. Ted didn't care for animals, but he had grown to love this one.

The house smelled clean to Ted. Wood and soap and expensive

fabric. New rugs. White tulips in a glass vase on the counter. They were in the kitchen and Claire had made herself a cup of chamomile tea. It was late afternoon on a raw April day and she had a dinner reservation that evening with her friend Nancy at the Jean-Georges restaurant in Pound Ridge. Nancy knew Claire planned to tell Ted that afternoon and promised to be at the bar with two large Stoli rocks, three olives, waiting.

Claire couldn't wait to get to dinner. But first, it was important to her—to the memory of their life together—to do this right. Her therapist had said this and Claire agreed. Also in a way that made sense for both of their "brands," as well as their status in New York in the years to come. This from Claire's legal team, which also had a PR component when working at Claire's particular fee structure.

That said, she was hoping for honesty, for an adult moment that might transcend their current distance and pain and honor the larger life they had shared. They'd given life, buried friends and parents, grown older, grown closer, and then drifted so far apart. She'd imagined the scene and saw that it could play out like a Hugh Grant movie, with the two of them smiling and ultimately hugging before the scene cut, an Elvis Costello track over the end credits.

Ted had also wanted it to go well. He, too, had imagined the scene, though he was using a different lens, different script, and different crew. He saw, from a distance, his magnanimity and understanding, saw Claire's reaction, how she would want him sexually and how he would refuse her, how he would make a joke about how he didn't want her to cheat on the man she was cheating with. And how they would laugh. Ted knew little about music and had not scored his credit sequence yet.

After playing with the dog, Ted didn't know what to do with himself. He'd tried not to look directly at Claire, instead picking up glimpses of her in his peripheral vision. He saw the tea. It bothered him for some reason. He thought, Chamomile tea is stupid. He then thought, That thought is stupid.

After a long and rather awkward silence where they could hear the ticking of the old wall clock in the kitchen, Ted said, "So." He'd meant to say more. He was sure he would say more. Something profound, something to put her on her back foot. But all that came out was "So."

"So," Claire said chattily enough, which annoyed Ted. He felt he was now on *his* back foot. This from a man who prided himself on his interviewing skills, which, if he was frank with himself, had waned over the years.

"Thank you for coming up," Claire continued.

Ted nodded. Claire felt it was going well so far. Ted felt it was going poorly. Which led him to try to get the upper hand.

"Let me guess," he blurted out, instantly regretting it, "you've met someone."

He said it with far more attitude than he'd meant to, which immediately set Claire on edge. She sighed, closed her eyes, composed herself. Soon I will be done with this man.

"Yes," Claire said finally. "I've met someone."

Ted hadn't expected to be wounded, to feel jealous. His breath came in shorter bursts and he felt a kind of anxiety come on. She was, he realized, all he had at this point in his life. He'd simply assumed that this way of being—the distance and the fights and the long stretches where they didn't speak—was how they would always continue.

Ted nodded. He needed time. He couldn't think of anything to say. He knew the answer to his question but needed to ask it.

"Is it serious?"

Claire nodded.

Ted was gripping the back of one of the cloth-backed chairs at the island.

"Who is he?" he asked.

Claire noticed that he lacked his usual flippant tone. She could hear his vulnerability and it threw her.

"You don't know him."

Ted stared at her, trying for . . . what, exactly?

There is a language that exists between longtime married couples, one of small looks and expressions, sighs and body language, the placement of the tongue against the back of one's upper teeth, that tells epic tales, mood changes, moments, lifetimes. Everything truly interesting happens without words, Ted believed. He told this to young reporters who never listened and always overwrote.

"He's not on TV, if that's what you mean."

Ted didn't know what he meant and said nothing, though he was relieved the man wasn't famous.

"He's a lawyer," Claire added, as if talking to herself. "Lives in the city. He's British. Has his own plane. Not that that matters."

Ted watched as Claire began to sip her tea, then stopped, wincing at how hot it was. She put the cup down and smoothed her hand over the countertop, cleaning off crumbs or dust visible only to her, neat freak, a thing Ted had watched her do a thousand times. Did this new man watch her do that?

Ted looked at the refrigerator. *Has his own plane. Not that that matters.*

"How long?" Ted asked.

She'd anticipated the question, as had her attorney, with whom she'd practiced this speech. Claire was eager to tell the truth about the relationship but her attorney advised her against that. ("We don't use the word 'affair,' Claire. That's a word that can cost us money.")

"A while," Claire said.

Ted nodded and chewed the inside of his right cheek, Claire noticing, a sure sign of his core anger building. She was ready. She was calm. She heard the rain on the gravel driveway, off the eaves of the roof, tapping against the windows.

They had met the way people used to meet, before online dating. Through friends. A bar in Harvard Square called the Boat House. A small place just up from the Charles River. Ted was working at the Boston affiliate of NBC, having moved up from Providence. She was Claire Ford then, graduate of Wellesley College, an account executive at the Boston office of Kenyon & Eckhardt. In the two years she had been there she had risen, done well. She worked on Coffee-mate, which regularly took her to New York. She dated often, though no one serious. It was a time of life, her particular beauty at twenty-four, when men would stop her in the street and hand her a business card or write down their number.

She saw Ted when he walked into the bar. The Van Morrison song "Into the Mystic" was on the jukebox. She was drinking a Miller Lite in a glass. She was wearing a pair of baggy Levi's and a white T-shirt. Her hair was up but she reached back and took the elastic out. She remembered it all.

Ellen had been talking. Ellen Tracy, Claire's roommate. They'd known each other at Wellesley. Ellen had an uncle who taught at Harvard and who had gotten them an apartment on Ware Street, a few blocks away. An airy two-bedroom for a few hundred dollars a month. It came with a parking space.

Ellen knew a boy from growing up in West Hartford. George something. He was living here now and worked in news. Had a new friend he wanted her to meet, a great guy named Ted Grayson.

Claire simply couldn't believe how handsome Ted was. His half smile, one side of his mouth turning up, like a forties movie star. He was wearing a white oxford cloth shirt with the top button open and the sleeves rolled up. He was tanned and she thought she'd never seen a better-looking man in her life.

Claire could see Ted looking at her. The four of them got to talking, drinking beer, and listening to the jukebox. What do you do? Where did you go to college? Where are you from? What kind of music do you like? Did you play sports? Claire asked Ted where he summered. It made Ted smile. "We have a place in Woonsocket," Ted said. "It's called our house." Claire liked the way he talked. She liked his voice.

Someone suggested they get something to eat, so they wandered up Mass. Ave. toward Central Square, deciding on Mr. Bartley's Burger Cottage. They ate burgers and laughed and Claire wondered if the others felt the electricity in the air, wondered if they noticed how she sat forward on her chair, leaning in, smiling and laughing and talking but really only to him.

After dinner, they left the others and went for a walk along the river. A July evening, the oppressive heat of the day gone, the air warm and soft now. The sky still not fully dark. Thick green grass stretched down to the river's edge, the odd firefly dancing above it. Claire talked the whole time, Ted the good listener. An hour? More? They found a bench and sat. The more guarded she wanted to be with him the more she seemed to say, to admit. How she wanted to travel with children, three of them, how she wanted to live near Manhattan, bring them up traveling to a new country each year, have a garden. Her mother had had a big garden and ... Is this dumb? she asked. No, he said. It wasn't dumb at all. It was wonderful.

It got late and he walked her back to her apartment. He seemed awkward and extended his hand to shake hers good-night. She loved that, would remember that. She went on a lot of dates and most guys weren't like that.

"Good night, Ted Grayson," she had said, smiling.

"Good night, Claire Ford," he had said.

She had wanted to kiss him. She knew she wanted to marry him.

She looked at him now, in the kitchen in the house in Bedford, still so handsome, freshly shaven, and for just a moment, the briefest movie clip sense memory, saw him again, as she first had. And just that fast it was gone. And what replaced it, what caused her an even deeper hollow, a kind of falling, was the thought that no one would ever see her again as Ted had once seen her, at twenty-four, so alive and lovely, so much time ahead of her, anything possible. Where had life gone? Where had he gone, this man she had once loved so deeply and now didn't even like? Where had she gone, that young woman who had so many plans?

Ted felt it, too. Something had changed. And it wasn't, to Ted's mind, simply age. The freedom and possibility of youth, of life in your twenties and thirties, had vanished, certainly for him. Perhaps there were fifty-nine-year-old men out there who awoke each morning, giddy at the prospect of the day as they swung their achy legs out of bed, mildly dizzy from sitting up too fast, wondering if the sharp pain along the left temple was perhaps a tumor. He doubted it, though.

What replaced these dreamy thoughts of what *could* be was what *could have* been. He was no longer young. He was never going to speak French fluently or play the guitar or become good at chess. He would never run a marathon, never serve in the military, never sail alone to Bermuda. He would never be the recipient of a standing ovation from his local school or Little League team or homeless shelter for the remarkable gift of money and time he had given over the years.

Life was in the rearview mirror now for Ted. It was no longer a time of beginnings. It was a time for endings. Endings to jobs, marriages, friendships. It was the time of life when, more and more, the news from friends was bad. Sure, so-and-so's kid just got a Fulbright or was clerking for such-and-such judge or got married or had twins or made partner. But more often came news of pancreatic cancer and heart attacks on paddle tennis courts or accidents on vacation. Claire, keeper of names and birth dates and whose child was working where and who had grandchildren and generally the person in the family who cared about others, usually sent the cards with a thoughtful note.

Life changes. This was the essence of news. Why did it come as such a shock to an anchorman?

"Do you love him?" Ted asked the refrigerator, staring at a magnet for a place in town called Plum Plums Cheese.

She had not anticipated this but welcomed the question. Because what she had found was not some sordid thing. It was daylight and clean. It wasn't an affair. She hated that word, the tawdry, lying, immoral nature of it. It was love. Fine, technically it was an affair. But for God's sake, she was barely married, ignored for over a decade. The confidence-sapping nature of her union with Ted. She'd had her opportunities over the years. Men, friends of Ted, in fact, had hinted in no uncertain terms that they would love to meet for a drink or dinner, neither word said in a way that remotely meant drinking or dining. She never accepted. She wasn't looking for this, hadn't gone looking for it. He pursued her (fellow squash player). And do you know what it was? It was talking, sweat soaked, after a good game of squash, Claire's favorite feeling, a post-exercise high, better than sex. They sipped from their water bottles and talked. He was funny. He had good legs. Well-muscled. She felt, after all these years, after all the emptiness, that she was owed him, that she had earned him.

And yet. It was quite another thing to say it out loud. To your husband. There are things that are said that cannot be taken back.

"Very much," she said, quietly but firmly, surprising herself.

It was the *very much* that turned Ted's head. This was not how he thought the afternoon would go. He stared at her, mouth open slightly. So lovely, Claire. How strange to see someone you know so well in a different light, to see her, perhaps, as this new man might see her.

"What do you love about him?" Ted asked.

Claire sighed, sipped from her tea, the water still annoyingly hot. She burned her tongue and blamed Ted. The hot water was Ted's fault because she'd only made the tea in the first place because she knew this would be stressful.

"Do you really want to hear this?" Claire asked, going to the $15,000 Swedish-made refrigerator with the triple-filtered pH-balanced water for an ice cube. She put the ice cube to her tongue and stood at the sink, her back to Ted. She dabbed at her tongue, felt the cold, the drip down her wrist. She stared out the window at the rain.

She loved this house. She loved her daughter and her friends and the boxwoods and the garden she'd worked, her dog and the tennis and squash club and the smell of her new Audi Q7 and Netflix and the feel of her Hanro underwear and the taste of strong coffee in the morning.

"I do," Ted said, Claire momentarily confused, as she'd forgotten Ted was in the room and also what he was saying *I do* to. Weren't these the two words that had gotten them into this mess?

Claire dropped the ice cube into the sink, her tongue numb now.

What do I love about him? Claire thought to herself, a smile broadening across her face. She didn't want to turn from the window.

She wanted to stand here and feel good in this moment, with all that was in front of her, continue to pretend Ted wasn't there.

It had been a difficult few years for Claire. Menopause had hit her like a brick wall. The night sweats, the mood changes, the turning inward. No support or empathy from Ted. She also felt the seismic shift of turning fifty three years earlier. It wasn't possible. Mail, suddenly, from AARP. Someone was sending her mail telling her she was elderly, that she would die soon.

So Claire thought long and often about the future. About the house. About Franny and grandchildren. About when those grandchildren would visit and what room they would stay in and what kind of light would come into that room and what sheets and blankets would be needed and how a crib could be set up and how Christmas could be celebrated in the Bedford house and how, in summer, Franny and her children could use the Sag Harbor house, how Claire could be there all summer with the babies. The image spread through her body like warmth.

Ted thought almost not at all about the future. Indeed, at this moment, while Claire imagined it all, Ted was staring at Claire's ass, admiring its impressively protruding roundness, under her black skirt. All that squash. Still remarkably fit at fifty-three.

Claire paused before she said it. Even after all they'd been through—the arguments, the distance and coldness, the therapy sessions, the walks with Nancy, who had urged her to leave years ago—she had no desire to hurt him.

"He's happy, Ted," Claire said, still looking out the window.

"Happy?" Ted asked, as if Claire had begun speaking in the clicking consonant sounds common to one of the Khoisan languages of central Africa. "Who over the age of forty is happy?"

Claire turned and looked at her husband, dumbfounded and sad-
dened by the words, a kind of epigraph for Ted's life, and saw him so
clearly, at a remove, in a way she knew he would never see himself.
She felt sorry for him.

"People, Ted," Claire said softly.

Ted felt like a schoolboy caught in the wrong answer, an answer
he was so sure of, and now the class was looking at him and laughing. *Ha-ha! Ted's a dumb fuck.*

Claire watched Ted scratch at the collar line of his shirt, pull
the collar away from his skin, his go-to nervous tic.

"What's his name?"

"Ted. Really. Why does that matter?"

"I'm just curious."

She knew what would happen, but she said it anyway, proudly.

"Dodge Ramsey."

Ted snorted. "Seriously?"

"Christ, you're a child."

"What? That can't be his name. That's the show that runs after
Remington Steele."

Claire folded her arms over her chest and sighed.

"What do you do?" Ted asked.

"What?"

"What do you do? The two of you?"

Claire would not be drawn in, though she felt the tension, the
adrenaline release, the beginnings of those awful feelings she'd felt
for so many years with Ted.

"Ted."

"What? I don't think it's an unreasonable question. Let me guess.
He plays squash?"

"As a matter of fact, he does," Claire said.

Claire's obsession with squash had been a curious sore spot for Ted, a kind of jealousy. There was something about the sport, the WASPy, Ivy League clubbiness of it, the exclusivity of it, that bothered Ted in an admittedly petty way. Ted had tried it for a time and, though a natural athlete, simply couldn't master it. Or even get reasonably good. It looked so simple. Hit the damned ball against the wall. But he flailed. And the more patient Claire was with him, the more annoyed he became. So he gave it up, lying and saying he didn't really like it. And now the fact that Magnum P.I. or whatever his name was played—and probably played well—annoyed Ted. Images of a younger man, a far better-looking man, a more virile man, flitted across Ted's mind. He saw his wife smiling at this new person, sweaty and curvaceous in her little squash skirt, flirting with him, holding his surely enormous penis. Dear God.

Ted nodded, a prosecutor who'd just gotten a witness to confess.

"Why is that surprising, Ted?"

"What else do you do, besides play squash? Do you talk about squash? Watch squash videos on YouTube? Is there a squash.com?"

He wasn't sure why he was asking these questions. He felt out of control. He kept nodding.

Claire looked at him as if at a deranged man. She sighed deeply.

"We do the things people do, Ted. We go for a coffee. We go for a walk."

"That sounds nice." More nodding. Too much nodding. He felt it building. "What else? What other fun things? Movies? Do you go to the movies? Or plays? Or hotels? Do you screw at hotels?" He had not expected to say this but the line pleased him.

Claire stared at Ted for a time. "Don't engage," the therapist had said. "Count to ten, chuckle to yourself at the words you want to say. Say them to yourself: prick, fuck-nut." The therapist laughed. Claire did, too. The therapist had left her husband as well.

Claire tried counting to ten but had only made it to four when the line came out.

"We've done pretty much all of it," Claire said.

It was her tone that stopped Ted. Flat. Honest. Not intentionally cruel, but still. He thought he'd hit a winner over the net and she'd rocketed it right back over, straight down the line.

Ted turned and walked across the kitchen, to the window by the back door. Bismarck thought it was time for a walk and scampered to Ted's side. Ted looked down, patted her. She seemed disappointed and walked back to her spot. Ted had disappointed all of the women in the family.

He looked out the window at the rain. Patches of frozen snow, hardened and dirt-covered, dotted the yards, the rain washing it away. Ted felt very tired suddenly, the fight seeming to go out of him.

"Does Franny know?" he asked, still looking out the window.

Claire had told Franny about a month ago, at a lunch they'd had in the city, Franny asking what had taken her so long, which precipitated an argument that ruined the meal.

"Yes."

This wounded him, too. In another life, another universe, one where Ted was a good father and caring husband, this never happened. Or, if it does, his daughter calls him. In that world Ted and Franny are thick as thieves, best friends. Lunch once a week. Calls just to check in, for advice, to share a joke. Franny would have called. "Dad, we have to stop this affair. We have to keep the family together." And Ted, magnanimous, would have planned a family getaway. The Sag Harbor house, maybe, before the season. Paris. The French Alps. A skiing holiday. Time together. Where have I gone wrong, Claire? Let's never break up our little family or we will be lost.

Ted hadn't realized that he had been staring at a spot on the floor, a knot in the wood of the wide-planked oak floors. He was also scratching his head with both hands. He had been doing this for some time now. He looked at his wife and saw it on her face; she was over him. And this stunned him. Here he'd thought—and he wasn't sure why—but he'd thought that the talk that evening would be just another fight, one of thousands, followed by their respective retreats, where Ted would heat up an artisanal burrito from Whole Foods, drink three glasses of Sancerre, and watch half of a Jason Bourne movie while Claire would order sushi, call her sister, and draw a bath. He thought she would admit to the affair but say it was over and that she really wanted Ted back. Hell, why choose happiness when you can choose thirty more years of fighting and being ignored?

Ted wondered how he might report a story like this.

TED: Our correspondent, Phil Barnes, is live on the scene in the Grayson kitchen. Phil, any sense of why this Ted Grayson fellow was so delusional?

PHIL: It's an enigma, Ted. Though he was a huge disappointment to both his wife and his daughter, withdrawing into his own world and caring little for others. Neighbors say he kept to himself. Colleagues had little to say about him except that he was a friendless, egotistical prick. His daughter, Franny, a journalist in her own right, said only

that her father had, and here I quote, ruined her life. His
wife, Claire, an extremely good-looking woman, has said
that Grayson changed over the years. She also said he was
a shockingly bad lover.

TED: A pathetic man. Thank you, Phil. Phil Barnes, reporting live.

Ted was thirsty. His throat hurt and he needed a glass of water.

"What else?" he managed.

"Do you really want to know, Ted? Or are you just being an
asshole?"

The way we talk to each other, in a marriage, a ruined marriage.
A way we would never talk to another human being.

"I want to know."

"We talk," Claire said, voice a bit quieter, less defiant.

Ted was looking at the sink and Claire saw him nodding slowly.

"What about?"

"That's none of your business."

She didn't mean it to come out this way but it was reflexive,
years of practice. She regretted the tone instantly, squeezing her
eyes shut and clenching her jaw.

Breathe, Claire.

Ted went to the sink, turned on the tap, and put his mouth up to
the end of the spigot. Then he stood and wiped his mouth on a dish
towel. A ball of anger built in Claire's stomach. A $500,000 kitchen
renovation, open shelves, Simon Pearce glasses an arm's reach away,
and he has to drink like a pig at a trough?

"Everything," Claire said. "We talk about everything."

"Really?" Ted said, once again finding his thirteen-year-old-boy voice. "You talk about LeBron James and race relations in America and the concern over the renminbi?"

And again, Claire wasn't having it. Her voice remained calm.

"We do, actually. He loves sports, cares deeply about social justice, and has clients in China."

Water dripped down Ted's chin. He felt it would be unmanly to wipe it, though he wasn't sure why he felt this. Once, a long time ago, Claire would have reached over and dabbed it, rolling her eyes at what a boy he was, finding it charming. Now the water on his chin repulsed her.

"Is this really a surprise, Ted?" Claire asked.

It was, but Ted said nothing.

"We don't talk. We don't do anything. You don't love me. And we stopped being husband and wife a long time ago."

His body tightened. He knew she was talking about sex. He'd assumed it wasn't important to her anymore. The notion of her as a sexual being, with someone else, thrilled by someone else, made him weak.

He was filled with embarrassment and rage. He was also surprised to find that he wanted to say *Claire, please, I love you and I miss you but I'm lost inside and I don't know how I got here and I desperately need your help.* But that's not what came out.

"Well," Ted began, unsure of where to go after that. "I hope you two are happy talking."

Claire stared at him. This petulance. How long had she put up with him? He drove her to these feelings, these awful, toxic feelings.

"We're happy doing a lot of things," she said.

Ted felt that he had long ago reached a point where he couldn't be surprised. He had seen so much of life, so much pain and ugliness. But this shocked Ted to the point where he opened his mouth to say something but nothing came out.

How best to respond?

She'd be expecting a blowup. Show class, Ted. Show some grace. Let her go. Surely after all this time together he wished her happiness. It didn't take.

He was staring at the pristine Carrara marble counter, the tulips in the glass vase, Claire's phone next to them.

Ted nodded slowly and, with a nimble quickness that recalled his days as a high school quarterback, scooped up Claire's cell phone and sidearmed it through the kitchen window, a sharp, urgent cracking sound from the Marvin window ($3,500 per window and there were twenty-seven in the house) breaking but not shattering, the phone exploding in two, like a space shuttle separating after liftoff, the disparate pieces coming to rest in a pile of dirty, mud-caked snow by the back door.

Claire looked from Ted to the window and then back to Ted, yet seemed not at all surprised. She stared at him for a time and then held up her phone.

"That was your phone, Ted."

All the news that's not even remotely fit to print.

High above Ninth Avenue, just north of Fourteenth Street, across from Google's New York offices, in the former mixing and baking rooms of the National Biscuit Company, sit the impossibly hip offices of scheisse.com. Once, decades ago, in this same space, underpaid men and women with heavy accents, from Russia and Ireland and Italy and Poland, takers of long subway rides from the outer boroughs, lugged sacks of flour and baked saltines and Uneeda Biscuits twenty-four hours a day, food to show for their labors. Now, within the exposed brick walls hundreds of nearly identical-looking people in their twenties and thirties, from fine universities, posted their own kind of sustenance to the masses, an endless feed of insipid online drivel, a kind of visual and verbal vomit, under the guise of journalism.

On the walls, high-resolution photos of Orson Welles's character in *Citizen Kane*. Cary Grant and Rosalind Russell in *His Girl Friday*. Peter Finch as Howard Beale, looking insane, from *Network*. Why it was just fictional characters no one ever questioned.

And above it all, the *scheisse* mantra: NO RULES. JUST CLICKS.

The stories on *scheisse* were the result of research that in some cases took almost thirty minutes, based, often, on reading something on another website and repackaging it. Story length usually topped out around two hundred words and almost all stories were accompanied by a link to a video, thereby allowing a fifteen-second commercial to run before it. Bylines claimed that twenty-six-year-olds with two months of writing experience were "senior political correspondents," though most would be hard-pressed to tell you the meaning of the word "gerrymander."

The site had originally been called *Gertrude&Alice*, a small New York blog on culture, art, music, and the rich and famous in the 212 area code. It had been started by two women from Princeton, Upper East Side kids with connections. It was buzzy and hip, one of the early websites that generated notice. It also made money. Which attracted buyers, one of whom was the only son of a German industrialist, a thirty-four-year-old billionaire named Henke Tessmer.

Henke bought the site, charming the women who started it, making them rich, and promising to keep the "mission" the same. He fired both of them within a week of taking over, several of the writers quitting in protest when Henke put up a giant poster of Virginia Woolf's head rather expertly photoshopped onto Kim Kardashian's body in the office. Thus was born *scheisse*.

Henke's mission in life was to shock. Nothing more. To shock in his appearance, his words, his actions. He spoke openly about his sexuality, flirting with women and men equally. "Gender is a construct of the West," he liked to say. He would barge into the women's room at *scheisse* to wash his hands. In the early days harassment suits were filed, settled, the employees long gone.

He claimed he had gone to Oxford and done graduate work at the London School of Economics, though he also claimed to have quit because he was bored. He inhabited a world of half-truths and gauzy reality. When the spirit moved him, he said he'd also done graduate work at MIT, Stanford, and the Sorbonne, all of which he'd apparently quit. There was little the world could teach him.

In almost every serious endeavor in life there are standard operating procedures. Not merely technical but moral, ethical. Law, medicine, journalism, plumbing. A code of conduct. A manual, codified over years of careful thought and experience. Henke did not hold to this worldview. He believed the world had changed in ways so radical that most people still hadn't grasped them. That facts were dead. That today you could write and say anything you wanted. He believed the internet generation would write the rules as they went along. Had he been in Philadelphia in 1776, he would have said, "Fuck the Constitution. Let's just see what happens."

This, he believed, was the essential difference between a place like *scheisse* and mainstream media. The old guard didn't get it and they never would. Fake news? There was no such thing. There was only what you could get people to click on. End of story. Perfect example: a story recently about an intern at Procter & Gamble who, while working on the P&G product Dawn dishwashing liquid, posted a tweet that read, *We're going to war with Greece. Who's with us?* The poor kid's autocorrect marring his thin resume for years to come. The typo was retweeted 1.5 million times in twenty-eight hours. Within three days, protests against the nation of Greece had broken out in a dozen cities around the world. *Scheisse* ran stories about P&G being a company that unfairly bullied a poor nation, knowing full well it was a typo. They stayed on the story for a week. The hits were spectacular.

Now. Let's talk about journalistic responsibility. The *scheisse* worldview assumed that everyone was an adult and as such had a responsibility to find the whole story. *Scheisse* had no interest in telling you the whole story and if you for some reason (say, the history of responsible journalism for much of the twentieth century) were under the impression that the words on the site were carefully chosen and vetted, reported, and sourced twice (*The New York Times, The Washington Post, The Guardian*, etc.), then you were a fool. Because what you didn't understand was the mission. The mission wasn't to inform. The mission was to sell to advertisers. Click, friend, at your own peril. *Clickeat emptor* (Henke's words).

He'd caused a stir at a TED Talk last year (titled *God is dead. And so is* The New York Times) by saying nothing was out of bounds. He demanded that the TED audience suggest stories or images too far gone.

Sex? Please.

Private moments in one's home that had nothing to do with news? Grow up. Everything is news.

The Pope on the toilet? I would pay a million dollars for that photo.

In his talk, Henke said, in part:

"There is a quote that guides me. It was said by digital media thinker Danah Boyd. She said, 'In the tech sector, we imagined that decentralized networks would bring people together for a healthier democracy. We hung on to this belief even as we saw that this wasn't playing out. We built the structures for hate to flow along the same pathways as knowledge, but we kept hoping that this wasn't really happening. We aided and abetted the media's suicide.' Now, I agree with every word except one. The last one. I would change the word 'suicide' to 'rebirth.' Mark this date. Remember this talk. Because you are alive at the birth of new media. Like any birth, it is messy. It screams and cries. It is afraid and cold. It knows nothing. *Yet*. But it will learn. It is the birth of an entirely new way of communicating. And I am not talking here about the digital age. That is a vehicle no different than the printing press and it bores me. I am talking of a far more profound shift in *how* we talk to each other, of *what* is allowable, of what is real and true. Because it is no longer the same. Empiricism is for dead men with beards in bas-relief on university library walls. I can prove or disprove anything. Because there are no more rules. No more guides. To some, it is profoundly disturbing. To me, to the people who work for me, it is liberating."

There was stunned silence, a few boos, and a smattering of confused applause. *Wired* magazine recently put Henke on its cover and called him the future of news.

Burrowed in a far corner, a view of the Hudson River on one side, a wooden bookshelf she'd found at a flea market blocking her view of her colleagues on the other side, sat Frances Ford, née Frances Ford Grayson. Franny was a seasoned veteran at age twenty-seven. She was the head of features (stories that could run almost a thousand words as long as they had photos and accompanying video). She had decided a few years ago to refer to herself in print as Frances. Her mother and a few old friends were allowed to call her Franny. She'd dropped her surname, initially because she wanted to make her own career and later out of sheer rage.

At present, Franny was trying to breathe. Her palms were sweaty. Her stomach nurtured a small bubble of tension. She wasn't sleeping well or enough. Her diet lacked fruits and vegetables. She'd stopped going to SoulCycle and hadn't played squash in months. Mostly she watched Netflix, ordered in sushi, and drank too much white wine.

She was on deadline on a potentially large story. Or so said Henke. He'd texted Franny and several members of her team last night, late. Apparently, Salma Hayek had experienced a minor wardrobe malfunction at the opening of a new restaurant in Los Angeles, thereby exposing a portion of her nipple. The kids in editorial were blowing up the video—just four seconds—and creating a GIF. There was clearly a quarter inch of nip—so said an unscientific mini focus group of four *scheisse* employees. Franny knew the nip would play big and that they could milk it (ha!) for more than one story. Why not an additional story, and by "story" Franny meant a video compilation of "Best Nip Slips" in history?

Franny was one of the original seven employees of *scheisse*. She had felt, at the beginning, anyway, that *scheisse* made a difference. She initially proposed longer pieces but they kept asking for shorter.

Still, she felt that she and her colleagues were at the center of entertainment and fashion blogging, of infotainment, the physical and literal center of everything important and fun that was happening in the world.

Did Franny really believe this? No. But it's what she told herself. She also told herself that she'd get a real job once her life began. She would be changed by love, perhaps marriage, by happiness, large, elusive, cloud-like thoughts that seemed reachable for others. There would be dinner parties and children's birthdays and the riches of life as seen in magazines, TV shows, and Subaru commercials. These images seemed to slip further away with each passing year, each empty hookup, each disappointing date, each late-night drink with like-minded friends whose cynical worldviews only confirmed that life sucked. This was not the plan.

Why did men suck?

Her father sucked. Greg sucked. She and Greg had dated for three months and he'd talked about moving in together and then last fall he texted that he wasn't over his old girlfriend and that they were giving it another shot but that he hoped he and Franny could stay friends. Franny had texted back. *Absolutely. Call me and I'll perform your bris.*

Dalton. Rippowam Cisqua Northfield Mount Hermon. Trinity College. American history major. She'd been a standout squash player. She and Claire still played together once in a while, Claire occasionally winning and leaving Franny in a bad mood for thirty-six hours.

It was that time of life when her friends were getting married. So many weddings. Two last year; three the year before; three invites so far for this summer. Now she would go dateless, or maybe with her gay friend Brian. She would turn twenty-eight in May and this, too, caused her mood to foul, as she fully expected to be married or at the very least seriously involved with someone at this point. And that further angered her because she felt that she should not need a man to be happy even though she wanted a boyfriend to be happy.

The prospect of nearing thirty frightened Franny. It didn't seem possible. She felt both far younger and far older, though she didn't quite know how to explain that. Twenty was a lifetime ago. Thirty was ten short years to forty and that both blew her mind and depressed her to the point of dizziness.

She'd recently stopped dating, stopped hooking up. No more Tinder or Bumble. Last New Year's Eve, with friends in Stowe, Vermont, she'd stayed at a small inn. While most everyone was in the tavern getting hammered, she'd rung in the New Year talking with an older couple in the living room, sitting by a fire. The three of them toasted with small flutes of champagne and Franny listened as the couple talked about the cruise they took on the *Queen Mary* for their fiftieth wedding anniversary. The man laid his hand over his wife's as she talked and didn't take it away.

After they'd said their goodbyes, Franny walked outside and stood looking out over a field of snow, listening to the silence of the night, inhaling the smell of the clean Vermont air, wood smoke and pine. So many stars, so far from city lights. Later, she went back to her room and took a yellow legal pad, and wrote as fast as she could think, the fleeting lightness of New Year's Eve hopes dancing across the page.

Read more.

Find peace.

Call Mom more.

Be a better daughter to her.

Be a better friend.

Find a new job.

Take time off.

Travel.

Learn French.

Get in shape.

Play squash again.

Don't be afraid.

Be clean again. Detoxify.

No hooking up.

Find someone.

Children.

Volunteer.

Silent retreat.

Dad.

Here she stopped, surprised to see the word.

An air horn blared. And even though she was wearing headphones, the noise startled and annoyed her. Someone had used the word "millennial" in a story. Henke's rule.

Franny hadn't planned to be at *scheisse* this long. In the few days that her post–New Year's high lasted, she promised herself she'd quit at the end of the year, get rid of her apartment, put her things in storage, and travel. Mexico, maybe. Or Guatemala. Maybe Vietnam. Someplace inexpensive. Someplace she could find . . . what? She wasn't sure. She just wanted to escape. Ironically enough, that's exactly what she felt the readers of *scheisse* craved. Did she buy into Henke's manifesto? Not really. But she did believe that old media was dead, that they didn't understand the new world and the way people consumed information, what they wanted *from* information.

Real life, Franny believed, was boring. It was traffic on the Major Deegan, on the 405, on the highways and byways of this vast land. It was a delayed, uncomfortable flight to Chicago. It was whining kids and an unappreciative husband. It was rote. A shower where you forget you were showering. A meal where you later had almost no memory of eating. The gurus and yoginis and SoulCyclists wanted you to believe that life was best lived *in the moment.* Horseshit, Franny thought. What people wanted was *the exact opposite.* And that was where the money was.

What the networks and the serious newspapers didn't understand was this: people didn't want more bad news. They wanted less. Because what was happening on their screens—their phones and tablets and desktops—was overwhelming, nonstop awful. And now it was everywhere. Constantly being packed and manufactured and made newsworthy, even though most of it wasn't. Breaking news: tax bill passes. Breaking news: Famous Actor out of rehab. Breaking news: last remaining midget from *Wizard of Oz* dies. Breaking news: little people community up in arms over use of the word "midget."

Yes, we wanted to know the news. Flood? Fire? War? Okay. Good to know. But let me show you this video of the singing monkeys. We wanted to go home at day's end, lock the door, sit down, and hold back the tide. We wanted to stop the world for a bit. Each of us retreating to a device of some kind to watch Netflix or Amazon Prime or HBO or some easy-to-swallow network sitcom or the shows where people sang and cried to a live audience and a panel of judges, as well as reality TV that went as far as it possibly could to shock. *The Real Erections of San Luis Obispo.* We wanted to sit on the oversized couch and hold that clicker and escape. We wanted to get into bed fully clothed with a bag of Cool Ranch Doritos and a liter of Pepsi and hold that iPad and read about *Jennifer Aniston's obsession with Greek yogurt* or *Surprise! Angelina Jolie's travel loafers are actually affordable!*

And it wasn't merely escape from the outside world. It was escape from ourselves. It was a muting of our inside voice. Once, people sat after dinner on the back porch, as evening gently overtook the day, watched the fading light, listened to the din of crickets, to a dog barking down the road, a train going by in the distance. Alone with their thoughts. The bravest thing. Today we would do anything to run from our own thoughts. The noise of our minds. So we check the phone, the text, the email, the alert. Why look inside for the answers when you can look outside? Hey look, a sale at J.Crew.

Thus, Salma's plump breasts. A salve. A momentary respite. The mother's milk (ha!) of escapism. Was that so wrong?

Henke appeared at Franny's desk, startling her. A thing he did, approaching people from behind, standing too close. He leaned forward, beefy, nail-bitten Teutonic hands on her desk, face close to her screen and Salma's mighty breast. He smelled of cologne, too much and too strong.

"Christ, Henke."

Henke ignored her, a man deep in thought, too important, too brilliant for the niceties of life.

"Tit for tat," he said. "There's your headline. That's why I'm a billionaire."

"You're a billionaire because of your father."

Henke turned and stared at her. "Yes, Frances, famous fathers, right?"

He turned back to the screen. "I imagine yours are better," he said.

He looked at her, smiled an ugly smile.

He did this. All the time. Not just with Franny. One never got used to it, but Franny would never give him the satisfaction of thinking she'd been shocked, offended.

"You'll never know."

It starts as a tiny heartbeat.

It had been three days since the broadcast, which had been on a news-quiet Friday evening, a typically lower-than-average ratings night. Ted had canceled his dinner plans and gone straight to the Manhattan apartment, taken a hot shower, downed a Big Gulp–sized Ketel One neat, popped an Ambien (happy birthday to Ted!), and gone to bed, waking ten hours later, feeling rather splendid.

The days passed and the world turned on its axis and humanity did what it always did: fought wars, killed one another, committed perjury. Professional sports teams did noteworthy things; powerful people had intercourse with people who weren't their spouses and got caught. Nature wreaked havoc. Unprecedented storms ravaged Caribbean islands. A cargo ship disappeared in the Indian Ocean. The Russian army blew things up. A drone strike killed the leader of a terrorist sect on a road from Damascus to Beirut. A blind softball pitcher in Oklahoma continued an uncanny streak of strikeouts for his local team.

And Ted's network reported on all of it, snippets of bite-sized news-like items that were neither helpful, informative, nor particularly interesting. Much of it seemed déjà vu–like. Haven't I heard this exact story before, like, a week ago?

The weekly Nielsens were in and they were superb. No one knew why but they attributed it to Ted's moving Triangle Shirtwaist closing. The hair-and-makeup girl was ancient history. It never happened. Ted was king.

And, to celebrate twenty years in the anchor chair, the network was launching an advertising campaign. They were releasing it Friday evening, during the broadcast, and running it all weekend during college basketball (males, forties to fifties) and the NCAA women's hockey Frozen Four (the moms of the players: a key Ted demographic). Ted had, over the past few weeks, watched the rough cuts with the marketing team, half a dozen earnest men and women speaking a language Ted didn't really understand. *Click rate. Digital extensions. Transformation imperative.*

The campaign was called "You know Ted" and it consisted of a series of TV commercials and web films. Shots of Ted over the years, around the world, at the anchor desk, interviewing heads of state and various popes, sitting forward and pointing at CEOs and mendacious politicians and third-world terrorists. Shots of Ted in war zones and in refugee camps, wading knee-deep in the ocean to help a father and baby off a listing raft, and his time in Bosnia, holding a baby, Ted having been hit by the tiniest piece of shrapnel in the history of warfare, perfectly placed and made for TV, on his cheek, a line of deep red blood mixed with dust and dirt. The first of many Emmys.

A song was purchased, at great cost, from an Austin, Texas–based alternative band called Explosions in the Sky. It was called

"Remember Me as a Time of Day." Ted found it haunting. They'd gotten a Hollywood star to be the voice-over.

"You've seen him, in good times and bad. In sickness and in health. In crises and crashes. When lives were at stake, when hope hung in the balance. He was there. And you were there with him. The times of your life have been brought to you by Ted Grayson." And then the big finish. "This is your life. This is Ted Grayson." And here, at the end, a shot of Ted and Claire, walking the English gardens of the Bedford house.

Simon Samson, head of the news division and Ted devotee, called a meeting of the news staff and introduced the campaign, showed the commercials to great applause, as Simon had made sure to film snippets of as many newsroom people as possible to boost morale. Young Murray with hair. Grace, Murray, Jagdish, and Ted working on a story. Producers, production assistants, camera operators. Even Ruth Silverman, the longtime receptionist, had a cameo.

Simon couldn't know for sure but his sense was that the commercials seemed to generate an excitement that permeated the newsroom. A renewed belief, perhaps, in Ted, in the mission of news, in their work. That it still mattered.

As they made their way through the newsroom, Ted and Simon stopped by the writers' room.

Ted did this from time to time, though less often than he used to. Weeks went by where he didn't talk with the writers, the producers overseeing the assembly-line–like machinations of the broadcast, ferrying the words that Ted needed to say to the teleprompter. The visits never ceased to thrill his writers. Like a parent in a large family who takes one child out for the day.

"Ted," Murray said. "How wonderful to be you." He'd meant only to think that but it slipped out.

They had been together since the beginning, Murray and Ted. Of the original nine writers on the news staff when Ted took over the anchor chair, Murray was the only one left. He'd been there for September 11, their finest hour, when none of them left for five days.

Grace had come on board three years ago, having completed a master's degree at Hunter College in social work. She took a job in the outpatient psychiatric unit at Elmhurst Hospital, Queens, and lasted exactly four days. She could write about pain. Seeing it firsthand was something else entirely.

Jagdish took the job on a whim. A friend of a friend who was a producer. None of them had expected to be there so long. But unlike so many jobs, theirs was new each day. And when large stories hit, they felt they were at the center of something. And, of course, Ted. Their proximity to Ted, to a man watched by millions of people. "For God's sake," Murray would remind them, "the president of the United States watches Ted. Which means he's listening to the words we are writing in this room."

Ted sat on the arm of an old couch. His spot. A Christmas morning excitement at having the great man in their office.

"What's the word, Gracie," Ted asked. "How's the world's greatest band?"

"About to go on tour. Fort Lauderdale, Miami, Tampa, Jacksonville, Greenville, Hampton, Columbia, New Orleans, Lexington, Philly, then to New York May first and second. I've got tickets to both shows."

Grace said this as a single sentence while putting Carmex on her lips, a thing she did ten to twelve times a day.

"You going?"

"Ted. Please." Grace smiled.

Grace had suggested a story last year about the band. Ted agreed and to this day it was the greatest assignment of Grace's life. It was the only story that she didn't have to do any reporting for. Ted brought her to the interview with Eddie Vedder, at the Mercer hotel in SoHo. Grace could have died that day and lived a full life. Grace's therapist felt differently but so be it.

"Jagdish. Getting any sleep?" Ted asked. Jagdish had a baby at home.

Jagdish smiled and walked over to Ted, holding out his oversized cell phone revealing a photo of a cherubic face, wide-eyed, loony smile.

"Look at that. What is she, a year?" Ted asked.

"Ten months."

"Tell me her name again."

"Sita," Jagdish said, beaming. "It means goddess of the harvest in Hindi."

"She's beautiful."

"Any advice?" Jagdish asked, smiling.

A second. Maybe two. Maybe a bit more. Ted wasn't sure what to say.

No. No advice, actually.

Don't love them too much.

Get ready to be hurt.

"You'll know what to do," Ted said kindly, half smile. He stood up.

"I just wanted to stop by and say . . . I don't think I say it enough . . . you guys make me look a lot better than I am."

"That would be impossible!" Murray shouted, though again, he'd not meant to speak.

Grace stood and walked over to Ted. She hugged him and Murray died a little inside. "Thank you, Ted."

Ted was unsure what to do, so he simply patted her back. The hug went on too long.

"Okay, then," Ted said. "See you tomorrow."

Murray had meant to mention Cassini to Ted. He hustled down the hall.

"Ted," he shouted.

Ted and Simon turned to Murray, looking at him as if at a crazy person.

"I forgot . . . Cassini, Ted." Murray was grinning.

"Is it getting near?" Ted asked.

Murray nodded. "Ted, we have to do something."

Simon said, "What the hell is Cassini?"

Ted started to say something but Murray jumped in. "The NASA probe to Saturn. It launched the year after we did. Almost twenty years ago. Pretty soon it's going to crash into the surface of Saturn. A planned death. What a way to go."

"Fascinating," Simon said, fake smile.

They turned and walked away.

"You canceled on me. Who cancels on an old woman?"

It was Polly, Ted's longtime agent and lawyer. Ted wasn't sure how old she was. Maybe sixty-five. Maybe older. Five foot four, perhaps, and "pleasantly plump." (Her words. "Ted I look like a goddamned pear. But a ripe one, I'll tell you that.") Never married.

Lived in a stunning top-floor apartment on Riverside Drive with her cat, Hannah Arendt.

"Polly," Ted said. "I didn't cancel on you. I asked that we move it a few days."

"'A few days,' he says. Like I'm chopped liver." They were seated at Ted's corner table at Cafe Luxembourg. Ted sipped a Ketel One, rocks, and Polly was chewing one of the three olives she needed for her martini. She chewed with her mouth open, unaware of the sound. Ted had never gotten used to it. They were waiting for their food. Ted had ordered salmon and Polly had ordered a steak with a side of mashed potatoes.

Polly raised her glass. "Happy freaking birthday." Ted raised his glass and they drank.

"How long you want to keep doing this?" she asked.

"Drinking? A while."

"I love Irish humor," she said without smiling.

"The job? What else would I do?" Ted said. "Maybe five more years."

"Do you still like it?"

Ted sensed a small change in tone. Polly was playing with the toothpick the olives had arrived on.

"I guess. Why?"

"'I guess,' he says. I guess. You're a queer one, Teddy. A little birdie told me there was a bit of drama on the set a few nights ago. The night you canceled, in fact."

"How do you know about that?"

"Boychik. I know about everything. That's my job."

"It was nothing. Lost my temper."

"Not what I heard." Polly looked at him, a mother's look of concern. "Tell me you're okay."

"I'm okay."

"Let's try that again and maybe this time mean it."

Ted grinned. "I'm okay, Pol. I hate birthdays."

"Who doesn't after the age of twenty-nine?" She sipped her drink. "Listen. Okay. Who's your first call when something like that happens? Who's your first call when anything like that happens? Aunt Polly. This is a person we're talking about. I fix things. So nothing blows up. Are they fixing this?"

"It's fine."

The food arrived. Ted ordered another drink.

"Another martini?" the waiter asked her.

"Sonny. I'm a Jew," she said through a mouthful of steak. "Which means I don't drink like my handsome friend here. But I will be having dessert so stay close."

That same evening, in Long Island City, a land far, far away from Ted's Manhattan, two women walked home from a liquor store, lugging a case of Pabst Blue Ribbon. They walked past the end of the Dutch Kills, the cold and wind keeping the stench and whatever else haunted those toxic waters heading in another direction. Along Forty-Seventh Avenue, past the Taxi & Limousine Commission, past the Extreme Sports Paintball & Laser Tag place where the bankers and ad agency people held retreats—team building, slumming it in Queens for a night.

Natalia walked with her sister, Laura. Her best friend. Laura was younger by two years but acted older. Alpha tough. They walked past the City Ice Pavilion, where sometimes, on a weekday, when she hadn't booked a hair and makeup job, Natalia would go by herself and skate for an hour or two. It always felt like being back in Zakopane, a resort town about two hours south of Kraków, in the Tatra Mountains of southern Poland. Her parents worked in the swank hotels in the winter and on farms in the summer. She'd grown up skiing, skating, snowshoeing with her father on his days off.

Natalia told her sister the story.

The network's human resources department had called and asked that she come in. Natalia assumed they would apologize, that perhaps she'd meet with Ted. Mostly she hoped to be brought on full-time, instead of her permalance position, which had no benefits.

She waited more than an hour before being ushered into the office of a woman named Donna. Donna was fiftyish, unsmiling, a person uniquely unsuited to be in human resources due to an unnatural lack of compassion, hardened, most recently, by an ugly divorce. Without making eye contact, Donna motioned for Natalia to sit.

Natalia sat silent, stone-faced, embarrassed. She wanted to cry but wouldn't let herself, her father's daughter.

Donna said nothing at first. She continued filling out the paperwork, checking it against something on her large, antiquated computer screen. The longer she was ignored, the angrier Natalia got.

"We're letting you go, of course," Donna finally said to her desk. She managed to look up, a grin crossing her overly made-up face.

Natalia hadn't been expecting this. She thought she might be reassigned. A morning show. Something. But not this. It came out fast. "Are you firing him, too?"

Donna's grin disappeared.

"Do you have any idea who you're talking about?"

"Yes. A man who called me a Russian whore. I'm neither."

"What?"

"He did."

"That is a *very* serious charge you're making."

"It's not a charge. It's the truth."

Donna was a born bully and sensed a weakling.

"Well, this is the first I'm hearing of it," Donna lied.

"Ask the people who were on the set."

"I did. And—"

"I thought this was the first you were hearing of it," Natalia snapped.

"I asked them, young lady, to describe what had transpired," Donna lied again, raising her voice. "And what I was told was that you had the audacity to give Mr. Grayson the middle finger, which people in this country think is a major offense."

Donna stared at Natalia, challenging her. Natalia felt her throat tighten, her eyes tingle. She'd never been fired from a job in her life. She wanted to pull her phone out, show the video. But Donna was picking up her phone, calling security. A panic-fear came over Natalia. She prided herself on her work ethic. Her father's work ethic. She had done nothing wrong. Fine, she had given the old man the finger. It had been a reaction, in the moment, because he'd screamed at her. Because he'd frightened her. Because she felt threatened. Her parents wanted her to come home, to find work in Warsaw, meet a nice Polish boy. But she was desperate to make it here.

A large security guard escorted her out of the building. He gently laid his hand on Natalia's shoulder. "It'll be okay," he said. Which was when she started to cry.

So that night, Laura's boyfriend, Filip, and his friend came over. They drank beer and rolled cigarettes from a pack of Drum and listened to Laura's iPad playing A Tribe Called Quest. When she wasn't working at Polish-owned coffee shops, Laura picked up work as a DJ. She knew hip-hop better than any white girl from Poland should.

Natalia could tell Filip's friend was hitting on her, but she had no interest and her sister would throw him off the roof if he made a move. She had her iPhone out and was showing pictures from Poland when she scrolled past the video she had taken of Ted. She played it for them and they laughed. She laughed. She played it again and they laughed again. Filip said they should play a drinking game. Play it and every time Ted said "Russian whore" they had to drink. Which they did three or four times. Her battery started to die. They moved on to something else. There was talk of going to a bar but Natalia wanted to find her bed. The others left and Laura and Natalia were alone.

Laura was the only one who hadn't laughed at the video of Ted. She said, "That guy's a dick. You should post that to your Facebook page. What are they going to do, fire you?"

Across the East River, in the wide-open spaces of *scheisse*, Franny and two of her colleagues watched Ted's new promo. It wasn't set to launch until Friday but someone had leaked it. They clicked on it and watched. One of them was writing a critique (175 words or less).

He was so young, Franny thought, as they watched. The shot at the end surprised her. She'd remembered that day. Her father and mother had just gotten in a huge fight about whether Franny should return to Northfield Mount Hermon, which Franny had not wanted to do, or move back home, go to school in the city. Ted was against the idea of quitting. Claire said he was being his own pigheaded Irish father. Ted said not everyone had had it as easy as Claire. Franny had watched the toxic verbal ping-pong, hating every second of it.

Now, watching, Franny found herself holding her shoulders high, felt an unpleasant tingling in her belly, a low-grade malaise creeping over her day, the blandness of the night to come, the weeks to come, her life in general. It seemed empty and hopeless. In fact, a few days ago she had received an unwanted email from a former roommate at Northfield Mount Hermon—Lauren—inviting her and her classmates to a reunion. Of course it would be Lauren planning the reunion. The invite, like so much about life these days, annoyed her. She responded no, saying she would be unable to attend, and then went to the class Facebook page, looked at some comments, saw some old classmates, and wrote what Lauren would feel was a mean, snarky, typically Franny Grayson comment. Franny thought she was being funny. Lauren thought she was being a bitch.

"He was hot, your dad," one of her coworkers said.

"Shut up," Franny had said. "I want your story in thirty minutes."

Here was the essence of news. A thing was happening right now, real time, and there were those who knew it and those who didn't. Most didn't. It was too new, too small. Those moments, before you know a thing—the spot on the X-ray, the middle-of-the-night phone call, the affair your spouse is having that you are still unaware of—these moments of blissful ignorance. This is where Ted and Claire and Franny lived.

Claire was in the city. She had gone to a SoulCycle class in Union Square, where she felt she more than held her own against the skinny twenty-five-year-olds with their perfect bodies and tight skin. They looked so young. How did they see her?

She left the class and walked through Union Square, past the farmer's market stalls, the smells of lavender and apples and pretzels and fish. She continued south to University Place, heading like a tourist to the spot Franny had suggested she go for a coffee. Franny had said she would try to meet her mother but that work might get in the way.

What is a mother to make of this? Here she was, in the city, so close to both her husband and her daughter, and she would see neither. A life shared and now this. The time Franny, age four, needed an MRI, Claire lying on her back, holding Franny, covering her ears with her hands for twenty-five minutes, Franny falling asleep. The car trip to Maine, Franny eighteen months old, a nose full of snot, unable to blow. No drugstore nearby. Claire put her own mouth to the child's nose and sucked, spit the snot out, Ted wide-eyed. Adapt and overcome, as the marines said. And what was a mother if not a marine. What wouldn't she have done for this girl?

And now, happy for Franny in her new life, her career, Claire still smarted at the selfishness of not meeting for a coffee.

She went in and waited in line. Reclaimed lumber on the floors and halfway up the walls. Exposed brick. Vintage light fixtures. A low techno-beat playing from unseen speakers. Tattooed baristas who looked like people from a photo shoot of people who work in coffee shops tended to high-end Italian espresso machines, calling out people's names as if it were physically painful to do so, their boredom at Sandra's and Oshi's and Brock's coffee order almost too much for them.

In front of her were two girls, early twenties. Both wore yoga pants. There was, about both of them, an open sexuality so foreign to Claire's life experience. Their bodies on display. The two girls were talking, almost at the same time, when one of them pulled off a sweat-shirt to reveal a formfitting tank top. Claire looked at the girl's bare shoulder. A purple workout bra just visible under her shirt. Claire watched as the girl listened closely to her friend talk about work, hair falling out of a bun, gold and brown strands creating a veil at her neck. A man will worship your body someday, Claire thought. You will lie in bed one rainy Sunday afternoon in late fall, the day quiet, after an hour of lovemaking. Mostly it will be lust then. A false love. An oxytocin-release love. A hormonal love. Not twenty-plus-years-of-marriage love. Not hold-their-hand-at-their-mother's-funeral love. But rather lust disguised as love. Youthful lust. Zero body fat lust. Remarkably rigid penis lust. Bright light lust. Not shades down lust. Not hope for barely any light lust. You'll want to see it all.

But know this, my round-bottomed friend, Claire wanted to say aloud. Know that he will worship your gift-of-a-body more than you, the person, the soul. He will conflate you and your body. It is what men do. He will partially listen to you. When you think that he's being sensitive and engaged, chances are what he will really be thinking about will be turkey sausage. Or a pair of big boobs in a tight sweater he saw on the subway. Or a female colleague who bent over a desk to reach for a sheaf of papers. He will fight his Neanderthal instincts to respond in a way that makes you think you have one of the few good men. The early days of your relationship will be the wonder days, where you can't believe it's happened, that you've met someone like this, when you sleep late on a weekend and eat meals at odd hours and wander the city and talk in bed until the sky gets light, your energy and craving for each other, for life itself, seemingly boundless.

But it will change. Slowly at first. Then powerfully. Children. He will see you differently and you will see it in his eyes. The way he doesn't look at you. The way he looks at younger women at parties you attend. How work and money and position will hold tremendous sway. How he will come home and talk only about himself, if he talks at all. How you will long for him to ask about your day. How your confidence and self-esteem, once so strong, will ebb. *Is it me?* you'll wonder. *Am I doing something wrong?* No, you're not. Which makes it all the worse. After the arguments, the fights, the ones that seem to happen more frequently as the years progress, notice how he comes up behind you at the sink, when you are doing the dishes, after the baby is down, you thinking about the laundry that has to be done, the shopping, feeling about as sexual as a lug wrench, when he, having caught sight of your ass, a distracted woodland animal, presses up against you, and reaches around to hold your breasts, when all you wanted was a "sorry," a hug that did not involve his hands on your ass. Is that so hard?

She wanted to tell the girl. Tell both of them. Be careful, she wanted to say. There's an accident up ahead. Avoid it. But they wouldn't listen. She also wanted to tell them that, if you were lucky, you might even meet a man like Dodge, who, you hoped, could save your life.

They walked through the Frick, Dodge occasionally brushing against her shoulder. He smelled like sandalwood. They looked at the paintings, an exhibit of Van Dyck. Claire stared, unable to comprehend that someone had moved his hand in such a way as to create what appeared to be alive. They walked slowly in the quiet, peeling off to look at pictures in their own time, Dodge ahead of her, assuming the stance of a regular museumgoer, hands intertwined behind his back, leaning forward at the waist. He loved art but was eager to get to dinner, to a glass of wine, to his apartment, where he could remove Claire's clothes.

Claire was staring at a particular picture, a portrait of two children. *Elizabeth and Anne.* The write-up on the wall next to the drawing told the history, how Van Dyck had become the favorite painter of King Charles the First of England and his wife, Queen Henrietta Maria. At the time of Van Dyck's painting, the royal couple had five children, Charles, Mary, James, Elizabeth, and Anne. Henrietta gave birth to nine children, two of whom were stillborn.

Claire read this and then read it again. She leaned closer. It hit her, the feeling, so fast, so suddenly, that her eyes welled. She blinked and leaned even closer. A docent startled her when he gently asked if she could not lean so close.

She was embarrassed, mostly because she had tears on her cheeks. Dodge turned to look at her but Claire quickly made her way to the ladies' room, where she sat in a stall with the lid of the toilet down, staring at her shoes, trying to muffle sobs with a wad of toilet tissue. So strange, she thought, observing herself. She's not a crier. Stoic. Strong. A New England Ford. Don't whine. Keep moving. And yet something about the painting, those two children.

After Franny, who was so hard to conceive, they had tried again. So many tests, so much disappointment. And then, the little miracle. A boy. Walt. An emergency C-section at thirty-six weeks. Stillborn.

The effect this has on a person. On a mother. The sadness of it. Do you compensate, perhaps, by loving your only child too much? Can you love a child too much? Can you give in too easily? Overlook traits and behavior that to someone perhaps a bit less wounded would be obvious? Do you, perhaps, spoil them? Act as a mother bear when the child's father raises his voice, even when warranted?

She stood and stepped out of the stall, washed her hands and splashed a little cold water on her face. She rarely wore makeup, the good fortune of high coloring and fine skin. She blinked several times, reapplied her lipstick, let her hair out of the bun she'd had it in and reset it.

When she walked out Dodge put a hand gently upon her shoulder, his face contorted with confusion and pain. "Are you okay?"

Claire touched his cheek, smooth from a recent shave. She was happy to see his face. She wanted to feel good. She wanted desperately to be happy.

They had dinner at a small Italian place between Madison and Fifth, a place where they knew Dodge. The food was very good. They drank wine and, later, espresso. They split a tiramisu. A short walk back to Dodge's five-thousand-square-foot apartment, where they slowly undressed each other. And then Claire lay down with a man other than Ted for the first time in over thirty years (fine, it was their seventh time). She was blissfully unaware of the calls from Franny, the texts. Or the texts from Nancy. Or from Ted. Or from her own lawyers, giddy with excitement at the potential ruin they could inflict on Ted. She hadn't remembered that she'd turned the ringer of her phone off at the museum, that the battery had drained to nothing. Dodge was whispering in her ear in the quiet and the dark.

It started as a barely palpable heartbeat. A minuscule speck of data among the two billion users of Facebook. A microscopic dot among the more than two hundred billion emails sent every day, the more than five hundred billion text messages sent every day, the more than three billion Google searches every day.

But it was alive.

A few friends of Natalia's saw it. A leaf going over a waterfall. It was nothing. Except then a friend of a friend emailed it to another friend, who happened to be a reporter at TMZ. Some famous newscaster dude losing his shit. It was funny. The reporter had it posted seventeen minutes later with a three-line story absent of facts except for Ted's name, a story that, owing to an alert, a reporter at *scheisse* emailed to his editor, who emailed it to Henke, who posted it. A colleague of Franny's texted her the Facebook link.

■   ■   ■

Franny had taken a bath. She had ordered Thai and was going to watch something mindless, pop three Advil, go to bed early, and pray for a good night's sleep.

She had just sat down on the couch, a towel still wrapped around her hair. She was opening the takeout, hitting the Netflix tab on her laptop, when her email started pinging. Her phone, too. Friends. Colleagues from work. Henke.

Franny watched it. Then she watched it again. If she had been able to scan her body, head to toe, like the yoga instructor told her to do, she would have found tension, fear, anxiety, tightness in the back of her head, tingling palms, a knot in her stomach, a sense of disbelief. She took a large pull from a glass of white wine she'd just poured. She watched again. Watched her father's face, her left hand covering her mouth. This man she knew so well, hated so much. She had refused his money, made it on her own in the world of media. Once, he was everything to her. And now . . . now he was a man who looked vaguely familiar on television, in ads on the sides of buses.

But for just a moment, barely measurable, he was her father. And Franny was terrified for him. She pitied him. Yes, he was rich and white and powerful. He had homes and influence, access and reach. He had cars and stuff and a thin, fit wife who was empirically beautiful. He had a lovely daughter who was—well, used to be—seen with him, the family, out at an event, smiling, the savage screaming and fighting on hold for the photos. Yet she also felt for him. Because it was a veneer. And it was all about to be taken away in a public and deeply humiliating fashion.

Franny saw the future. They were going to crucify him. She needed to call her mother. She needed to call the office. She needed to get on the story.

If Claire had walked from Dodge's king-sized bed with the impossibly soft Frette sheets and stood naked at the large windows with the extraordinary view out onto Central Park, all the way across to the Beaux Arts wonders of the West Side—the San Remo and the St. Urban—she might have spied her soon-to-be-ex-husband walking briskly around the Jacqueline Kennedy Onassis Reservoir, on his second of two laps. But she did not. She was busy lying nude, enjoying the postcoital bliss of new lust.

Ted felt no such bliss as he made the southern turn around the reservoir in Central Park. A low-grade tension wouldn't leave him.

He was thinking about a story they were preparing on Congress, on the division between the parties. He'd seen some of the interview footage, the representatives and senators talking about the divide. One of them said, "Something fundamental has shifted. I believe the democracy itself is in peril." They were using that line as part of the teaser campaign.

It seemed true to Ted. The way we interacted now, how we saw each other, as a member of a political party, a cultural group, an affiliation, a sexual identity, a devotee of a TV show. Instead of personality traits, quirks, hobbies, these labels had come to define us. Cable talk shows—comedy, news, the lines blurring—and their easy, crude, relentless, school-yard-bully trouncing of pretty much everything they disagreed with. Others didn't merely have a different opinion. They were wrong. They were bad. There was anger and self-righteousness and why aren't you listening to me because I am right. Sarcasm had replaced hope. Cruelty and judgment had replaced empathy.

And what of the great hope of social media? Of technology? That it would bring us together? Sure, there were remarkable blogs out there. People were, in some spaces, connecting and growing and creating. But the hope that we would find common ground with strangers, people with whom we disagreed, that we would find a common humanity, see the truth that we are all the same, deep down, had failed. The technology was new. The traits and insecurities, the biases and anger and hatred that we brought to it were not. Technology hadn't failed. Humanity had.

This was not something we expressed, ever, to anyone. Because the assumption from people's Instagram pages and Facebook pages and Twitter feeds was that they lived rewarding, happy lives.

Look at Glen's goddamned vacation photos at the Grand Canyon! Look how annoyingly happy he and his beautiful family are! They're fucking perfect!

But, of course, what's not seen in Glen's vacation photos and iPhone videos, what's never seen, is the moment right after the photo, when Glen screamed at his teenage son, Jared, for hitting his younger sister, Missy, and making her cry, Glen overreacting and calling Jared a "little prick" and threatening to smash Jared's face in, Glen's wife, Mary Pat, reacting badly to this behavior from her dickhead husband, and also because she much preferred Jared to Missy, who had, in Mary Pat's mind, always been a problem child, Mary Pat shouting at Glen and the rest of the afternoon at the South Rim of the Grand Canyon ruined, everyone in a mood, wishing only to get back to the crappy motel, pack, get on the plane home, lock the door to their respective rooms, dive into their screens, to their solitude, to their own world.

The nation was angry. And it had a new and wonderful tool to express its anger.

Without realizing it, Ted had stopped walking and was staring up at the sky. Joggers made their way around the cinder track in the fading light, their footfalls making an earthy sound, a country sound. Quieter in here, the earth cooling, wisps of cold air circling up, the trees exhaling. Ted could hear his own breathing.

Screw the third lap. Time to get home, a hot shower. He'd order in from Five Guys, a treat to himself. Watch *Tinker Tailor Soldier Spy* for the fifth time. He was feeling good. His phone buzzed. It was Lou. Something about a video on the internet.

The quality of mercy, the English poet wrote, *is not strained; It droppeth as the gentle rain from heaven upon the place beneath.*

Maybe back in 1620s Stratford-upon-Avon that was a thing. But this was New York City, America, the World Wide Web, in 2016, and, well, the quality of mercy was indeed strained. It was broken, actually. It was a punch line on Comedy Central and a relentless stream of scathing tweets and comment sections. The quality of mercy didn't make for good ratings and, hey, someone had to pay, someone had to take the blame.

The quality of mercy no longer fell as a gentle rain. It slashed down like a toxic rain, like an acid rain, like a storm of shit upon the crown of whoever had the misfortune of making a mistake. Of having a bad day. Of being captured doing something selfish or rude or foolish. It didn't matter who you were. If you were in power all the better. If you were famous, then the masses were giddy. People like Ted? Rich, powerful, a white man in a world grown tired of their reign? Mercy? We think not. How about merciless? How about unrelentingly cruel and savage? Yes. Yes, that would do nicely.

Ted goes viral.

The emergency call involved Ted, Lou, several network lawyers, PR people, and Tamara Fine, the president of the network. The head of the twelfth floor, as they liked to say. Where the CEO sat. She'd been with the network less than a year. Prior to this she was head of Sky TV in London.

Most of the people on the phone felt that the situation was containable. The PR people—on a years-long retainer with the network that Tamara wanted to reevaluate—felt that initially the story would cause problems but it would ultimately blow over. Ted, they felt, was too much of an icon and had too much equity in the hearts and minds of TV-watching America.

Tamara listened as Ted explained what had transpired the evening of his meltdown, soaking in a bath in a $4 million home in Bronxville, a ritual before bed, holding her cell phone with one hand and a cold bottle of Sierra Nevada with the other. She was a good listener. She believed this was the secret to business. To life, really. She had taken an improv comedy class in college. Two people, standing on a stage, given a topic by the instructor. Go. The trick, she learned, was not to think of the answer while the other person was talking. The trick was to listen so carefully that the answer formed itself organically. Just listen, the instructor said. You'll find the answer.

So many people wanted to speak, to talk, forming their sentences while others spoke. Tamara listened and waited. But now, on this call, she listened and was bored because she saw how this ended. Movie watching was hard for Tamara. TV shows, too. She saw the plot points, saw the end, well before it came. She'd taken a first in maths at Cambridge and was fluent in French, Spanish, and Japanese. She'd been a competitive swimmer and still swam two mornings a week at the Field Club pool.

She lifted a wet leg out of the tub and admired the shape and tone of it. She briefly toyed with the idea of pleasuring herself but felt she should listen. She had a decision to make. Tamara's job, as she saw it, was simply this: to see into the future. To see what the world would be a month from now, a year from now. To read the landscape as it was being written and formed. To date in her career she had been exceptionally good at it.

What should she do, head of a large, plodding American network, an old-school newscast that was losing one million viewers a year but that still made substantial profits? Should she stand behind a man who'd been with the company for twenty-plus years, a loyal and valued employee, the face of the news division, the nightly news leader half a dozen years in a row? Should she mount a campaign of apology and support? Or should she realize that Ted's time was over, that the past meant nothing now, that he had committed a cardinal sin in the new world; he, a rich, famous, privileged person, had been caught on camera spewing his wrath.

She knew her answer. But she needed to wait for the emergency board meeting tomorrow. In the meantime, it was agreed that an apology was needed. Ted said he would write it. Tamara hung up, called Maxwell, her head of PR, and told him to draft one instead.

Murray was in early. He liked the office before the phones started ringing. The newswriting staff worked most nights until seven or eight, so most people didn't start arriving until nine or ten, unless they were on the morning show.

He sat with a large Dunkin' Donuts coffee, black, and read the paper versions of *The New York Times*, *The Washington Post*, and the *Daily News*, and, presently, the *New York Post*, which he leafed through quickly, holding its pages as if they might have dirt on them. In all of the papers he scanned headlines, read the first graph of a story, sometimes more, looked at the photos, read the captions. He saved the *Times* book review and crossword for lunch at his desk.

Papers finished, he should have begun work on a long piece they were preparing on an upcoming United Nations assembly. Instead he watched the video again. He'd seen it, of course. Everyone in the newsroom had the previous day, when it had broken. You heard it as you passed an edit bay, as you passed one of the kitchenettes. You heard it from a desktop or an iPhone. Reactions varied. Lots of men laughed. It was the clueless laughter of man-boys, of white guys, frat guys, former lacrosse players, men whose façades projected an All-American decency but whose deeper beliefs were far less attractive, especially about women.

Nice tits.

See that ass?

I'd fuck that.

Laughter all around.

They saw nothing wrong with these comments. So Ted let off a little steam. Lighten up. What's the big deal?

The three of them had watched it together. Grace, Jagdish, and Murray.

"This does not strike me as the Ted Grayson I know," Jagdish had said.

"We don't know the context," Murray had said, desperate to protect Ted.

Grace shot him a look.

"I'm just saying," Murray said sheepishly. "Maybe the girl . . ."

"Woman," Grace said. "She's a woman. Not a girl."

"Sorry. Woman. Did she say something to him, piss him off? We don't know the context."

"Maybe she was having her period, Murray. You know how annoying that can be for men."

"Oh my," said Jagdish.

"I'm just saying . . ."

"Why do you fight so hard for him and not her? Why do you assume she's to blame when he used those words?"

Grace didn't wait for an answer, though Murray didn't really have one. Not one he would ever share, anyway. His only answer was that he simply couldn't allow himself to believe that the Ted Grayson he had worshipped for twenty years would be capable of saying that.

So Grace worked on a story about Syrian refugees, Jagdish had wildfires in California, and Murray worked on his long piece about the UN. They spoke little the rest of the day.

Jagdish and Grace walked in together that morning and Murray briefly wondered whether they were having an affair but then recognized the thought for what it was: the thought of a jealous man who hadn't had a girlfriend in many years.

Murray looked up, his version of "Good morning."

Grace and Jagdish took off their coats and settled in, stared at their computer screens. Each went about their tasks, quietly tapping away at keyboards, cross-referencing facts, double-checking population numbers, casualty statistics, the spellings of names in Urdu, Hindi, Mandarin. The speed at which fire moves. The number of people a wooden boat normally holds, the amount of time a body can survive in fifty-eight-degree ocean water. Arcane, seemingly meaningless things that were the backbone of news. Unalloyed facts. Truth. The last stronghold of democracy. Or so Murray believed.

Murray was in the middle of writing this sentence—"While the Russian ambassador was later found to be drunk during his speech . . ."—when he looked up and said, "He made a mistake."

Grace and Jagdish looked up at him.

"What was that, Murray?" Jagdish said politely.

"He'll apologize," Murray continued, as if to himself, as if trying to convince himself, as if he hadn't been shocked by the video and deeply disappointed. "I heard talk . . . They're going to do an apology."

"That would be wise," Jagdish said. But Murray wasn't really talking to Jagdish. He needed Grace to make it right.

"Grace," Murray said.

"What?"

"It was a mistake."

She was staring at a spot on the floor. She stood suddenly. "I'm getting more coffee. Anyone?"

Jagdish shook his head.

"Grace," Murray said again, more urgently.

She turned and faced Murray.

"A mistake? Have you lost your fucking mind? I was on the phone with my sister last night, who urged me to quit in protest."

"Grace," Murray said. "Let's not overreact . . ." He knew it was a mistake, a poor word choice, the moment it was out.

"Don't you dare," Grace said, angry.

"I'm sorry . . . I didn't . . ."

Grace stared at him and said, "You have no idea what it's like to be a woman."

And she walked out.

It was Christmas morning at Fox News, CNN, MSNBC. The websites—TMZ, Vice, Huffington Post—were giddy. They'd caught a great white. Their anchors and bloviators, their consultants in psychology and sociology, on anger management, on brain trauma (a story that surfaced briefly claimed Ted had suffered a head injury years before during a car accident; although the story was totally without foundation, CNN reported it for seventy-two hours). They spoke with earnest expressions, exactly like Ted would have done had he been reporting on some poor sap who had made a mistake. They played their roles, one talking of how we can't rush to judge, the other talking indignantly about a nation's trust, about anger, about white privilege, about how we really know so little about people in power, about misogyny. They spoke with the surety of people who knew nothing.

Tamara woke early and went to the pool to do laps. So she missed Hal Winship on the first hour of the *Today* show. Some smart producer had gotten him in and there was Savannah Guthrie showing Hal the video of Ted on a large screen behind them and asking him the question "Should the anchor of a major network news organization speak this way?"

Before Ted sat in the chair, Hal Winship invented the chair. Hal invented the news. Hal was better in every way than Ted and his phony, coiffed colleagues. Hal was eighty-two with the hairline of a twenty-year-old. He was Harvard when Harvard turned out diplomats, philosophers, and presidents, not bankers and twerps who built websites.

He had covered everything. Moon landings and coups and assassinations and hijackings and armistices. Live. On the scene. No makeup or graphics or theme music. Just raw footage and skilled writing. Nothing but Hal and his chain-smoking producer, Leonard "Boots" Feeney, and a network that believed news mattered. Until it didn't believe it. Until the networks were taken over by corporations intent on packaging the news, profiting off the news, entertaining instead of informing, when they became obsessed with the three words that would be the ruin of civilization, according to Hal. Marketing. Advertising. Branding.

"No, he shouldn't," Hal said. "I have to be honest with you and tell you I think it's a disgrace. I don't know what's going on over there but I'm sure Mr. Grayson will apologize."

"Have you been in touch with Ted Grayson since this video came out?"

"I haven't. I'm retired and they don't really reach out to me anymore."

"If they did what would you say?"

"I'd say grow up. I'd say a real man never talks like this. I'd say beg this young woman's forgiveness and the forgiveness of your audience, especially the female viewers."

"Hal Winship. You're a legend and we thank you for being here this morning. Coming up, Al Roker introduces us to a hundred-and-two-year-old pogo stick champion. This is *Today* on NBC."

And Ted?

He had seen the video Wednesday evening, when he'd returned home for the emergency call. He had watched it, again and again, holding his hands against his forehead, as if trying to keep his brain from falling out. It was like he was watching someone else. He didn't remember it. He couldn't have said it. His voice, his face. It wasn't him, he wanted to say. If he could just explain. He had a bad night.

Within an hour there was a video trending on YouTube of Ted screaming at the girl, and Hal saying "It's a disgrace," all to a techno-funk beat.

.   .   .

You could watch the counter on YouTube by hitting refresh every few seconds. Forty-eight hours in and it was at more than two million views. By week's end it would be five million. The comments were unrelenting and savage. Some were sarcastic. Some were funny. Some suggested he should kill himself. By Wednesday the comments section would be disabled by YouTube customer service, in large part because a repeat commenter was threatening to kill Ted. The troll gave Ted's Bedford address. The Bedford Police Department put a patrol car in front of Ted's house.

Newspapers, the weekend newscasts, TMZ: all had stories. Someone from TMZ had gotten Ted's cell phone number and called, asked for an interview. He'd hung up.

It would go away, he told himself.

Simon Samson waited for Tamara to speak. But all she did was stare out the window.

For almost seven minutes he'd made his case on Ted's behalf. He'd brought numbers from the marketing department showing Ted's value to the network. He'd had Roy someone-or-other, the head of advertising, call around to some of the largest advertisers of the broadcast, among them Pfizer (Viagra), Eli Lilly (Cialis), Procter & Gamble (adult diapers division), and Johnson & Johnson (Imodium) to get them to write letters on Ted's behalf, about how they wouldn't pull sponsorship. The general reaction to this request being "Have you lost your fucking mind, Roy?"

Simon Samson was head of the news division and had been for almost twenty years. He'd been brought in at the end of Hal Winship's tenure and watched—after Hal's retirement—as the once-preeminent network news broadcast in America slowly went down the toilet with Hal's handpicked successor, George Beebe. George was a fine reporter but Hal had, in a rare judgment misstep, relied too much on the old-boy network, on a friendship, to put George in the anchor seat after Hal's remarkable twenty-eight-year reign.

Six months in, ratings plummeted. Simon was brought in to revamp the news division. He and Ted had worked together in Boston. He convinced the network to let George go and put Ted in. Young, handsome. They focus-group tested Ted and he did surprisingly well.

Simon had urged Tamara that the sound move was to run a carefully scripted and produced apology show. Not merely an apology at the end of the broadcast, but a program about Ted, where you saw him with Claire and Franny, where he apologized on camera to Natalia. Simon had not run this idea by Ted yet but, considering the alternatives, was confident he'd agree to it.

Simon had ended his talk (he'd been up late the evening before and had risen early this morning, scribbling notes, speaking aloud as he shaved) with something he believed in his soul. That Ted Grayson was the last of the great American newsmen, that he *mattered* to the eight million men and women who tuned in each evening, that he was a valuable part of their day. And if Simon could speak on a personal note, he believed Ted was a good man who messed up and simply needed forgiveness. We're a forgiving people, Tamara, Simon had said. If this had happened twenty years ago, the event would have been laughed about over drinks that evening, the poor intern or whoever was subject to a powerful white man's temper or ass grab, inappropriate comment or random erection, would be given a gift certificate to Keens Steakhouse and an autographed eight-by-ten glossy of Ted. Here, Simon smiled and tried to chuckle but it sounded as if he were choking.

Done, and rather satisfied with his speech, Simon sat back and waited. He was a man used to getting what he wanted.

Tamara had listened, looking at Simon from time to time but mostly looking out the window of her office, high above Midtown Manhattan.

"Do you know when I stopped listening to you, Simon?"

She turned and looked at him now.

"It was around the time when you were telling me what a great newsman Ted Grayson is. Do you know what I started thinking about instead? I was thinking about how you guys don't know the end of the movie. Now, I could tell you the end but I also don't want to ruin it for you. You have no idea what's outside waiting for you. I can't believe I'm sitting here listening to a middle-aged white man tell me that I should forgive another middle-aged white man who makes eleven million dollars a year and called a poor immigrant a Russian whore. You'll have to forgive me, but as a forty-four-year-old woman who for most of twenty years of her working life has endured comments about my tits, ass, face, and gender from people exactly like Ted, I think I'll give empathy and forgiveness a pass. I've personally used up all my forgiveness chits to men behaving badly."

Simon said nothing, though his mouth did open a bit involuntarily.

"Your expression suggests that wasn't the answer you were hoping for," Tamara said.

"Christ. A little harsh, aren't we?" Simon finally managed.

"Are we?" she snapped back. "If I had my way I'd cut him loose now, publicly, ugly. I'd distance myself so far from that kind of behavior that it would make your head spin. I'd have his seat filled and wave goodbye to his impotent, incontinent viewers and take the hit for a few months until they got used to the new male anchor's young handsome face or the new female anchor's remarkable legs, which we would showcase in most every shot, so that in six months' time people would say, 'Ted who? I think he died.'"

And for a moment Simon thought it was over.

"But unfortunately, despite my title, job description, and unusually large salary, I have a vagina, which in this board's view means I'm incapable of making a major decision. The board wants him to stay, by the slimmest of margins, I might add. They want the apology. And it better be fucking good."

The initial response to that evening's broadcast was positive. In Ted's ninety-second apology at the end of the broadcast, he spoke of the women in his life. Of Claire and Franny. "I am not merely a newsman. I am a husband and a father to a daughter. My words were ill chosen, offensive, and I deeply regret them."

Calls came into the network switchboard. Older women, mostly.

"I believe in Ted."

"If he were my son I'd wash his mouth out with soap and then give him a good dinner."

"We all make mistakes. My husband used to yell at me and we've been married forty years!"

But that small sampling wasn't the audience that mattered, the coveted golden children. The millennials, who had never and would never watch an evening news broadcast at 6:30 p.m. They were too busy staring at their phones.

No one had thought to reach out to Natalia.

The end was already happening. Ted just didn't know it yet.

A video had been posted on YouTube by "Dick Man 1989" that showed footage from the new Ted promos, except it had the music from the movie *Doctor Zhivago* and a spliced-together version of Ted saying, "You Russian whore . . . you Russian whore . . ." over and over.

What a lovely party.

Bhutan, Ted."

Diana was talking. Ted was fairly sure her name was Diana. She was the host of a charity event, an evening Ted did not want to be part of but which Claire had urged him to attend, in part to support her fund-raising leadership for the something or other, and, more important, Claire said, to put a good face on "us" and "you." They had not gone public with news of the divorce yet.

A small group of photographers, alerted by Claire's fund-raising committee (for the homeless, it turned out), had gathered at the head of the long driveway to Diana's home in Westport, Connecticut. What better way to fete the generous donors and bring awareness to homelessness than by hosting an exclusive event at a ten-thousand-square-foot home on three acres of waterfront property hugging Long Island Sound?

"How bad is this going to be?" Claire asked Ted in the car service from Bedford to Westport.

They were each looking out their own window.

"The party?" Ted said.

Claire waited.

"They've got it under control," he said finally, though he didn't believe they did. "They" being the network's PR team, working with external forces at blogs, websites, and news outlets.

Claire's legal team (which Ted was paying for) felt the timing of Ted's faux pas was ideal for their upcoming settlement hearing. "Goes to character, Claire," said her lead attorney, an angry woman who fake laughed a lot. "If he verbally abused this makeup woman, what did he do to you?"

What had surprised Claire when she finally heard the news, listened to her voicemail messages, spoke with Franny, turned on the TV, scanned the web, was her own reaction. Defensiveness. A need to protect.

She knew exactly what had happened. She'd bet a dollar ($20 million, actually, when the settlement was done) that he was in a mood that evening and snapped at the poor girl. He was many things, her husband. Annoying, cold, inconsiderate. He was depressive, moody, and controlling. But a misogynist he wasn't. She'd watched the video of his explosion and had never known him to use that word.

"Ted," Claire said, looking at him. He turned. She saw it on his face. She saw that he didn't think it was under control.

Claire's hair was down. He preferred it down. She had on a simple black dress, sexy shoes that looked expensive. Her lips were tastefully glossed and she wore For Her by Narciso Rodriguez. It was a scent she had worn for years. Ted had bought it for her, a long time ago, at Franny's suggestion.

"They're working on it," he said, looking out the window.

Ted sensed a softening in Claire. Maybe there was hope. Maybe her Englishman had disappointed her.

"You look very nice," Ted said. He didn't know he was going to say it.

"Thank you." She turned back to the window, embarrassed by the compliment. "You should be receiving the divorce papers early next week. Hoping we can sign soon."

Ted saw them as the car pulled closer to the long driveway. A police officer standing next to a motorcycle at the entrance. Maybe ten people, mostly women, holding signs, chanting.

"Ted must go!"

Ted and Claire watched, in a kind of slow motion, as the car turned into the driveway, the driver's window lowering, the noise of the protestors entering the car ("Shame on you, Ted Grayson!"), the singsong chant, the police officer looking in back, seeing who it was, nodding them in, the driver's window going back up, near silence, a look between Claire and Ted, Claire blinking fast, then back to their respective windows, not a word spoken.

"Bhutan," Ted repeated, staring at Diana. She was so thin. "How do you mean, exactly?"

They were standing inside a large white tent, three sides of which were closed, the fourth open to the Sound. Space heaters kept the place warm. Black-suited waiters offered hors d'oeuvres.

"It's the new 'it' place. Stunning. The people, the mountains, the culture. You and Claire should go. Everyone's going."

"Are you going?"

"I have no plans to, no. Why?"

"I just . . ."

"They have something called the Gross National Happiness. Isn't that adorable? Measuring happiness. We have something similar here in Westport. It's called Gross Miserable People." Here Diana winked. "Do you read *Departures*, Ted?"

"I don't know what that is."

Diana laughed too loudly and hit Ted on the arm, nearly spilling his drink.

"It's a magazine, you freak," Diana said. "American Express publishes it monthly. Do you have an American Express Platinum card?"

"Yes."

"Then you get it in the mail," Diana said.

"Oh. Sure." Ted still didn't know what she was talking about.

"I know the editor." Diana said this with the same gravitas she might have said, "I know Sting."

Ted made the face he felt Diana wanted him to make, nodding appropriately.

Diana continued to speak about *Departures* magazine and its editor and the stories it told about the places and hotels and experiences available only to the very rich. Ted managed to mute Diana's voice in his head and instead simply stared at her mouth moving.

Ted overheard snippets of conversation from different groups around him.

"A federal grand jury indictment . . . the man's going to prison . . ."

"They found a tumor on his rectum."

"He's heir to a Dijon mustard fortune."

He couldn't spot Claire. They had walked in together, smiling, each looking away from the other, Claire stopping to say hello to someone, dropping Ted for what Ted knew would likely be the rest of the evening. Ted had gone for the bar, where Diana cornered him.

A casual perusal of the fifty or so guests showed a fairly uniform group: white, middle-aged, attractive, fit, well-dressed, smiling, sexually devious, deeply wealthy, unusually successful. They were members of an elite club, a club to which they were desperate to belong and yet, here, now, to which each felt like an outsider.

"I keep them," Diana said.

Ted had forgotten what she was talking about.

"The magazines. I collect them. Keep them on the shelf. I think they're a wonderful reference for travel, food, fashion. Very beautiful."

Ted found this sad for some reason, a peek into Diana's empty life. But then, Ted thought, who was he to judge her happiness? What was he but a worthless piece of shit? The story wasn't going to be contained. This thought hit him full force, his brain releasing an array of chemicals causing him to feel mildly nauseated, cold, sweaty, tingly, afraid, and profoundly sad in a matter of seconds. He was getting texts from Simon. The initial small bump after the apology had worn off and now Ted was center stage on social media, naked, alone, and being beaten to death. No one was coming to his defense.

He took a large gulp of his champagne. Ted suddenly wished he could hold Diana, whisper to her, *You are good. You are beautiful. Love yourself.*

Diana smiled and said, "Ted likes the shampoo."

Ted was confused and feared she was commenting on his hair

and possibly his bald spot, though he couldn't imagine that she could see it over his advanced height. He suddenly hated Diana.

"The shampoo," she said, touching her glass to his. "The champagne. It's not just for breakfast anymore." She emptied her glass and winked.

"Oh, Ted," Diana said. "You'll have to excuse me. That's Leopold and Faustia Freudlich. And they gave vastly more than you." She smiled and hit Ted's shoulder, raising her eyebrows, flirting. "Don't go anywhere."

And she was gone, across the tent, a knower of names and where people's children had gone to college, of who was marrying and divorcing and moving and dying. A woman, in other words. Arms wide, welcoming the world and life experiences, showing up, trying. Whereas men—and perhaps it was just Ted—preferred to be left alone, at home, wandering the house, going from room to room, often standing in a room having forgotten the reason they'd walked in in the first place. This was called life over fifty for the American male. Why would you want to go out when there was a fridge full of sandwich fixings, cookies in the pantry, and a Bond marathon on Bravo?

Ted looked out over the party. He was alone now, the others paired off in conversation. He turned briefly back to the bar but realized he didn't want anything. Most times people approached him. He was, and had been for a goodly portion of the past twenty years of his life, the center of things. If he was in a room he was the focus of attention. Even in interviews with world leaders and rock stars. He was the one asking the questions, leading the conversation.

He should mingle, of course. This is what one did. He turned and mistakenly made eye contact with a couple he'd met before but whose names escaped him. They were wide-eyed and making a beeline for Ted, who, without realizing he was doing it, raised a finger and pointed to the water, though he had no idea why. He started walking away, smiling at them, watching as their smiles changed to confusion as he slipped behind the bar, beyond the tent, to the broad, lush lawn, toward Long Island Sound, where not another soul stood.

He walked and became aware of his own heavy breathing, watched as his polished shoes sank into the thick grass. He was reminded of ball fields, of running out to center field, running out to the twenty-yard line to start a game from scrimmage, the feeling of lightness and anticipation, the confidence of knowing he would play well, adjusting his cap, snapping his chin strap.

It stayed light later now. Still cool but a sense of spring in the air, the smell of the grass and the flowering trees, the colors of daffodils and crocuses. The sounds of the party faded and were replaced by the water hitting the rocks at the far edge of the property.

He stood and looked out over the Sound. What if he removed his clothes and waded into the water? He was a good swimmer. He imagined the shock of the water, temperature in the low forties at this time of year. His body would adjust. The stroke of swimming so natural and miraculous, moving through the water with grace and speed. The idea of running to the edge of the lawn and removing his clothes pleased Ted enormously. But here, quite suddenly, and for no reason he could think of, the image of his father lying in his last bed came to him. Ted winced at the image, his father's head leaning off to one side of the propped-up pillows, lips pursed, parchment skin pulled tight to his face, the beginnings of a skeleton. It was a hospice just outside Providence. This was ten years ago. Ted's mother had died the year before, his father never really recovering, alone in the house. He was a lifelong smoker who didn't believe in doctors and let the coughing go until it was far too late, when all they could do was give him a morphine drip. Ted and his younger sister, Susan, sitting in the room for days. Susan was going through her second divorce, drinking too much, as always.

Long days in a room with a dying man. Adjust his blanket. Place an ice chip under his tongue. Smooth his hair. Watch the nurses come and go. Notice the clock on the wall, the barely audible tick. Notice that time slows down. Ted would stand at the window and look out at a parking lot as he listened to his father's breathing, the long delay between labored inhales and exhales. How does a man's life come to this, to this place? There was a small closet in the room and the door was open and his father's pants were on a hanger. His pants and a check flannel shirt and an old beige cardigan and a heavy parka from L.L.Bean that Claire had sent him many Christmases ago. And his shoes. Scuffed brown shoes, size nine-and-a-half.

A job with the railroads. First New York & New Haven and later Boston & Maine. Assistant operations supervisor. Overnights to Worcester, Nashua, Portland, Bangor, Montreal. He would bring Ted model trains with the company's logo on the side.

"I run those," he'd say.

Later, as the railroads faded, his father was forced to accept a buyout and a reduced pension after their labor union lost a protracted court dispute. For a time, he tried cleaning-supply sales, traveling New England in a much-used Ford Falcon station wagon. He'd stay at Howard Johnson motor lodges, sitting in a booth alone in the evenings with a glass of beer and an evening newspaper, chain-smoking unfiltered Lucky Strikes. He'd bring back saltwater taffy for Susan and chocolate lollipops for Ted. They had horses on them. Cars. The Apollo missions. What were those evenings like, alone, a day with no sales, days when no one would see him, days when he'd leave a card, keep smiling, get back in the car, keep going. He never said, *I just don't find the work fulfilling. I'm thinking of taking a year off to find myself, do more yoga, maybe talk with a life coach.*

He should have been sitting next to him, holding his hand, talking to him. He just couldn't bring himself to do it. It felt like a bad movie. So he stood at the window and looked out. And that's where he was when his father died. With his back to him.

They buried him on a bitterly cold day in January.

Six months later, Susan—Zee, Ted called her, his nickname for her, or Zeebee—was swimming in Little Compton. She drowned. That's what the report said. She'd been captain of her high school swim team. An early swimmer. A little fish. Their mother put her hair in pigtails. This doe-eyed girl. Ted had driven to Rhode Island to identify her body. The memory caused Ted to cover his face with his hands, to rub his face as if to rub the image away.

It was this image that Claire saw when she looked over from the small group she was standing with, laughing, making small talk, feeling wonderful, feeling pretty and wanted and alive and hopeful for the first time in years. She saw Ted standing alone with his hands at his face and wondered if he was crying and for a moment, for just a moment, she felt herself start to go to him.

He turned and started back to the tent, hands in his pockets, head down, unaware he was being watched.

"You must know the Freudlichs, Ted."

Diana was back, thankfully. She popped a small toast point with a baby shrimp and pesto into her mouth, scanning the party.

"I don't know them personally."

"Leopold is a descendant of Archduke Franz Ferdinand. He grew up in Paris. They have a home there, in the Sixth. Do you know the Sixth, Ted? Of course you do. They live half the year there and half the year here. They have a place in the Carlyle. He's never worked a day in his life. He paints. She's a dominatrix."

"I'm sorry?"

"A dominatrix. She flies around the world. Very high-end clientele. She tried to show me the ideal blow job technique once using a peeled banana. But I was hungry and I ate the banana. What would Freud say, Ted?"

Diana chuckled.

"Doesn't her husband mind?" Ted asked.

"No. She bought more bananas. Ted, I should do stand-up. For Chrissakes, I'm joking. No, Leopold is gay. They've been together for thirty-five years. Best marriage I know."

"Sounds like Claire and me."

Here Diana raised her eyebrows. She looked like she was going to say something but stopped.

"Thank you for coming to this, Ted, especially considering your new status as feminist pariah. I joke. Also for your paltry donation.

Ten grand more would've killed you? Ted, they're poor. They're homeless. Do you find it hard, Ted?"

"Do I find what hard?"

"Dirty," Diana said, flirting smile. Ted was lost. "Caring," Diana said, switching gears fast. Ted said nothing.

"Your catatonic expression and weird silence tell me yes, you find it hard. Let me tell you what happens to me. I watch the nightly news. Not yours, by the way. The shootings. The racial divide. The refugees from the wars we ignore. The pain is overwhelming. What are we to do? With the information? With the outrage? Is voting enough? Throwing a lovely and perfectly planned fund-raiser? Because I don't think it is anymore. I feel like something fundamental is breaking. Now that could also be the recent change from Lexapro to Wellbutrin. I have this nonstop buzzy thing in my head. My question is this: Are we worse people than we used to be?"

Ted opened his mouth to respond, but Diana said, "Don't speak, Ted. You looked like you were going to speak and it was a rhetorical question. I think the ugly truth is that we've always been awful. Humans, I mean. Not just the rich. I'm funny, Ted. And I think you're partially to blame. You, the media. This new world we are living in? Every conceivable horrible image is at our fingertips, being pushed on you every minute of the day. You don't do news. You do horror. The nightly horror, with Ted Grayson. What is to be done? I am a woman of substantial means and I feel powerless. Should I tweet my outrage, Ted? Should I tweet it? I'm no Luddite. I like technology. But fuck Twitter. Toxic trash. I say that, I might add, as a substantial investor. Should I go on a TV show, on Fox, on MSNBC, and shout about it, go for cheap applause? Tell me what to do. Because most times, knowing I can do nothing . . . I drift. Ted, I was four pages into the devastating piece on reparations on *The At-lantic*'s website when a pop-up ad appeared for Fossil watches. Do you know what I did? I clicked on the ad, spent five minutes looking around the Fossil site, bought a beautiful messenger bag. That site led me to another site about handmade bicycles, which led to a story about a company that does high-end tours of Italy, which led me to book a trip next summer to Italy. Which I'm so excited about. How's Claire?"

Claire was a schoolgirl at a dance with the handsomest boy. Here, on the lawn, in a dress she loved, heat lamps under the white tent keeping the evening chill away. She had long ago buried any hope of feeling this way again. She was surprised to find it still there. Surprised at how wonderful it felt.

Claire had known Dodge was going to be at the fund-raiser. But she still felt the electricity in her when she saw him. This secret of theirs. She would conduct herself as she always did. She'd simply stand in this small group, chatting, feeling Dodge's eyes on her. The way it made her stomach tingle, the tips of her fingers. She felt like someone in a novel, a Virginia Woolf novel, the young girl having the affair. Which one was that? *Mrs. Dalloway*, maybe. Or Tolstoy. She was Anna. Dodge was Vronsky. The illicit affair, being wooed by this dashing man, slowly succumbing to it, as Claire had. Not looking for it. Telling her suitor no, in fact, that she was a woman of high ideals who refused sordid things. But the attraction was too powerful. Anna's/Claire's awful husband. Count what's-his-name. Older and unattractive, though Claire still found Ted annoyingly and effortlessly handsome.

Had she been a good wife? She asked herself this from time to time. Had she played any role in the marriage's ultimate ruin? Could she have reached across the divide? At her angriest, she was sure it was entirely Ted's fault. But late at night, not quite sure of herself, she wondered if she weren't at least partially to blame, if she hadn't superimposed her ideals of what he should be, ignoring the things he was. No. Wait. This was getting away from her. Also, didn't Anna throw herself under a train at the end, after ruining most everyone's lives? She was thinking about Anna under the train, furrowing her brow, when she saw Ted and Diana strolling across the lawn toward their little group. This couldn't be. Diana wouldn't do that. Wait. Yes, she would, the tramp, the slut. Claire could see it all on Diana's face. Were Diana and Ted having a thing? She knew Diana would but, somehow, she also knew that Ted wouldn't. Yes, he'd had flings, but she knew they meant nothing to him. Why was she standing up for Ted's flings? Diana and Ted were ruining Claire's reverie. She closed her eyes, tried to retrace the path, to find that good feeling from a moment ago. It was gone. Claire looked over at Dodge, who was looking at her. He had a smile on his face, a man in love.

"Is that him?" Diana asked, looking past Ted.

"Who?" Ted asked.

"The man she's leaving you for."

Ted stared at Diana before he turned and followed Diana's gaze. There, across the lawn, under the white tent, in a group of six people chatting harmlessly, Claire among them, Ted saw him.

"Dodge Ramsey," Diana said. "Some kind of international

lawyer. He's a lord or something. A viscount, whatever that is. Has his own plane. But then, who doesn't?"

Ted watched his soon-to-be-ex-wife gaze at her boyfriend and it was so clear, so startlingly obvious, that she loved him. Ted felt a wave of jealousy and anger. Dodge looked happy. *He's happy, Ted.* He was smiling and talking and he was the center of the conversation, people laughing at his witty stories.

"Poor Ted," Diana said.

Ted turned to see Diana staring at him.

"How long have you known?"

"A bit."

Diana's eyebrows went up like a cartoon. "Bit late to the story, aren't we, Captain Anchor Boy?"

Ted didn't know what to say.

"C'mon," Diana said. "Let's have some fun. Let's see how awkward we can make this."

She slipped her arm through Ted's and led him over to the group.

"Who needs a drink?"

It was Diana. She had Ted and a waiter in tow, the waiter holding a tray with flutes of champagne.

Ted shook hands with two men who smiled and both said it was nice to see him again and yet Ted had no memory of ever having met them. He air-kissed another woman who also seemed to know him well and then shook Dodge's hand, which seemed quite strong. He didn't know what to do with Claire, whether to kiss her, shake her hand, or ignore her.

As the waiter left, there was a moment, just the briefest time, when the air was wonderfully thick with tension. And it had nothing to do with Claire and Dodge. It had everything to do with Ted. Ted and his video. He felt it in the way that they didn't look at him and instead examined the grass as if they were turf specialists. But Diana was too expert at working a room to let the awkwardness last.

"He's going to ban the immigrants and cut off Medicare for the elderly now. What do we think? What are we going to do?"

A few of them turned to Dodge, who had a wry smile on his quite handsome face.

"We were just talking about that," said the woman. Ted felt he ought to know her name. Jane. Jan. Pam. One of those.

"Dodge is a human rights lawyer," Claire added, looking at Dodge.

"A small cog in a large wheel," Dodge said with Hugh Grant charm and posh public school accent.

"What about you, Ted?" Dodge asked. "How do you see the situation? As a newsman, I mean."

Ted blanked. He blanked and wondered if Dodge was asking about the Syrian refugee crisis and the battle for Aleppo or about the evacuation of Muslim women and children in mountain towns in northern Afghanistan. Or was it Nigeria and the ethnic slaughter by Boko Haram, the long lines of women and children on dirt roads there? Or the civil war in Myanmar? Or South Sudan? Or the Democratic Republic of Congo? Or Donbass, Ukraine, where more than ten thousand fatalities had occurred? He didn't know. They had done so many stories lately and now they were all washing together for Ted, the colors and textures and faces and locations and details fading into one another. This from a man who once prided himself

on names and dates and history. Now he read the words on the
prompter. He then turned it over to the reporter on the scene. Or
was it the Somali civil war? Maybe Aleppo. He just kept thinking of
the word "Aleppo" and the images of a seemingly endless stream of
humanity walking along the road to nowhere. Also, hadn't they done
a series of stories lately on poverty in Guatemala? Ted was blinking
quickly. He knew he needed to say words, that words needed to
come out of his mouth.

"I think we've only seen the start."

Ted hoped this was vague enough to keep the conversation going, though the confused expressions suggested otherwise.

Dodge, English grace at the ready, rescued Ted. "I think that's
exactly right, Ted. I would add, though, that . . ."

And here Ted tuned Dodge out. Why was it that lately, a man
who had made his living talking, easily and fluently and intelli-
gently, was finding simple speech so difficult?

For a time, Ted had tried to read, to keep up with the important
books, fiction, nonfiction, the biographies. He had, long ago, been a
reader of *The New York Review of Books*. They still arrived at the
house and were stacked in a neat pile by Rosa, their cleaning lady.
But Ted almost never read them. Nor *The New Yorker*s, *The Atlantic*s,
*The Economist*s. The piles grew, stress-inducing symbols of his lazi-
ness, his intellectual wanting. With each Netflix series and each
SportsCenter, he fell further and further behind, a man who had faded
in a race, miles behind, the energy gone. He also found he simply
had no attention span. The books were too depressing, too long, too
boring. They sapped him of hope. His concentration had waned,
especially in the evening, after a glass of wine, an internal drifting

mechanism took over his operating system. He watched sports. He rewatched movies he'd already seen.

The breeze must have shifted because Ted caught the smell of the ocean. It caused him to turn his head and look out at the water. Ted had wanted to buy in this area. They'd found an old house in Southport that Ted loved. But Claire had preferred Bedford. Which was probably just as well. This area had become, to Ted's mind, an unholy place, once a quaint artist town now soiled by the moneyed vultures of private equity. Ted did not express these thoughts to anyone, certainly not his hosts, who were now feeding him truffles, which Ted found exceedingly delicious. Ted found himself smiling, which his drinking companions took to be a sign that he found Dodge's good-natured ribbing funny. Ted had, in fact, missed a good forty-five seconds of conversation and wry commentary from Dodge. And now everyone was smiling and looking at Ted waiting for a response.

"Well, Ted?" the woman next to him said, smiling. "Dodge wants to know. Are you mad as hell?"

Ah, yes. Howard Beale. *Network*. I'm mad as hell and I'm not going to take it anymore. The lunatic anchorman.

"No," Ted said finally to Dodge, trying for lighthearted, but hearing an edge in his voice. He looked at Claire, who was staring at him, wide-eyed, worried.

"Surely, though, Ted. There must be evenings during your show when you just want to scream or tell the real truth." It was Dodge.

Ted found himself blinking more quickly, felt his nostrils flare. Who was this little shit to tell Ted what he thought? Yes, Ted was a roiling ball of gastric goop inside, but he was still Ted Grayson, still the man who had sat across from presidents, dictators, and terrorists and challenged them in interviews, thanks to Lou's questions and Ted's hard stare (two-camera interviews, so they could get Ted's stare).

"I think we do just fine," Ted said.

Dodge was clueless and on the edge of a good drunk and plowed ahead.

"Prescient, though, *Network*. No?"

"How so?" Ted asked, instantly regretting it, seeing the fat softball down the middle of the plate he'd just lobbed.

"Why . . . the end of network news, of course. News as entertainment. The vaunted anchorman now a relic of a bygone era, a time long ago when people actually cared about what you said."

Dodge smiled, enormously pleased with himself and this splendid party, his plane, perhaps the thought of Claire's marvelous rump. He gulped at his drink.

Really? You pompous English twat. Twenty-two million Americans watching one of three networks every night. Ted nodded, smiling, finding his calm.

"I remember who you are now," he said, smiling at Dodge. "You're the man who's fucking my wife."

He had him. Ted had him. The small group reeled. Claire closed her eyes. The woman next to Ted gasped.

But Dodge . . . Dodge never broke his easy smile, his English charm.

"Well, yes," Dodge said. "Yes, that's right. But then, someone had to."

It was Diana who laughed out loud.

．　　■　　■

Diana stood with Ted in the driveway, waiting for an Uber, smoking a cigarette she'd bummed off the waitstaff.

"Well played, old sport."

Ted couldn't tell if Diana was serious or not. She took a deep drag, held it, then released the smoke from her nostrils, a seasoned smoker.

"You think it's over, don't you? Your . . . life."

She wasn't looking at him. She was looking across the lawn, toward the road. It was quiet now; the hum of the party seemed a long way away. Ted had lent Diana his sports coat to fend off the night's chill.

"It's not," she said. "This is what it is for people like us. The money. The . . . stuff and the houses and the . . ." She trailed off. "How do you explain to people that none of it means a thing?"

She took a deep drag.

"He fucks other people," she said, as if to herself, looking out over the lawn. "All the time."

She turned now and looked at Ted. "What's wrong with you guys?"

Her voice was different. Lower. It wasn't trying so hard.

"We give you *every*thing. Children. Our body. Our love. And you treat it like it's . . . like it's nothing."

And here her voiced cracked, on the word "nothing." And it seemed as if she was doing everything she could not to cry. She snorted, flicked the cigarette across the stone driveway, widening her eyes, looking up to the night sky, to the stars, to the hope of an answer.

Diana wrapped Ted's coat tighter around her. She was an actress backstage, after the play had ended, tired from the week's performances, almost herself again, but part of her left on the stage, as if a bit diminished.

She took a deep breath. And in doing so it was as if she reverted back to something. Someone. Ted wondered what it would be like to really know Diana.

"She's gone, Ted. You fucked it up. But you'll be fine. It's not like you're a hedge fund manager who actually did real harm. Or a lying politician. I mean, what did you do? You called someone a Russian whore. If I had a nickel for every time I did that in a day . . ."

Diana looked at Ted and he had the distinct impression that she was deciding whether or not to suggest a room next week, midday, at the Four Seasons.

A black Cadillac Escalade pulled into the long drive, the tires crunching along the gravel.

Ted said, "Why aren't we happy?"

Diana looked at Ted for a time, a half smile on her face, as if trying to figure out if Ted was serious.

"Sweet Ted. You really are lost, aren't you? Only a buffoon or a morning talk show host asks that question. This is America. We're lucky, not happy. We're rich, which is better than happy, better than everything. We're healthy. Look at my teeth, Ted. It's like a perfect photo of teeth. Cost me thirty-five thousand dollars. Happy? I mean . . . that's like asking if there's a God. Here's what I know. I don't care for abstracts. I like a planned day. So tomorrow late morning I'm getting on a private jet and flying to Telluride to meet my perennially erect husband, who will have 'secretly' had sex with his twenty-two-year-old assistant. We'll ski. The kids will do what they do. Smoke pot, copulate with similarly spoiled private school teenagers, stare at their phones as if they were the face of Jesus incarnate. Happy? What a funny little man you are. But with the help of prescription medication and a small handful of made-up stories I tell myself in the moments before sleep, I stay sane."

The driver got out, opened the back door for Ted. Diana handed him back his sports coat.

She snorted. "'You're the man who's fucking my wife.' Why can't you tell the truth like that on your little newscast? You'd be a star."

#TEDGRAYSONISAWHORE

The world continued to make news and Ted continued to report on it each evening. But his own world was closing in. He was becoming the story.

Protestors had begun appearing in front of the network headquarters in Midtown. At first, when the story broke, it had been a small group of mostly women, a few signs. But a movement had grown. Dozens of protestors arrived each morning. They had created a website with a GoFundMe page. Volunteers showed up by the busload and set up tables and hot coffee and donuts. Building security, at the network's behest, had tried to disperse the crowds and force them off the sidewalk but that backfired spectacularly when a guard pushed a young woman too hard, the woman slipping and falling on the sidewalk, opening a small cut on the back of her head that required stitches. The young woman was fine, but the video and still photos that followed—Ted's large head in a split-screen with the young woman with blood on her face—simply poured gasoline on the already growing fire.

The head of the National Organization for Women urged a boycott of Ted's newscast, launching #TEDGRAYSONISAWHORE.

The Russian Consulate in New York issued a strongly worded statement demanding an apology from Ted and Ted's network, saying both had defamed Russian women.

Rachel Maddow did an entire show on Ted, expanding the subject to misogyny, the power struggle between men and women, female pay inequality, and the continuing danger white men posed to women and society as a whole.

The *New York Post* ran unflattering photos of Ted, face contorted, with headlines like this: SKANCHOR MAN; TED MAN WALKING; and, somehow finding a photo where it looks like Ted is laughing, HO, HO, HO!

A new episode of *South Park* had a newscaster character named Fred Whiteman yelling at a blind nun, tripping the woman, and stealing her Bible.

Advertisers were being urged by some groups to boycott Ted's newscast. They met in hastily called meetings, high above Manhattan's filthy streets, behind closed doors, trying to assess the PR risk in being associated with Ted's broadcast versus the benefit in reaching a wonderfully impotent, incontinent audience. Morality versus money. It was an easy call. Corporate America stayed with Ted.

At *scheisse*, Franny sat in meetings to discuss what stories they were focusing on. She listened as people talked about "Ted Grayson." People in her group covering it, writing about it, researching Ted's life. She didn't know what to do, to say. A story formed in her mind. She knew how to tell it. She knew all the facts, all the players, the timeline. It was the story of her life. Ultimately, of course, she said nothing. She stopped going to meetings. She wrote her stories. And as luck would have it, an NFL player had been caught on video pushing down women and children while trying to escape a false fire alarm in a Las Vegas hotel. So, there was a good story for a week or so.

If only he hadn't taken the anchor chair. He blamed Claire. Of course, he blamed Claire for everything bad, including Pearl Harbor, the Kennedy assassination, and any time he burned his mouth on hot soup. Claire was to blame.

Ted had told himself the story that Claire had wanted him to take the job. Fame, money, entrée into the world of Claire's money-eyed West Hartford people. Claire a third-generation Miss Porter's girl. But that was bad reporting. Check the facts, Ted.

The affiliate in Boston had given way to a job in Washington, where Ted covered the Pentagon. He and Claire had rented a Federal-style town house on P Street in Georgetown. It had a run-down, musty charm. The fireplace worked and Claire loved having a fire in the evening. After Franny's bath, Ted would come home and the three of them would sit close to the fire, Franny in her pajamas, the kind with the feet in them, a zipper up the front, her plump, round body, bath-smelling body plopped in her father's lap.

Ted remembered the night he came home and told Claire. He was later than usual and Franny was asleep and Claire was roasting a chicken in a Le Creuset they had received as a wedding present. Claire's comfort meal. "I was thinking of roasting a chicken," she'd say. It meant family. Ted hadn't known what a Le Creuset was and made fun of it, referring to it when Claire mentioned dinner. "Will it be in the Le Creuset?" Ted would ask, needling her. "You know I must have it in the Le Creuset, otherwise I can't eat it."

He asked about Franny. Claire told the small stories of the day, the things Franny had said, interactions with someone at the supermarket, at the dry cleaner's. She had been an early talker, blurting out whatever came to her mind, obsessed with all things pink. "I like your pink pants!" she'd yell to a woman in line at a coffee shop.

Ted listened with a smile on his face. He would sneak into her room when he went upstairs to change out of his suit, peek in on her, put his face close, smell her skin, her breath.

Ted kept a bottle of Stolichnaya vodka in the freezer and took it out, poured himself a small glass. He poured Claire a glass of white wine. He always waited with personal news. He held it, drew it out, the surprise of it. He knew and Claire didn't and in that knowing he felt something exciting. Maybe that's what had drawn him to news, to the knowing of a thing when so many didn't.

"I talked to Simon today," Ted said as casually.

"You talk to Simon every day," she responded, sautéing green beans.

"They're moving George out of the chair."

George Beebe, Hal's replacement.

Claire looked up. "What? Why?"

"Bad ratings."

"But it's only been six months. What do they expect after Hal?"

Hal Winship's thirty-year tenure as the most trusted man in America had come to an end the previous year. George Beebe was Hal's handpicked successor. A good man and a fine reporter, he was an unfortunate choice for the anchor desk. He had a crippling fear that the teleprompter would go down and blinked so often that the network routinely received calls wondering if George was having a stroke.

"It's New York. They want ratings, not news."

"That's a shame."

"Yup."

"Who are they replacing him with?"

"They've offered it to me."

If one went back, if one could go back, could somehow look at a life, a marriage, and see the plot points, the X-ray on the light box, then one could see this moment as the beginning of the end. This, to Claire's mind years later, was the moment Ted began to change.

"Are you kidding?" Claire asked. "You're not kidding, are you?"

"No," he said, trying to suppress a smile.

"What . . . how did it . . . ?"

"Simon came by at lunch. Said he was taking me out. Said George just wasn't cutting it. That they'd focus-group tested me and that I'd done really well. Like, really well. And they wanted to offer me the chair. It's a one-year contract worth five hundred thousand dollars. And if it goes well . . . there's more."

Ted's salary at the time had been $85,200.

Claire was confused. She wanted to be excited for him but she needed to understand the change. He loved being a reporter. He loved the work and the writing. The chair wouldn't be that.

"Are you sure this is what you want?"

"It's the chair," Ted said, wide-eyed, smiling. "You know how many guys would kill for this?"

"I know. I think it's great. I just ... you'll be reporting less."

"I'll be able to do both. Special assignments, things like that. And it's New York, Claire."

She hugged him. Or rather, he hugged her. A huge bear hug, picking her up off the floor.

The phone rang. It was someone from the network. This was another plot point, another shadow on their marriage X-ray. Their little bubble of a family, their small world and needs, just each other and time, a chicken and some wine, some strained carrots and time to talk and be, was slowly, imperceptibly, being taken away. A small fissure. But they couldn't see it ...

After the move to New York, they talked about a brother for Franny. But she'd learned with Franny that she had a unicornuate uterus. Only one fallopian tube worked. Much scarring from the first pregnancy. A doctor on the Upper East Side told them their chances were extremely slim but that she'd had success with a procedure she'd pioneered. They met with doctors, in vitro specialists. It was exhausting and expensive and unromantic.

But again, it didn't happen. A year, two, three. Coming home from work midmorning to have sex, bright winter light showing every blemish on their bodies, faces turned away from each other, trying to concentrate, Claire desperate for it to work.

Ted closed his eyes, imagined women from the office, pictures from dirty magazines and websites. But he felt guilty doing this. And really, all he had to do was look at Claire, at her lovely face. "Kiss me," he always said, in the moment before he could no longer hold back. He whispered it, embarrassed at the need for something so seemingly unmanly ... so ... he didn't know the word. Claire knew. And kissed him, deeply, passionately. Knew she had that power over him.

It was a boy.

The months during the pregnancy, the planning, the euphoria of finally getting pregnant, changed Ted, Claire thought. He was softer, more caring. When she got up at night to pee, he bolted up. "What's wrong?" he'd ask. The way a pregnancy alters your worldview. Names considered and discarded and finally settled upon. You think about the person, what he will look like. It will do her good, Ted and Claire thought. A brother to care for, to share attention with, fight with, watch cartoons with. They will have bunk beds. Franny had trouble going to sleep. She was afraid of the dark, needed a nightlight, the door opened all the way. Ted and Claire had to keep their door open, too. She had an owl that played music, soothing piano music, on a loop. Over and over it played as she lay there, struggling to relax. Ted would sneak up and watch her sometimes, his heart breaking at this small person struggling so mightily with life.

Claire never looked more beautiful than when she was pregnant. Her coloring was high and healthy in her cheeks. Her breasts swelled and she liked the way her body looked, fully female.

Ted was nine minutes from going live when his phone rang. It was Nancy, Claire's friend.

"Ted. She's fine, but she lost the baby."

Ted did the news, though he remembered little of it, then drove to Westchester Hospital and brought Claire home. She sat holding Franny, silent, tears running down her face. She wouldn't eat. Ted put her to bed, put Franny down. It was raining. He walked around the house and checked the doors and windows, the small leak in the guest bedroom he'd caulked the previous spring.

He sat up for a long time, looking out the window, listening to the rain, sipping a chilled vodka. Claire's ob-gyn had come by the hospital room. She said, "The baby wasn't viable. He wasn't ready to be born."

Walter. They were going to call him Walt.

Save the date for the ten-year reunion!

It was Franny's idea to go away to school.

After the move from D.C. to New York. Then the move to Bedford and private school there. By then she was seeing a therapist twice a week, taking fifteen milligrams of Lexapro, and not talking to Ted. The more they reached out to her the deeper she seemed to disappear into herself. Sometimes it felt like other people were tuned to a very low volume and she couldn't turn it up. Her brain ran a constant interference, like a foreign government scrambling a channel. Nobody knew her. Not really. Not deep down, not what she felt and thought, who she was. The anger seemed to come from nowhere, overtook her.

She tried not to let others see that side of her. Not at school. Not at squash. Not at parties that she began getting invited to. She was pretty and fit and a cool kid. True, she would sometimes break a squash racket, swear on court. But she won most times. Her coach felt she was fiery. Other players thought she was a psycho (their word). The tantrums turned into more. Hitting her parents. Throwing a shoe across a room, scratching herself until she bled. She was twelve when they began losing control of her.

■   ■   ■

Sometimes a person had patience. Sometimes you could find it within yourself, after a long day, to sit and listen, to withstand the storm of screaming and thrashing, the hitting. Withstand the umpteenth door slam, withstand another tempest, yet another evening ruined. You tried. The therapists for her. The family sessions. The schools. The camps. The nights of talking with Claire about it. But the more you tried, the further away she seemed to go. The therapist said it was the opposite, that she hated herself. That she desperately needed her parents and that what she was really feeling was a profound anxiety and fear, bordering on terror. So you tried harder. But the job, the responsibilities of it, the travel, the nights and weeks away, at exactly the time she needed you most.

Sometimes a person had patience. And sometimes you didn't.

Sometimes you said, *You miserable, spoiled brat.*

Sometimes you said, *What in God's name do you want from us?*

Sometimes . . . no . . . no, that couldn't have happened . . . you said . . . no . . . you must have imagined it. But you said it.

One night, in the seemingly perfect home in the quaint town, the European cars safely in the driveway and the doors locked and the fireplace going and the house cleaned by immigrants and the good Bordeaux breathing and her iPod and MacBook Pro blinking and her squash outfit washed and folded and her backpack ready and her trip to France for the summer with friends planned, she screamed again and again and the house was a terror zone and Claire was trying to calm her but occasionally shouting herself and Ted trying but out of gas, out of patience, images of his own upbringing in Woonsocket, his own parents, how hard they worked and provided, never complaining, and here was his own daughter, his mother's granddaughter . . . screaming *I hate you I hate you I hate you* . . .

"Oh yeah?" Ted said, too loud. "Well, guess what, I hate you, too."

And the house went quiet. And Claire put her hands over her face. And Franny stared, mouth hanging open. Because the therapist was right. She hated herself and feared she wasn't lovable. So she pushed and pushed and tried to make it come true. And she knew, in that moment—even if it was just a moment—that he meant it.

Ted tried. Until he didn't. He started working later, traveling more. Often, by the time the broadcast was over, after they'd prep for the next day, a dinner or drinks, he'd opt to stay in the city at an apartment the network rented for him.

But there were many nights when he simply didn't want to go home. When he didn't want to deal with Franny, fight with Claire. Where he simply wanted to retreat to the apartment, change his clothes, wash his face, and open a cold bottle of beer. He'd watch a Rangers game. Make a bologna sandwich. He didn't know what to do with her. So he did nothing. He thought that would be the least harmful thing.

Ted missed all of the meetings with the therapist. That's how Franny saw it. In truth, Claire and Ted had met with the therapist, who had suggested that it might be more productive if Ted not be in the family sessions. Franny's anger was so complete that she would likely shut down if Ted were in the room.

Her father's lack of attention was a gift. It prepared her for her teenage years, the fumbling emotions of other kids. She may have been a mess inside, but she learned to maintain a steely face to teachers, bullies, opponents on the court.

There was talk of Bedford High School but Claire had her sights set on New Canaan Country Day School or Greenwich Academy. Ted wondered aloud why they were paying $42,800 a year in property taxes for a school system they didn't use. This struck Claire as insensitive and Franny as typical of her father.

Franny's friend Emma Beckett had started at Northfield Mount Hermon the year before and loved it. Claire was against it, felt she wanted to keep Franny close. It was Ted, to Franny's surprise and then dismay, who thought it a good idea. Franny's main goal in life was to get her father's attention by doing things he didn't want her to do. She questioned any idea he agreed with. But leaving was too strong a pull. She had to get out of the house, to get away from her parents, whose only desire was to help her.

She hated it. Hated every minute of it. She was profoundly homesick but couldn't bring herself to admit that. She discovered the great joys of smoking pot and music she'd never listened to before, the Grateful Dead and the Jam and the Smiths and Simon & Garfunkel and when it was very late and her roommate was asleep she would put her headphones on and listen to Vince Guaraldi's version of "Moon River" and cry herself to sleep.

■ ■ ■

Junior year. Scott Landau. His great-grandfather had started Stride
Rite shoes. Scott played hockey and acted like a person who knew
that money could buy you out of anything. He turned Franny on to
cocaine. Just once in a while. Nothing serious. A few lines. Sometimes more. Also Ecstasy, which Franny thought was quite pleasant.
Again, not all the time. Not, like, a problem or anything. Special
occasions. All-night drives to New York City and a room at the Bowery Hotel or Soho House, where his father was a member. Friends of
Duncan's from Dalton and Horace Mann, rich kids, parties at absent
parents' apartments on Park Avenue, in the Hamptons. It felt like
touring with the Rolling Stones. It felt too good to let it stop. The
dopamine surge, warm and happy. The serotonin kick that elimi-
nated the need for food or sleep, everything and everyone alive and
sexual and there for the taking. The downside being the fall after it
wore off. Nausea, chills, headache. The feelings of paranoia, distrust
of people, and fear of your surroundings. Though at this particular
time in her life, she felt that way most days stone sober.

She woke up vomiting more. She missed Work-Job. Everyone at
Northfield had a Work-Job and you couldn't miss it. It was the one
decent thing her roommate did for her. Lie and punch her in on
those mornings she couldn't get in, after a long night, those bitterly
cold western Massachusetts winter mornings; when to have to make
pan after pan of scrambled eggs, pancakes, bacon, was out of the
question. Lauren someone. She was clingy and a little weird but she
seemed to care about Franny. Franny had woken up one night to
find Lauren staring at her.

One night . . . no, more than one night . . . she passed out, waking in a half-conscious state, with Duncan on top of her, one of Duncan's friends laughing.

Would Franny Grayson come to the reunion?

These thoughts crossed Lauren's mind as she crafted a witty invite for the reunion for the class of 2006 from the Northfield Mount Hermon School. She knew from Facebook and Instagram that Franny worked at some kind of website.

As for Lauren, she was a social worker who helped run a not-for-profit clinic in Greenfield, Massachusetts, for families in crisis. She also took an Armenian folk dancing class every other Tuesday evening in the basement of the Armenian church, though she herself was not Armenian but a New York Jew, a line that always got her a laugh at parties. She ran road races and 5Ks in the foothills of the Berkshires and once did a Tough Mudder with a group of friends to raise money for the clinic.

She had loved NMH. Loved the clean life, the outdoors and the sports, the healthy people and open attitude, the acceptance. Sure, there were cliques but that was any school. After Harvard (Divinity, honors), she returned to Northfield to work as a residence counselor. The time there, both as a student and as a counselor, had formed her. She'd found a sense of place and belonging. Which was why she sat in front of her computer in her office at 7:30 on a Tuesday evening in March. It was cold out, the last hints of light in the western sky. Ahead of her an evening alone at home with Peepers, her cat, and *American Idol* and a book and possibly a burrito of her own making. On paper that might seem lonely to some. Not Lauren.

Though with the cursor blinking at her, taunting her, it did, for a moment, seem a bit sad.

No. No, it wasn't sad. I'm doing fine, she thought. I have my books here and my motivational apps and my stuffed animals. Yes, some of my colleagues make sarcastic comments. Yes, I try too hard sometimes, come on too strong, get asked by people to give them space. If that's the worst you can say about a person then I'd say that person is doing all right. And yes, maybe a person sits in their car at night and watches a colleague through their window. Just to see them, to feel connected to them, to know what their life is like. A few times. A half a dozen times. Maybe more. People do that. Don't they?

Lauren opened Franny's Google image page. Photo after cool photo of Franny at parties and art openings and galas, speaking on new media at TED NYC. She hadn't aged. She just looked prettier, had nicer clothes. She looked like someone in a movie. Her middle name was Ford. Frances Ford Grayson.

Lauren hoped Franny would attend. They hadn't been close but to Lauren's mind they had been friends. They talked. Well, Franny talked, Lauren listened. So much drama. So much going on. It had been a hard time for Franny. So angry, all the boys, the drugs. She'd met her beautiful mother a few times and even her famous father. Just once, that terrible snowstorm. Maybe time had softened her. Maybe they could be friends. A kind word. Something small. Anything.

She wanted to strike the right tone. She didn't want to be made fun of. She didn't want to be rejected. She just wanted people to come back in June, when the weather was so lovely in western

Massachusetts, when the lawns would be lush green, freshly mown, when the campus would be quiet, the kids gone, the dorms used for alums. She attached a link to their class's NMH Facebook page, where people could comment on whether they were coming, and hit send.

Frances, we have an assignment for you.

They sat in Henke's office: Henke, Franny, and Toland. Glass walls on three sides, views to the open floor plan, employees plugged in, headphones on. Out the windows, views of the West Side Highway, the Hudson River, New Jersey in the distance.

Franny didn't know Toland would be there. Toland Figg, New Media Guru. That was her title. Toland was partial to formfitting skirts, tall leather boots that looked expensive, and snug agnès b. sweaters. A collection of noisy bracelets, all silver, on her left wrist, maybe fourteen of them. You heard Toland coming before you saw her. Very little makeup, her high coloring and unusually blue eyes enough of a palette. She did like shiny lips, though, Franny noticed. Long stunning blonde hair that she played with often. She'd previously worked at the William Morris Agency in Hollywood and seemed to know everyone. She had a law degree from Stanford, had briefly directed (rare for a woman) and been nominated for an Academy Award (though it was in documentary shorts, so no one really knew or cared). She was thirty-six or possibly fifty-four. It was impossible to tell without an MRI.

Rumor was that Henke never made a major decision without

Toland weighing in. Rumor also had it they slept together, though most found it idle gossip, as they felt Toland was simply out of his league. Henke was Germanic, blondish (though he frequently dyed his hair bright colors), squat, muscular, but it was gym-bought. He was not a natural athlete, moved with none of the grace of one. He had been a chubby boy, bullied at his private school in Berlin, someone who dreamed of reinvention, of high school reunions where the former bullies were now overweight tax attorneys or insurance salesmen or German railway officials, while he showed up driving a Tesla, a lingerie model on his arm, smiling at the strudel-eating wives of his former tormentors.

"We have a story idea for you," Henke said to his computer screen, after Franny had taken a seat.

"Henke," Toland said.

Henke looked up, as if awakened, and stared at Franny, blinking, reorienting himself to the non-digital world.

"What do you think?" Henke said.

Franny looked to Toland, who rolled her eyes.

"You haven't told me anything yet," Franny said.

Toland said. "We'd like you to write a story about Ted Grayson."

The feeling was one from grade school. The fear that came during recess, when the mean girls had massed, after lunch, and stared at her, waited for her, taunted her. They'd picked her out, randomly at first, but then because they saw she was afraid. Until she hit one of them one day. The leader. Slapped her hard. They didn't bother her after that. But the fear didn't go away.

Scheisse was running stories every day, reposting every few hours. Photos taken as he exited his apartment building, hailed a cab. The iPhone footage of him screaming. But they wanted more.

Franny wanted to leave. She wanted to go outside and walk.

"No," she said, too forcefully, responding more to the voices in her head than to Henke and Toland.

"I just . . . I'm not sure I'm the best person for this," she continued.

"Who better?" Toland asked sweetly.

"I'm not exactly an impartial reporter."

"We don't want impartial. We want passion. We want something no one else can get."

No, she thought again. And yet here was a mild excitement at the prospect, like the moment before jumping off a high diving board, before running into the ocean at Cape Cod, the water so cold.

He'd never do it, Franny thought. "I can't imagine he'd agree to it," she said out loud.

"I can," Henke said. "The network will want it. They'll need it, in fact. A story by his daughter. The real Ted Grayson."

"I don't think you want that story," Franny said too fast, looking at Toland. But Toland was already three moves ahead. So Toland said nothing and let Franny do the math.

"Wait. You want me to write a bad story about my father?"

"No one said that," Toland said. "We want the real story."

Toland came closer, sat on the edge of Henke's desk.

"I think what we're talking about here is shame," Toland said, though for a moment Franny didn't know if she was talking about her or her father.

"In fact, that may also be the title. 'Shame.' Or 'Shame on you.' This is the irony of the world we live in. There is no shame. People will do anything, say anything, post anything. And yet when we see transgression of epic proportion, we must shame. We're primitive.

We must publicly stone. It's the baseball player who bet on the games. The athlete who doped. The congressman who exposed himself to a Girl Scout. It's the progeny of Chinese billionaires and Saudi kings. It's the morally lost. It's not new. It just seems new because we cannot help ourselves. That's who we are. It's Shakespeare. He did it all. He did it first. We're simply in reruns with his work under different names. We love watching because it's not us. Because we know how easily it could be."

And here she looked at Franny.

"We know our own demons, don't we? Deep down. We know we are capable of selfishness, meanness. But we haven't been caught. And these poor suckers have. This is about the search for redemption in a world that won't forgive unless you die. We take pity on Reagan now because he's long dead. Nixon. People talk about China instead of Watergate. What would be interesting is redemption while you're still alive. Isn't that what so many people want? To be forgiven?"

Franny had a tic. She ran her index finger across her thumb, picked at the skin. It had caused the nail of her thumb to grow in bumpy. A dermatologist had told her to stop picking at it. But she couldn't. To the point where she would sometimes wear a Band-Aid because the skin would become raw and exposed. She did it now, felt the sting of it.

She stood quickly and opened the door.

"Okay," she said.

Ouagadougou.

North Dakota, he'd say to her.

Bismarck, she'd reply.

Mogadishu, he'd say.

Somalia.

She was five, six, nine.

On drives. On walks. On the couch on cold Sunday afternoons, when Ted watched a football game, watched golf. Franny would plop down next to him, just to be near him. Why are they doing that? she'd ask. Who's that guy? Why does that man have a zebra shirt?

Sri Lanka, she'd say to him.

Please, he'd answer. Colombo.

Both of them staring straight ahead, at the TV, trying not to smile. Claire would watch them. In their own world.

Burkina Faso, he'd say.

Easy peasy, she'd say. Ouagadougou.

You just like saying Ouagadougou, he'd say. Ouagadougou, he'd say in a ridiculous voice, over and over, making her laugh.

Ted showed her maps, showed her the places he'd been,

explained countries and peoples and languages and history. If he'd been a bricklayer she would have memorized the composition of mortar and the differences between burnt clay bricks and sand lime bricks. She was a wonder to her third-grade classmates and teacher, who had no idea where Burkina Faso was. Franny showed the class on a map whenever she got the chance. "My father's been there. Ouagadougou is the capital," she'd say.

And then one day she let go of his hand.

Ted had thought it a mistake and went to take it back, reaching for it blindly, looking ahead. And then, looking down for her hand, saw her pull it back, though she continued staring straight ahead. His mouth opened to say something but he stopped himself. They continued on, into the school, the rush of parents and students, the comforting chaos of the morning drop-off, the overheated school, the smells: paint on the radiators, pencils, construction paper, and glue. Past the collages outside each classroom, the kindergartners and first-graders on the first floor, the bizarre drawings and little worlds worked on and cared about by the Trevors and Juanitas and Charlottes and Josephs. And outside her classroom door, he knelt down and she kissed him quickly on the cheek. Not the bear hug around the neck that lasted ten seconds, followed by holding his face in her hands, talking about how she would see him after school, followed by the slow walk into the classroom, where she turned around and waved, smiled and waved, blew him a kiss. Now, a quick peck on the cheek and she was gone, into the room, talking to a boy who was coloring (Patrick?) and then a girl with glasses (Penelope?), slipping her backpack off, hanging up her coat. A person. He stood for a time, looking in, half hiding himself, when the 8:30 bell rang to signal the start of the school day. He had been waiting for Franny to turn back and look at him. The teacher came to the door, surprised Ted was still there. She smiled and closed the door, and Ted stood alone in the hall.

He stopped outside the school's entrance, stood on the old granite steps, worn smooth in the middle from years of small feet. She was a little girl. A tiny little thing and Ted would yell sometimes, lose his temper. The shame of it. The disgust. A wave of regret at lost moments when his impatience and smallness of character, his inability to rise above the parenting situation and minor stress—the "daddy-daddy-daddy" voices and lost shoe and late for school and phone ringing, work calling, rainy morning when he simply couldn't attach the long lens to his mind's eye. When he couldn't laugh at it all. When he didn't understand that it could end. That it would end. That it would be lost.

Who are you again? Oh yes, my daughter.

Tamara's office, the twelfth floor. Ted, Simon, Tamara, a network lawyer named Camilla, and a PR guy named Maxwell.
He'd written Ted's apology.

Tamara was staring out the window. Everyone was waiting for
her to speak. Ted had presented the email he had received from
Franny and Henke formally proposing the story.

"Max?" Tamara said to the window.

"I like it and I don't like it. I like it for the obvious optics. I don't
like it because *scheisse* is a rag and Henke Tessmer makes Rupert
Murdoch look like Bill Moyers. I like it because we need women
and the girl—sorry, what's your daughter's name?"

Ted stared at Maxwell, pure disgust.

Simon said, "Franny. Frances. She goes by Frances."

"Anyway. She's an unknown quantity. I don't like it for that reason.
I worry about inflaming the story. I also worry that the story is getting
away from us. The best PR is to do nothing most days, let the speed of
news and new scandals bury us deep under them. But nothing's doing
that yet. So, I say, with regret and fear, that we should let her write it.
With one condition that I can't see them ever agreeing to."

"Which is?" Tamara asked.

"We have to see it first."

"They'll never agree to that," Simon said. "What news organization would?"

Here Tamara turned from the window and stared at Simon.

"Of course they will," Tamara said. "Because they're not journalists. They're entertainers. They want the booking. They want the show. Max. Call Graydon Carter. Tell him we can offer him an exclusive on Ted, with his daughter and his wife, the women in his life. Then call Frances Grayson and Henke Tessmer and tell them we'll give them their story if we see it first. If not, *Vanity Fair* is in an Uber on their way to Ted's house and Annie Leibovitz is riding shotgun."

Tamara looked at Camilla.

"I'll have a contract for them end of day," Camilla responded.

"Thank you, everyone." Tamara stood and Camilla and Max walked out of the office.

"Ted." It was Tamara.

Ted stopped. So did Simon.

"Bryce is taking the chair tonight. Take the evening off."

The two men were confused, little boys told it was bedtime when the sun was still out.

"What?" Ted said.

"Bryce is taking the chair tonight. Friday night. Low ratings night. Don't worry."

The words "Don't worry" did not have the intended effect on Ted.

"Wait a minute," Simon said, clearly annoyed. "Whose idea is this?"

"Mine."

"Well, I don't like it. She's, like . . . eleven years old."

"She's twenty-six years old, thank you very much, with a law degree from Yale."

Bryce Ringling had come from a Chicago affiliate six months ago. Tamara had taken a shine to her.

"I think part of getting past this moment is the consistency of seeing Ted in the chair. So I say, as head of the news division, that Ted's in the chair tonight."

"And I say differently," Tamara said evenly.

"Yeah, well, news is my call."

"No, Simon," Tamara said, raising her voice. "The moment your man called an immigrant a Russian whore he made it my call."

Tamara loathed raising her voice. She preferred intimidation by silence, by being smarter than everyone else. She turned and walked to the window, *ujjayi* breath. A long breath where the inhale and exhale are equal in length. In through the nose, out through the nose, the back of the throat. It was called ocean breath in yoga class, because of the sound, but Tamara had looked the word up. It meant victorious.

"You have the flu, Ted," Tamara said. "That's what we're going to say. Let's hope you get better."

Last Christmas Eve. That's the last time Ted had seen Franny. Claire had an open house every year, starting late in the afternoon. Drinks, food Claire had prepared for days. Old friends and their grown children. Over the years the numbers dwindled. Friends getting older, moving to warmer climes, their children marrying, starting traditions of their own.

Franny had left early Christmas morning with her then boyfriend, to visit the boyfriend's family in Boston. Tom someone. A no one who'd followed Greg. It hadn't lasted long.

Before that? The wedding of a family friend the previous June.

Before that? The previous Christmas.

Ted heard about her life from Claire.

Franny had called Claire two nights earlier.

"Hi," Franny had said.

And in one word Claire knew something was wrong.

"Hi," Claire had said, trying to counter Franny's tone and mood with lightness, motherly cheerfulness. "How are you?"

"Fine."

Silence.

Claire was pouring pine nuts into the Cuisinart. She was making pesto.

"Oh hey. You know who I saw recently?" Claire asked, not waiting for an answer. "Claudia Paine."

Franny hadn't thought of that name in years. A junior high school friend. Sleepovers. Summer camp three years in a row, a place in New Hampshire on a deep lake. The name made Franny smile.

"Really," Franny said. "How is she? Where is she?"

"She's good. Lives in Los Angeles. Makes documentaries. She's married. Has two little girls."

She has my life, Franny thought. The life I want. I'm almost twenty-eight years old and I am nowhere. These thoughts pulled Franny down into her dark place. It was 8:30 on a Tuesday night and she was drinking a glass of white wine and pacing her apartment and realized she hadn't eaten any dinner.

"She said to say hello. Gave me her email address to give to you."

"Oh. That would be great." Which was, of course, a lie. It wouldn't be remotely great. She wouldn't email.

Claire started to say *I'll send it to you*, but Franny cut her off.

"They want me to write a story about Dad."

Claire paused, looked at a block of Parmesan cheese on the counter.

Please tell me you're calling to say you're not going to do that, Claire thought.

"Oh," Claire said instead. "Is that a good idea?"

"Probably not. But I'm doing it."

The place was Franny's choice. Breakfast at Noho Star. It was Franny's go-to spot. Ted had wanted to do it at his apartment. The network didn't want him out, but they discussed it and being seen with his daughter, they felt, was a plus.

Ted arrived early and was seated with his back to the room. He'd brought a newspaper but found he couldn't concentrate. He was nervous to meet his own daughter.

He scanned the paper—stories the broadcast would reference that evening. Afghanistan. Iraq. Syria. NFL concussions. Ted read the first paragraph of many of the stories and then moved on, drifted, got bored. All of it—the news stories, the editorials and op-eds, the movie reviews, the local news horror and accidents and subway shutdowns—felt like something he'd read before, heard before, seen before. Nothing felt new.

Ted put the paper down when he saw his own photo and a small story that he chose not to read. He drank more coffee, even though he didn't want any.

*   *   *

Franny stood on the corner of Bleecker and Crosby smoking a Marl-boro Light. She hadn't smoked since before New Year's Eve and was mad at herself for stopping and bumming one off a construction worker who wanted to give her two and kept smiling at her.

She just needed a moment. More and more she found that she just needed space, mental space, a little time to think and be quiet. She couldn't seem to find it, though. The phone buzzed and pinged and never seemed to stop. She couldn't turn it off. The smoke felt filthy and delicious and soothing. Her palms were sweaty even though it was chilly out, a wind tunnel on this corner.

In the window of the Bleecker Street Bar, a lone man sat drink-ing a glass of beer. He was wearing a fuzzy red suit. On the bar next to him was a large Elmo head. It was a little after 9:00 a.m.

She dropped the cigarette, stubbed it out, and took a deep breath.

"For fuck's sake, Franny," she said in a whisper.

She reached for her phone and walked around the corner to the restaurant.

Franny was fifteen minutes late, her cell phone on her ear as she walked in. She looked at Ted like she might look at opposing coun-sel at a deposition.

"What does it matter?" she said into the phone. She looked like Claire. "It's Gisele. Run it. Use the line."

She sat, put her phone down, and looked at Ted.

"Hi," Ted said.

"Hello."

Franny took off her coat.

"Work call?"

She nodded. "We have a video of Gisele Bündchen kissing another guy."

"Isn't she married to Tom Brady?"

"Yeah."

"So she's cheating on him?"

"We're not sure. The guy she's kissing . . . we can't tell if it's on the lips or on the cheek. Also, it might be her personal trainer. Or her brother-in-law. Or a cancer survivor from a benefit she did. But we think it's a model."

"Huh. So, wait. Was she cheating?"

"She might have been. But it doesn't matter. It'll be viewed fifty thousand times by lunch. Tweeted and retweeted twice that. And we'll have attached five different ads to it that make you watch them before you watch Giselle suck face with a guy who's not Tom Brady. It'll be picked up by every tabloid and blogger in the Western Hemisphere, every fashion blog, sports site, every twenty-four-hour news show. We paid ten grand for the footage and will make twenty times that. That's the news business today."

It was the way she said it. The little girl trying to sound confident.

Ted did his slow Ted nod, leaning forward, elbow propped on the table, index finger across his upper lip, eyes squinted. The look millions of Americans knew and trusted. It was a thing Franny had always hated. She felt condescended to.

The waitress appeared.

"Can I start you out with coffee?"

Franny checked her phone.

"No-foam, nonfat latte," Franny said to her phone. Then a quick fake smile to the waitress and back to the screen.

We spoiled her, Ted thought. We spoiled her and loved her too much. Or not enough. We did this. We made this. But then Ted was part of a generation where it was impolite to look at a cell phone while you were talking with someone. For Franny's generation, it wasn't. And it didn't seem to bother the waitress one bit.

The waitress said, "Do you need more time or are you ready to order?"

"I am," Ted said. "But do you need more time, Fran?"

Franny looked up at her father. A couple of beats. *Fran*. Don't call me Fran. You've lost the right to call me that. But she said nothing.

Then to the waitress. "Egg-white omelet with mushrooms and asparagus. Thank you." Back to the phone.

Ted said, "Scrambled eggs and bacon for me, please. White toast, dry. Thanks."

The waitress collected the menus and left. Franny put her phone down and sighed.

Who is this person? Ted wondered. This stranger.

The morning she was born. Claire's water had broken at midnight the night before and she had a fairly easy labor. When the doctor pulled the baby's head from Claire, she gently turned Franny and Ted saw his daughter's profile for the first time, a perfect little Botticelli cherub face, fully formed. My God, Ted thought now, wanting to reach over and touch her. Ted hadn't realized that he had a mildly idiotic smile on his face at the memory.

Franny mistook Ted's smile for sarcasm and drew on a deep well of hatred for her father. Her phone buzzed and she picked it up with an urgency that suggested she was awaiting test results. For just a moment Ted was tempted to take it from her, as if she were a teenager. As she listened to the person on the other end of the phone, she held up an index finger to her father. She got up and walked out of the restaurant. Ted watched her out the large plate-glass window.

The food had arrived but Ted hadn't touched it. He wanted to wait for Franny, who was still on the phone outside. He also found he wasn't hungry.

When she came back she looked at her food, then his. "Why didn't you eat?"

"I . . ." And here Ted reverted to his old self, the one afraid of a Franny explosion. He was about to say *I wanted to wait for you*, but he knew that would make her feel guilty and her guilt would manifest itself as anger at Ted when, really, she was angry at herself.

She sighed, annoyed. He could see the inner workings.

"It's fine," he said. "I'm not that hungry anyway."

She was chilled and put her coat on. She picked up her coffee mug and held it with both hands.

Franny's phone buzzed, a text. Ted's buzzed at almost the same time. They both looked and saw links to *scheisse* with a photo of the two of them taken not twenty minutes ago through a window, sitting together.

"Wait. What is this?" Ted asked, confused.

"Fucking dickhead."

"What?"

Franny was shaking her head.

"It's my boss."

Ted stared at Franny and Franny saw that he was actually hurt.

"I didn't know they were sending a photographer," she said, hating the sound of her voice here because she thought she sounded thirteen.

Ted nodded, his slow nod, his *I'm disappointed in you and will withhold my affection and love for you.* At least that's how Franny read it.

"I have to get back," she said.

There is an unpleasant secret of family life. It's not found in movies because it doesn't hew to a narrative we care for. We are told, instead, that there is always time, always another chance, if only we try. That we can mend relationships. That is a lie. Because with enough pain, with enough time, we close the door on those people and we do not let them back in. We move on. Ted could see it on Franny's face. He was a stranger to her. He had caused her too much pain. Knew so little about what she felt and wanted and needed and hoped for.

The image came so fast and so clearly that Ted was forced to sit back in his chair. The image was this. Franny, in Ted's hospice room, watching him die. He sees the scene as if apart from it. He knows she will feel pain and regret and the thought of his death causing her pain forces him to wince. The film continues in his head. The scene switches to Franny, older, children of her own, children who would never know their grandfather, who would hear little of him. Franny going on with her life. He would be forgotten, as if he hadn't lived. The waitress asked if he wanted more coffee. He managed a nod.

"Your mother told you? We're getting a divorce."

"I know."

"She met someone."

Franny said nothing.

"Have you met him?" Ted asked.

"Yes."

"I hear he has his own plane. Not that that matters."

Franny looked at her phone. She seemed unable to not look at it for more than a few seconds.

"I'm sorry," she said, "but that's between the two of you."

"Me and Dodge or me and your mother?"

Franny ignored him.

"So you'll do an interview?" Franny asked.

"Whose idea was it?" Ted asked.

Franny looked up, a lock of hair falling over her face. Ted wanted to push it back behind her ear.

"Why does it matter?" Franny asked.

"I'm just curious."

"My boss."

And something about the answer relieved Ted.

"And what did you say when he asked?"

"How do you know it's a he?" she demanded.

"Fine. What did you say when your transgender boss asked?"

"It's comments like that that got you into this mess."

There was something about her expression, her voice, a meanness, and it's out before Ted can stop it because he's under attack, has been under attack and he is so tired of being hit again and again and here his own daughter . . .

"*Don't* lecture me," Ted said in a hard voice.

It came out too loud. People a few tables away turned and looked.

They had played this match before, many times. And, of course, Franny couldn't help but react.

"Whatever." Her face contorted.

How did he inevitably do this to her, make her feel this way?

"Anyway," Ted said, trying to move past it, like it never happened, a thing Franny hated. "I was just curious."

"I said I . . ." And here her New York confidence deserted her for a moment. "I said you'd never do it."

On Franny's plate, next to her untouched omelet, sat a wedge of orange. Ted watched her pick it up and pull the rind off. And then he watched as she began pulling off the tiny white pieces of pith, almost obsessively. Ted ate an orange the same way. That's how they peeled an orange when she was little. It drove Claire nuts. "I want Daddy to peel it," Franny would say.

"The network thinks it's a good idea," Ted said.

"Is that a yes?"

The waitress brought the check. "When you're ready," she said.

Franny had her credit card out. Ted reached for his.

"Don't worry about it," Franny said, not looking at him. She felt she'd not been brave enough. She was starting an internal monologue of self-laceration. She needed to leave.

"Franny," he said.

"It's *Frances*! For Chris*sakes*."

It was a screech so painful to Ted's ears because it was Franny at four, Franny at seven, Franny at eleven, when she was out of control, wide-eyed. She stared at her lap and Ted looked out the window and they waited for the moment to pass, like it had never happened.

And then, in a quiet voice, Ted said, "Sorry. I was just saying that . . . the network has a condition."

She had started gathering up her things. Her cheeks were flushed. The same thing happened to Claire.

"What is it?"

"They'll want to see a draft."

"No."

The waitress returned with the check. Franny signed quickly, a woman about town. She stood, grabbing her large leather bag. It looked expensive.

She looked like she was about to go when she stopped and looked at him.

"Do you really want to do this?" she asked.

"Do you?"

Say no. He wanted her to say no. Say something nice.

"It's my job."

He watched her go. He waited for her to turn around as she left the restaurant. She never did. She walked out the door, her phone to her ear, made a left, and was gone.

Kandahar Province, Bravo Company,
Third Marine Battalion.

Two months ago, during February sweeps, they went to Afghanistan for five days of frontline reporting. If by frontline reporting you mean many miles back from any activity. They wanted the ground soldier's experience. They'd run promos with Ted in a khaki shirt from the last time he was at the front. "An exclusive look at the frontline experience. Ted Grayson. Front. And center. All next week."

They had waited for a Marine Corps platoon to return, Ted and his small crew. It had been raining for days. Cold and rainy. They had waited all night, well into the morning. When the soldiers did return they were soaked and exhausted. They seemed distant. Ted and the crew waited as they went to the tent that served as the mess hall and ate. After a while they filed out, some to their tents, some for a smoke. And one, a lieutenant, stood off to the side, leaning against a rock, looking out over the camp and the hills beyond. He looked to be about twenty-five or twenty-six. Handsome kid. All-American look. Ted looked at Lou, who was looking at the kid, too. They knew. He was the one. He was the face of the story they wanted to tell.

Ted walked over to him.

"Mind if I talk with you, Lieutenant?"

Most times this was all it took. They recognized Ted, smiled automatically. Not this one. He just stared at Ted.

"I'm Ted Grayson."

The kid kept staring and it was unnerving. Ted saw in him a strength of character, a rawness and honesty, that was intimidating. What he had seen, what he had been asked to do, what he would have to live with.

Ted said, "What's your name?"

The soldier pointed to his name, above his left breast. *Kelly*.

Ted had done a stand-up after a package showing footage gathered by a local camera crew who'd gone to the front. The military wouldn't let Ted near the front and the network forbid it for insurance reasons. All they needed was a soldier talking about how important the war was. For the package. Ted was tired and sick of the place. He wanted to get on the plane and go home.

Ted tried again. "We were just hoping for your thoughts on how the fight was going, on what it means for you to be here, for the folks back home."

The marine stared for too long and finally said, "Well, sir. Here's what I think. You know what you look like? In your little flak jacket and shiny helmet? I think you look like an asshole. Sir."

It happened. The number of interviews that go wrong, that amount to nothing, that end up not being used, subjects who don't want to be asked questions. It happened.

It's just that they had been rolling. The camera had. That's how you do it. You have to roll. It's not scripted. You can't go again. So you roll. Picture and sound. Ted was wearing a lav. A lavalier mic on his shirt and it picked up everything. It picked up the kid. Ted had forgotten about it.

But now it was online. Someone had leaked it. And it was everywhere.

You look like an asshole. Sir.

Old news.

The talk had been scheduled for six months. Despite the fact that it was to be held at the nation's leading school of journalism, no one from the school seemed to have the remotest grasp on the news itself and how Ted speaking to graduate students might play. The paparazzi, though, were very much aware and made leaving his own building that morning difficult.

From the back of the car service that the university had sent, Ted could see the crowd in front of Lerner Hall at 116th Street and Broadway, and he was praying it was a just another group of spoiled, self-righteous twenty-year-olds protesting the male-centric curriculum or the paucity of vegan options available in the dining commons. But he knew it was for him. The driver was looking at the crowd and Ted watched him put two and two together, watched him turn back.

"You are the TV man, Fred!" he said, in an accent Ted couldn't place, though he guessed Egypt.

The man grinned, wide-eyed, as if Ted were an astronaut.

"Ted." Ted smiled back.

"I have a story for you. For your news. Atom bomb."

"What's that?"

"Atom bomb. The weather. Global warming. The crazy weather is because of all the atom bomb America tested. You research. Is true."

The car came to a stop by the curb, where a woman with an especially large head, mid-forties, smiled and waved like a crazy person. The driver held up his cell phone and before Ted could say anything the man leaned back and took a selfie of his own lunatic smile and Ted's furrowed brow. He tapped his phone a few times and said, "I put it on my Facebook."

The back door of the car opened, startling Ted, and the woman with the large head leaned halfway in.

"Atom bomb, Fred," the driver said. "Look it up."

"Hi, Ted!" the woman shouted. "Margo Litt from the School of Journalism. We spoke on the phone. I'm sorry, did he say 'atom bomb'?"

Margo had a forced smile on her face. Despite the cold, small beads of sweat dotted her hairline and upper lip. She shouted, as if Ted might be hard of hearing. Also, perhaps, to be heard above the noise of the chanting protestors outside. She kept moving farther into the car, one leg kneeling on the seat.

"Atom bomb, yes," the driver said. "Global warming atom bomb."

"I see," Margo said to him. "Okay, then." She turned to Ted. "We've got a larger-than-expected crowd, as you can see. Several networks are here as well." This was said in a shout, despite the close quarters.

"She was Polish, though," the driver said. "The girl. Not Russian. Also not prostitute."

"Very factual," Margo said, laughing too hard. "I like that. Shall we go?"

Margo maneuvered herself out of the car, ass first, Ted following.

The crowd was chanting, singsong, "Hey, ho, this we know, misog-y-ny has got to go."

Ted knew crowds. War zones, protests, the Arab Spring, the quicksilver energy of crowds protesting, how it could change from good to bad, from positive to violent, in seconds. This one felt bad.

He followed Margo as students held up their smartphones and recorded the man of the hour. Margo was still smiling but it was a nervous smile as they moved through the crowd, many of the students grinning when they saw Ted, the magic of seeing a TV personality. One of Ted's great strengths had always been his power to impress in person. Taller, broader shouldered, more handsome. *He doesn't seem like an angry, spittle-mouthed prostitute hater.*

They were joined by two of Columbia University security officers who, it seemed to Ted, were trying very hard to look serious and intimidating, though their ill-fitting uniforms didn't help.

The day had dawned sunny and clear but the weather had changed and it was colder now and windy, slate-gray sky, small patches of still-frozen black snow along the corners of the walkway, along the shrubbery, hearty daffodils giving fight. Ted was underdressed, Jack-Kennedy-sports-coat-only. The cold never bothered him but he'd gotten a chill and shoved his hands into his coat pockets. The officers led the way.

"Ted, thank you so much for coming today," Margo shouted. "We're thrilled to have you, though I should tell you that it's entirely possible we may cancel the talk, due to enormous pressure online. We'll know shortly. There's an emergency meeting of the deans.

The student union has called for a boycott, which has only made ticket sales go through the roof."

Initially, Ted thought that a particularly large bird had shat on his back. But when it happened again and then again, he knew he was under attack. He heard the gasp from the crowd. "Oooohh!" He heard Margo Litt mutter, "What the . . . ?" He felt something hit him squarely in the forehead and he thought, My God, they've assassinated me. But guns don't have onions and what was happening was that someone was throwing pierogi as an act of Eastern European defiance. People were laughing now as the airborne pierogi landed with a disgusting plop, most harmlessly exploding onto the pavement.

Margo, clearly under pressure from a long morning, turned and shouted to the crowd. "You selfish, cocksucking little pricks!" (This, as with everything in the new world, was captured on a phone, uploaded to the internet, and would later require an apology and ultimately her forced resignation from a job she loved.)

One of the security guards had tried to rush into the crowd but didn't get far. The pierogi hurler had escaped, a story he and his buddies would tell for years to come, a defining life moment at reunions thirty years hence. "Dude. You *nailed* that guy. What was his name?"

Margo and Ted made their way to the entrance of the hall and were joined by two of Margo's colleagues, one of whom handed Ted and Margo paper towels to wipe off the stray beef and onion from their clothes. No one seemed to have a response for this, though the assistant laughed. Margo turned on the assistant. "I don't know why an Ivy League–educated graduate student would throw an Eastern European dumpling at a grown woman! And I don't find it funny."

They walked quickly now, through a key-card-access door that took them down a long corridor to the backstage of Roone Arledge Auditorium. Ted had met Roone once. A legend. Brought sports to prime time. Games used to be played only in the day. The man invented *Monday Night Football.*

Ted was watching *Monday Night Football* on the night of December 8, 1980, with his father, at home in Woonsocket. The New England Patriots versus the Miami Dolphins. Ted was working at WPRI as a news writer, just out of school. It was late, after 11:00. The Patriots were driving, the score tied.

Howard Cosell said, "We have to say it. Remember, this is just a football game. No matter who wins or loses. An unspeakable tragedy confirmed to us by ABC News in New York City. John Lennon, outside of his apartment building on the West Side of New York City, the most famous, perhaps, of all of the Beatles, shot twice in the back, rushed to Roosevelt Hospital, dead on arrival. Hard to go back to the game after that news flash, which, in duty bound, we had to take."

Ted and his father turned and looked at each other. The impossibility of it. The electricity of it. The house phone rang and it was Ted's friend Rick, from down the street. He'd been watching the game.

"Are you watching this?"

He was watching. The nation was watching. They were hanging on Howard Cosell's voice, his words. He told the nation. Imagine that. The enormity of that. Of the knowing before others. The responsibility of it. Of how you share news people will never forget. That knowledge. That power. Ted wanted to be that person.

They arrived at a large room backstage. Several students sat around a fortyish woman with long, wild, graying hair. She had olive skin and large green eyes and was the kind of woman who made you slow your pace in the street. Ted knew the face. Elena Wolff.

Elena looked up and smiled.

Margo said, "Elena. My God. They pelted us with pierogi."

Margo and Elena hugged.

"At least they were fresh, not frozen," Elena replied. Her entourage laughed as well. Ted noticed that there was a young man in the group. He was wearing makeup and a dress.

"Where are my manners," Margo said, remembering Ted was in the room. "Ted, meet Elena Wolff. I'm sure you know her work."

Elena beamed, a smile Ted mistook as flirtatious.

"Of course," Ted said. "It's a pleasure to meet you."

"Ted," Elena said, eyes squinted, an enigmatic look. *So nice to meet you.* Or, perhaps, *Wow, you're a cock.*

Elena Wolff held a chair in women's studies at Columbia and lectured on gender in journalism at the graduate school. She'd authored four or five books, all best-sellers, and routinely made the talk show circuit, where her easygoing style, quick wit, and sharp mind cut other guests to pieces.

"Elena's filling in for Hugh Frankel," Margo said.

"What's that?" Ted asked.

"Should the talk go forward, we've taken the liberty of changing moderators."

"What happened to Hugh?"

"The women reporters' caucus felt that two white men onstage sent the wrong signal about the school, reporting, and the future of news."

"Yes," Ted replied, confused. "But the talk is titled, 'News: Where We've Been.'"

"Fair point. But the ship has sailed."

Elena stood and her entourage stood with her.

"Ted, if you'll excuse me. This was a last-minute ask and I should prepare. I want to watch your YouTube clip again."

Noisy college students began filing into the auditorium. Ted watched them from the wings of the stage. Elena was off in a corner, backstage, huddled with her staff.

Hugh Frankel appeared and walked up to Ted.

"Hugh," Ted said.

They shook hands. Hugh looked pale.

"Ted, I'm so sorry."

"What's going on?"

Hugh had been a reporter for *The Washington Post*. He was maybe ten years older than Ted. He had covered the fall of the Berlin Wall as their Moscow bureau chief. Two Pulitzers. Now he taught a class or two, accepted a comfortable stipend, and tended a lovely garden on weekends with his wife at their home in Stonington, Connecticut.

"The inmates are running the asylum. I just got off a conference call that would have made you vomit. They don't want to do the talk."

"But . . ."

"They want to make a statement."

"To the press?"

"No. Ted. A political statement. They want to take a stand."

"On what?"

"On you."

Elena walked over, on her way to the stage.

"I'll introduce you, Ted. Then we'll chat. This is going to be fun." She smiled and then walked onto the stage to huge applause.

"Ted," Hugh said. "You're about to be ambushed."

Two massive screens sat behind her. On one, live tweeting. On the other, live commenting from the journalism school's Facebook page.

"We live in an extraordinary time," Elena began. "Perhaps all generations say that, but we are witnessing history every day. The speed of technology, the ability to communicate, the power of the masses to influence government and corporations, to map out the way we want to live, has never been more real."

Applause and hoots. Tweets, real time:

Power to the people!!!

You tell them, Elena!

Fuck Ted and the old guard!

And on and on.

"This afternoon's talk was originally titled 'News: Where We've Been.' But we know where we've been. John Cameron Swayze and a newscast sponsored by Camel cigarettes. He interviewed baseball players and they spoke about how they loved smoking Camels.

David Brinkley and Chet Huntley and Walter Cronkite and Hal Winship. Now. The names I've listed. There isn't a vagina among them."

They laughed and cheered.

Hugh had gone. And now Ted waited alone. Who says the word "vagina" out loud? Ted wondered.

"Women in America," Elena continued. "Women around the world. We are second-class citizens. Paid less. Asked to do more, in the home, at work, to look good, to look sexy, to be an object, to be quiet. And who demands this? Men. Men in charge of companies. Fewer than one in five members of Congress are women and yet we are fifty percent of the population. The vast majority are Democrats. Republicans simply won't elect women to leadership roles. What about corporate America? Surely that's a place where all you need is talent, right? Well, listen up, future journalists. This quote is from a recent issue of *Fortune* magazine. The headline: 'Female Fortune 500 CEOs are poised to break a record in 2017.' Wow, I thought. There's hope. There's change. Thank God. Except, in this country, in this time, 'poised to break a record' means that, out of five hundred CEO positions in America today . . ."

And here Elena Wolff, seasoned speaker, paused and looked out over her audience. "Twenty-seven. That's less than five percent."

Huge, sustained boos. The tweets coming in so fast they were tough to read.

"We need women telling our stories. We need gay men telling our stories. We need transgender people telling our stories. We need people of color telling our stories. Not just male reporters. Not blonde bombshells on Fox playing nice and sweet and showing off their legs, playing the cock tease. We need real women who have balls—yes, balls! For too long the world's alt-history has been told to us by a single faction."

Laughing and cheering.

Women with balls! Love it!

#WomenWithBalls

"Real women and men who are in touch with their female goddess to redefine how we tell our stories. War and violence and crime and poverty and inequality. That is what they have made. That is what they did with their turn at power. Destroy and demean. Double D. Precisely the bra size most men prefer."

Laughs and hoots and cheers.

"In a moment, I'm going to introduce . . ." The boos built, the chairs slammed.

And here Elena Wolff held up her hands, barely suppressing a smile, magnanimous in her condescension.

"Please . . . everyone . . . please. We are defenders of free speech here. As long as it's correct free speech."

A roar of approval.

"I'm joking, of course," she said.

She sipped from a glass of water.

"Freedom of speech is a myth. We are under the impression that we can say most anything we want in this country. Print most anything we want. But we can't. Nor should we be able to. And in this new world, this constant geyser of words, commentary, counterpoint, scream, anger, vitriol, threat, sexual aggression, misogynistic cruelty, we must stand up, not to free speech, but to despicable speech. Hateful speech. Dangerous speech. Just as Oliver Wendell

Holmes did. Oh. But wait, says the ACLU. Who are the arbiters of this so-called taste? We are."

Applause, hoots.

#FUCKYEAH

#ELENAGENIUS

"We are the arbiters. We are the people who stand on that wall of words saying *not on my watch*. Not on my watch will you savage a young gay man and tease and humiliate him to his own suicide, as happened last year here at Columbia. Not on my watch will you body shame an author simply because she is clinically obese, as happened in California three months ago. Not on my watch will you post Nazi images on the Twitter page of a Jewish writer who reported on the rise of anti-Semitism in France, as happened two weeks ago. Not on my watch will you call a young, poor immigrant a whore."

They began chanting. They stood on their seats. Some hammered their seats. Some had brought thunder sticks, the inflated plastic bats used at football games. It was the Colosseum. It was a war cry before battle.

Ted stood in the wings, brow furrowed, confused at what was happening. He looked out over the sea of faces, these young people, so sure of their own rightness and moral superiority. Perhaps this was the nature of being a college student, a belief that all who'd come before you simply didn't understand the world now.

Ted didn't recognize himself in the faces. Didn't recognize any semblance of the world he had experienced to date. Theirs was a worldview that seemed to lack even basic rules. Dating, sex, religion, government, work. Rules, they believed, were created by straight

white men and hence the root of all evil. They believed only in
technology and identity. Who needs God when you have Google?
Who needs community when you have FaceTime?

Ted's experience was different. Ted was reared on Froot Loops
and Frosted Flakes and Yodels and Ring Dings and Chips Ahoy! and
liters of Coca-Cola. Cheeseburgers from Howdy's and corn in cans
and blade steak and instant mashed potatoes. Food was, during much
of Ted's youth, something made quickly from boxes that one simply
added water and heat to while watching *Gomer Pyle, U.S.M.C.* or
McHale's Navy or *F Troop* or *Hogan's Heroes* or *Rat Patrol,* programs
created by traumatized World War II vets who didn't know what
trauma was because the word hadn't really been invented yet so they
self-medicated with brown booze and cigarettes and jokes about
pain and long evenings on a screened-in porch looking out at the
neighborhood's quiet darkness, cicadas going, wondering what all of
this meant, what it was for, before going to bed in pajamas and waking to do it all over again.

How to explain to these little know-it-alls that Ted's mother, like
so many other mothers in greater Providence, thought it was a good
idea, when Ted was three and four years old, to put him in a harness
and tie the harness to a tree in the yard, near shade, and a small
sandbox, and Ted's mother, holding Ted's younger sister, leaning out
a screened window to toss little Teddy a baggie with a cut-up orange
in it. Today Ted's mother would be front-page news, shamed and
ruined. Back then, what harm?

The Twitter feed scrolled. One caught Ted's eye.

Ted Grayson is how Hitler got to power.

Ted couldn't believe it. He turned to a young man with a headset and a clipboard who appeared to be the stage manager. "Did that say . . ."

"Hitler? Yup."

Ted and the boy exchanged a look.

"Godwin's Law, dude," the boy said.

"What's that?"

"Godwin's Law. I think he was some lawyer guy. He said that if an online discussion goes long enough, at some point, no matter what the topic, someone will compare someone else to Hitler."

"That's insane."

"We had a woman in here last week who'd written a controversial book about gardening and race. Same thing happened." The kid shrugged. "It's just what happens now."

Elena Wolff began introducing him.

"Ted Grayson is a twenty-nine-time Emmy Award nominee and twelve-time Emmy winner. He is the anchor and managing editor of Continental News Corporation's nightly broadcast and has been for twenty years this fall. He has reported from every continent and most every major war, hurricane, flood, and tragedy in the last two decades . . ." But the noise grew, Elena becoming a silent movie star, her lips moving but no sound.

Ted thought of his parents. How glad he was that they weren't alive to see their son, their good boy, flayed like this. How hard his father had worked his whole life. How he never visited foreign capitals, except with the army. How he never complained. How he looked around when he was in line at the grocery store to see if the person behind him had fewer items, letting them go first. How he pointed out to Ted, as they drove past bus stops, that some people weren't quite so lucky as the Graysons, to have a car, waiting in the cold and the rain for a bus to take them to a job, a second job, home late at night. How he looked out for the older couple down the street. Shoveled their walkway. How Ted's mom brought them soups and lasagnas. How they knew everyone in the neighborhood. How his father hummed in the car in the summer, one hand on the steering wheel, one bent arm out the window, stopping at Fisher Dairy for an ice cream cone for Ted and a coffee frappe for Dad. "I don't see why not," his father saying with a smile and a wink. And that's all Ted needed to know he had a place in the world, that he was loved.

What had happened to kindness? Maybe Ted should Google that.

Elena had to shout above the noise, the boos, the "You *suck*, man," as she said, "Please welcome Ted Grayson."

Elena waited for Ted at the two chairs by the two microphones. She made no effort to meet him halfway. No effort to take a few steps toward him. Ted would have done it, had he been the host. A small gesture, a few steps toward a guest, to make someone feel welcome. Elena waited, looking at Ted with a smile that felt more like a smirk. Ted walked out onstage as scores of people in the crowd turned their backs to him.

It felt like a long walk, his legs heavy. More and more students turned their backs, the noise deafening now. Ted reached his hand out to shake Elena's but she seemed to decide, at the last minute, to not shake his hand, to put her head down and sit. Ted was left with his arm extended, looking like a presidential candidate on *Saturday Night Live.*

He heard someone laugh and yell "You douche!"

Ted sat and adjusted the microphone.

Elena said, "People . . . please. Could we please have some quiet."

They listened to her.

"Ted. Do you believe that a fifty-nine-year-old white man with misogynist tendencies is the best person for millions of people to trust?"

The crowd exploded, laughing, cheering.

Ted stared at Elena, who held his look. She was not intimidated. She was a bully and she wanted to bury him. To embarrass him. She wanted revenge for the Russian whore.

He was running his tongue against the back of his lower teeth. He hands tingled. He tried to speak. He was saying words. "I don't know if that's a serious question . . ."

But no one could hear him. Elena raised her hands, halfheartedly spoke to the crowd, "Please. People . . ."

But they were too far gone now.

"If I might . . ." Ted tried. But they weren't going to let him speak.

Elena turned to him, leaned in, put her hand over her mic. "Network news. Where we've been. That sounds like a punch line to me, Ted."

"Are you going to do anything about this?"

"Ted, there's no camera here. There's no diarrhea medication sponsors. You have no power here. And if you think I control this you're dumber than I thought."

He shouldn't have, but he stood. He was so angry. So sick of this *Twilight Zone* existence. He stood and he took a step toward the front of the stage. He was squinting at the roar, at the chairs being slammed in a kind of rhythmic primal war cry. For God's sake, he'd given a hundred speeches. Commencements and panel talks and interviews. He was a man used to being listened to. *Just listen to me. You invited me!* He held his arms out in front, trying to implore them. "Please . . . please," he shouted through the storm. But no one heard him, a small cry in a tornado. It would be the photo on the tabloids and websites, Ted, wide-eyed, arms out, "like Christ on the cross," said one website. "Except no one was hoping for his resurrection."

And that's when Ted saw Franny.

Franny had a seat on the aisle, ten rows back from the stage. Most everyone was standing now, many with their backs to Ted. Those who did face him chanted wildly, shouted obscenities, raised their signs in protest. Several Columbia police officers entered the back of the hall and hustled to the front of the stage. The crowd booed. Franny stepped in the aisle to leave. She wanted to leave. She needed to get away from this. And it was here that Ted saw her. They looked at each other for a time. And what surprised her, what confused her, was the desire to run to him, to get him off the stage. But she did nothing. She stood frozen.

A woman standing next to her turned and smiled. She had been cheering loudly at everything Elena was saying.

"Guy's a dick, right?" the woman shouted above the crowd.

Franny just looked at her.

The woman noticed Franny's small notebook, her scribbles.

"You writing a story or something?"

Franny nodded.

"Make sure you screw him over. He can't treat women this way, right?"

"What way?" Franny said, annoyed at the woman, at her know-it-all expression and condescension, at the fact that Franny completely agreed with her, *was* her.

"He called her a whore."

Franny nodded. It came out fast, hard, adrenaline-angry. "What the fuck do you know about anything?"

The woman's expression changed as she backed off into the crowd.

Franny watched her father turn and confer with Margo Litt, who had come onto the stage. Watched as Margo spoke to the crowd, who were delirious with their sound and fury. Watched as Margo and Elena and Ted walked offstage, the women—and here Franny wasn't sure of her own memory of it but it felt this way—walked away from Ted, ahead of him, leaving Ted alone, a final look over his shoulder at the mob.

In Midtown, Tamara was following the event on Twitter. Maxwell, her PR head, was messaging her. "This is getting out of hand."

Tamara texted back. "You think?"

Talk to me.

M urray." It was Grace.

Murray looked up from his screen, mid-sentence, still in the story he was writing. He looked at Grace, saw that Jagdish was looking at him, too.

"We wanted to say something," Grace said. She looked over at Jagdish, and Jagdish nodded. They had gone out for a coffee after work the day before. They'd talked for an hour and a half. They felt it was the right decision.

"I'm resigning," Grace said.

"I am also," Jagdish said. "Respectfully, Murray."

Murray nodded.

Grace had stayed up the previous evening and written her thoughts out.

"There is a part of me that loves Ted," she said. "Truly. But what he said, the word he used, the way he used it. He demeaned that woman. That's not okay. Ever. It's 2016, Murray. If we condone this, then we are part of it. I . . . we . . . want to make a stand. We want to be on the right side of history."

She looked at Jagdish. "What she said," Jagdish added. "I cannot say it better."

Murray scratched his scalp and sniffed his fingertips.

"Okay, then," he said finally, nodding. "Ahh, just . . . send me an email, make it official. I'll forward it to HR. We'll do an ice-cream cake or something for your last day."

He put his head back down, stared at the keyboard, and began typing. Grace and Jagdish looked at each other, confused and a bit hurt that Murray was being so cavalier.

Perhaps it was the pressure of watching Ted annihilated in the media, this man who had been so good to Murray. Perhaps, too, it was the sense of foreboding, that his job, his industry, certainly the evening news, was coming to an end, changing in ways he simply didn't recognize or understand.

"That's it?" Grace said.

Murray nodded, typing, staring at his screen.

Grace and Jagdish gathered their coats.

Jagdish said, "Murray. We're going for soup. Can we get you anything?"

"If you do this, they win. Okay?" Murray said too loud.

"If we get soup?" Jagdish said.

Murray stood. "Not soup! They! They win if you do this. If you quit. Don't you see? They win!"

"Who wins?" It was Grace. "What are you talking about?"

"I'm talking about everything that is wrong with America, the world, *us*, today. Mark Fucking Zuckershit. Sergey fucking Brin douche!"

"Elegant," Grace said.

"Just listen, please!"

"No, Murray!" Grace found her voice, her footing. "I'm done listening to men tell me—"

"You sanctimonious shits!" Murray shouted.

Their mouths opened involuntarily, Grace and Jagdish.

"I see. I see. Ted is bad and you are both good. Both so right. So you'll walk. Simple. I get it. You're *news* writers, for God's sake. When is a story *ever* simple? How old are you two, ten?"

"You're rude. I'm not listening to this." Grace again, heading for the door.

"You're so afraid to live." He was talking to Grace now.

"No I'm not!"

"You have your band. You know them. But only so you don't have to do the real work of knowing an actual person, trusting a person. Why do that when you can pretend?"

She was wide-eyed now and wounded.

"I know you because I *am* you, Grace. I'm just like you. And just as afraid. And I died when I saw that video of him. Because I love him. Because I believe in him. And I want to quit, too. I want to walk out that door and have cameras turned on and take a big crap on him. Because he doesn't get to do that. But he did. So what now? I owe him this. The hardest thing about a relationship isn't the I do part. It's the I do when you don't want to. Walk away now and the forces that won't let us make a mistake win. The sanctimonious assholes who criticize him like they've never made a mistake win. You are so much better than that. You make him better. Your work and writing and passion. You are amazing. And without you, without both of you, this newscast is the lesser. I'm the lesser. He's not going to survive this. It's over soon. To walk out now is . . ."

And here the energy seemed to leave Murray completely. He exhaled and sat down.

"I'm sorry I raised my voice," he said, staring at his keyboard.

Grace and Jagdish looked at Murray, waiting.

Jagdish said, "Murray."

"What?" Murray stared at his desk.

"Would you like some soup?"

He looked at them. "Are you coming back?"

Jagdish looked at Grace. She didn't answer right away.

"How about a mulligatawny?" she said to the floor.

"Okay," Murray said. "And some oyster crackers, please."

He began typing.

Ted woke early, after another night of not sleeping well, and had, around dawn, fallen into a deep and wonderful sleep for about an hour. He lay in bed for a time, unable to find the energy to get up, the regret and shame taking a foothold the moment he opened his eyes. He considered going to the gym in the building and riding the stationary bike for forty-five minutes and then doing light weights, rolling his fascia on the foam roller, then taking a relaxing steam, all of the things a high-priced personal trainer he had hired a year ago—two years ago?—had urged him to do but which he almost never did.

Ted had shaved and showered but had yet to dress. What he was able to achieve was making a pot of coffee, though the basic movements took time and he was aware of all of them. Now he stood at the window and looked out over the park.

He thought life would wait for him. While he was in the bubble, in the anchor chair, the most trusted name in network news. He thought life would wait and that there would be time to fix everything. Claire and Franny. He thought there would be time. But people had failed to wait for him. They had gone on living.

Paris. He thought maybe he and Claire would go back to Paris. They'd been, before Franny was born. They had stayed at a small hotel in the Sixth and gone to the same café each morning for coffee and omelets. It overlooked the church at Saint-Sulpice. There was a fountain and they would sit for a long time after eating, Ted leafing through the *International Herald Tribune* and Claire staring at the fountain between writing postcards to friends.

"I want to come here with kids," Claire had said back then. "Wouldn't that be fun?"

Ted had looked at her and smiled. He loved her voice and her face and her hope for the future, for what life could be. So he thought they'd travel when he was done with the job. He thought it was just all on hold, that it was all just waiting. He thought the distance and the arguments and the years of empty evenings and lost weekends would somehow not matter and that they could travel, first-class. Do Greece. Do India. The South of France. They'd have plenty of money. They'd have time. Christ, maybe Franny would have come out of whatever funk she was in and come with them. They would have a lifetime of stories and memories. He thought the things that happened to other people wouldn't happen to him.

Ted realized he was blinking rapidly, standing at the window, not seeing anything. He thought they'd been following him. Claire and Franny. He thought they'd been waiting for him, only to turn around and find them gone.

He'd missed her graduation from high school. By then they were so far estranged he thought it wouldn't matter. He was on assignment in Kosovo and there was a Pulitzer Prize–winning photo of Ted from that time, after a shelling had taken place, holding a four-year-old girl who was covered in dust, cut on her face, bleeding. Ted and Lou had been on the outskirts of town, on their way in, when the bombs went off. If they'd been ten minutes earlier they would likely have been killed. The screaming of the survivors, the screaming of those who were trapped and would die. The lack of infrastructure, of emergency medical workers. From out of buildings came neighbors, digging through rubble by hand. Lou wanted Ted to record. And he did. But in the middle of it someone handed him the girl. Lou got it. A photographer from Reuters snapped a few pictures. One of them—the one that won the Pulitzer—was on a credenza in Ted's living room. One of dozens of photos chronicling the remarkable career of Ted Grayson. Here was Ted on the set, in the anchor chair, with the twin towers behind him in flames. Here was Ted in Zaire, Cambodia, Afghanistan, Iraq. Ted at G8 summits in Berlin, London, Oslo. Ted with George H. W. Bush. Ted with Bill and Hillary Clinton. Ted with George W. Bush. Ted with Tony Blair. Ted with former Chinese president Hu Jintao. Ted with King Bhumibol Adulyadej of Thailand. Ted with Bono. Ted with the Pope.

▪   ▪   ▪

Claire had called the evening before. Ted assumed it was something to do with the upcoming meeting to go over the divorce agreement. He was tired. He didn't feel well. The tweets and comments never ceased, and yet he couldn't seem to not look.

"How are you holding up?" she asked.

"Well, according to the latest tweet from Gloria Steinem, I'm everything that's wrong with the twentieth-century male."

"Yes. She was on *Good Morning America*. What's the network saying?"

"Not much."

"You've heard about the petition."

"Yes."

Claire could see him, knew his furrowed expression. He didn't understand. He didn't see what everyone else did. Dodge had said to Claire, "You know he's going to be fired, yes?"

She hadn't. She never imagined it could come to that. She and Dodge had gotten in a small argument over this, actually, Claire surprised and hurt by the words, surprising herself by saying that Ted was a good man.

"Ted," she said now.

He wasn't sure what to say. He wanted to get off the phone. He felt he needed to get to the office. He had to talk with Simon. With Tamara. They could fix this.

"Yeah."

"This thing with Franny. Is it a good idea?"

"It wasn't my idea."

"Just please be . . . careful."

"With what?"

"With her feelings, Ted."

"Her feelings? Claire, I don't know if you've seen the news lately but I'm the anti-Christ. I think there's a better-than-average chance they'll fire me. And I'm supposed to worry about a reporter's feelings?"

"No, Ted. You're supposed to worry about Franny's feelings."

"You know what I meant."

"Do you want me to be there tomorrow?"

"I've been interviewed before, Claire."

"Not by your daughter you haven't."

She arrived on time and looked around the apartment like it was an open house, like she was considering buying the place. Ted tried to think when she was last there. He wasn't sure. But it had been a long time. She looked out the window as Ted hung up her coat. Ted poured coffee and brought it to her. He didn't know how she took it.

"Nice view."

Ted said nothing. He sipped his coffee. Had it started? My God, how strange, he thought. What were other fathers doing with their grown daughters right now? Holding a grandchild? Going for a walk? Catching up over lunch?

Franny turned her attention to a lacquered credenza set against one wall, a faded silver mirror above it. Both items looked expensive, surely the work of an interior designer. A large bowl with hand-painted Mandarin lettering sat in the middle of the credenza. It was filled with books of matches, souvenirs from hotel bars around the world. Ted had been to eighty-seven countries at last count, a number he was proud of. Though more often than not his experience of a country, a city, was that of a banker in for a meeting. He saw the airport, the inside of a high-end hotel. He was driven places. He never wandered the streets. Never got lost and had to ask directions. Never stumbled upon a quaint restaurant. He'd gone to these places not in search of real stories but confirmation of a narrative they believed to be true. They rarely looked beyond the obvious. Poverty in Africa. War in Sudan. Corruption in Bucharest.

Sitting atop the credenza in a row, the framed photos of Ted Grayson, famous person. Franny leaned forward, examining them. And there, toward one end, in an elegant, tarnished old silver frame with Claire's initials etched at the bottom, was a photo of Claire and Franny at Claire's parents' place on Cape Cod. A place called Sandy Neck on Barnstable Harbor. The old lighthouse and the house next to it had been in Claire's mother's family since it was built, as part of a girls' summer camp in the early 1900s. Claire had gone every summer, spending days at a small boat club learning how to swim and sail and play tennis. It looked like an Edward Hopper painting.

In the photo, Franny must have been around four. They were on the beach, Claire sitting, Franny standing, showing Claire a shell. Late afternoon light. Claire had one tanned arm around Franny's waist. Their heads close together. Franny's chubby thighs. Ted took it with an old Nikon he'd had for years.

Franny leaned closer. "Sandy Neck?"

"Do you remember it?" Ted asked.

"The water was cold."

"Always."

"And there was no electricity. Buckets of water to flush the toilet."

"Yup."

She turned and looked at Ted. Her phone buzzed. She took it out and looked at it instantly.

"Gaston Fouquet called you a great man," Franny said to her phone.

"What?"

"The leader of the far-right-wing party in France."

"I know who Gaston Fouquet is."

"He tweeted that you're a great man. You stood up to political correctness and called a whore a whore."

"She wasn't a . . ." Ted shook his head.

"I'm just quoting Gaston Fouquet, who was quoting a story on Breitbart that claims they have evidence that Natalia was a prostitute. Except they won't release the evidence because there is no evidence. We reached out to her. She wouldn't talk."

"That's insane."

"Which part?"

"A story that they know is a lie?"

"My boss says there are no lies. Just what people are willing to read and accept as the truth."

"Well, that's about the dumbest thing I've ever heard."

"He says we're not responsible for the truth. That that's the individual's responsibility."

"Let me rephrase my earlier comment. *That's* the dumbest thing I've ever heard."

"Henke's a billionaire."

"Henke's an asshole. I've heard him speak. What are you doing at that place?"

He'd not meant to say this last sentence out loud. But he couldn't help it.

The reaction was swift and angry. "What are you doing at *your* place?"

Ted walked to the kitchen, both composing themselves. Nothing changes in a family.

He poured himself more coffee. His fourth cup of the morning. From a bag on the counter he took an Entenmann's Pecan Ring that he'd had delivered. Franny had liked them a long time ago. He brought it into the living room and put it on the coffee table.

Franny looked at it like it was something she might see at the Museum of Natural History.

"What is that?" she asked.

"A pecan ring. You used to like it."

Ted cut a hearty wedge and stuffed it in his mouth. It wasn't nearly as good as he'd remembered. Stale. Flaky. Cheap sugar taste that hurt his fillings. Maybe two pecans.

Franny took her iPhone out and opened the voice record app. She held it up, showing it to Ted. "Okay if I record our conversation?"

"Sure."

Something about the question, the phone sitting there between them, caused a little flood of sadness in his head, his stomach. Franny had reached into her giant bag and pulled out a yellow legal pad on which she had scrawled what appeared to be many questions.

"What I like to do is write the questions out and then forget them," Ted said. "Just . . . have a conversation."

Ted had conducted thousands of interviews. So to him this just seemed like a mentor's guidance. To Franny, it was what large swaths of Brooklyn and Scarsdale and Silver Lake and West Hollywood and talk show hosts like Dr. Phil called a "trigger." She closed her eyes with all the subtlety of a daytime soap star. The reaction, one Ted had seen half a million times from Franny, caused him to roll his eyes.

Franny sighed. "Can we . . . I like to do it with notes. If that's okay with you."

"Fine."

Every word, every step forward, seemed misconstrued, a slight, an offense, a land mine.

"Do you think you're going to be fired?"

It was a right cross that landed.

But Ted was good at this. Good at poker face, at answers where the words don't really say much.

"That's not my decision," Ted said.

"I understand that but that wasn't my question," Franny said. She was looking at the notes. Had she scripted it? Did she know what he would say?

"That's the network's decision."

"But what do you think will happen? If you were Tamara Fine, what would you do?"

Ted had, of course, considered this many times. He didn't know

Tamara well. A lunch, two dinners, maybe. She was clearly smart. For that reason, Ted felt the smart move would be to put him back in the chair. Advertisers liked Ted.

"I'd try very hard to make the right decision for the network."

Franny nodded and let it go. She looked at her legal pad.

"Why should a sixty-year-old white male impose his worldview on a nation of such diversity?"

"I'm fifty-nine."

"Sorry. Why should a fifty-nine-year-old white male—"

"I remember the other part. I'm not hard of hearing yet. Is that a serious question?"

"Of course. Why?"

"Well, it seems a little like 'Have you stopped beating your wife?' Seems to me like a statement."

"And *I* would say that that is part of your problem. The problem of older, rich men. The sense of entitlement."

"You went to private school most of your life. Am I missing something here?" Ted was trying to sound light but the question, and her tone, annoyed him.

"That's not the point. The point is that you impose your opinions on others."

"I don't believe I impose my opinions on anyone. We report the news."

"Yes," she said, ramping up. "And every time you decide what to report on, or what not to report on, you impose an opinion."

"You mean like suggesting that Tom Brady's wife is having an affair."

He hadn't mean to say it like he did. He wanted it to sound light, funny, to break the tension. But it came out too hard. He saw her react, saw her face contort. She took a moment.

"I don't equate what our website does with the nightly news. We're not the problem."

"Who's the problem?"

"You. Your kind."

"My kind?" Ted asked.

"White men. You've had, what, like two thousand years in power? Now we have global warming, epic poverty, and race riots. How's that working out for you guys."

"I apologize for being white and male. It was not my choice. When the network wants to replace me they will. That's not my call."

Franny was smirking, slowly shaking her head.

"Well this is fun," Ted said.

She was home from college, spring of her freshman year. A long weekend. She treated the house like a hotel, coming and going at odd hours, saying little, taking the spare car. Claire had asked if they could have dinner together, the three of them. She would make Franny's favorite meal, a spicy shrimp pasta. The Sunday evening before she had to head back.

Claire had taken a bath, gotten dressed, had put music on. Ted had opened a bottle of wine. He was reading briefing papers on the G8 summit meeting in Italy that he was flying to the next day. Franny had said she would be home by 6:00. She texted at 6:30 to say she was running late. It was just after 7:00 now.

It's fine, Claire had said. *She's nineteen.*

He watched Claire go about making the meal. Peeling the shrimp, pressing the garlic, chopping the parsley. She did it with such care and attention to detail. Children never saw that. You got no credit for the invisible work of parenting. The late nights. The 3:00 a.m. pee when you checked on them, made sure they hadn't fallen out of bed, that their blanket was still on, that the temperature of the room was just right. Crusts cut off sandwiches.

He watched her and looked at his watch and sipped his wine and found himself getting angry. Angry at Claire for trying so hard. Angry at himself for not trying hard enough.

At 7:30, Claire called Franny's cell. It went straight to voicemail. She tried again twenty minutes later. Same thing. Claire put her phone down and moved the saucepan with the shrimp sauce in it, slamming the pan. Her back was to Ted and she stood looking out the kitchen window, a pose Ted had seen a hundred times.

"It's ruined," she said.

She turned and walked to the door, grabbing a fleece. She needed to walk in the garden. She needed the cool air. She needed to see her plants, to whom she gave so much care and attention, who flourished, who seemed, in their quiet way, to appreciate it.

Franny walked in a little before 9:00.

Claire and Ted were in the kitchen.

It was Claire who reacted first. Ted remembered that.

"Where have you been?" she shouted.

"I lost track of time, I'm sorry."

Claire looked at Franny's bloodshot eyes. "Are you stoned? Is that why you're late?"

Ted took a few steps to get a closer look. Franny put her hands up, pulled a mock-surprise face. "Whoa, Ted. Calm down." She smirked. Or maybe she was smiling. It seemed like a smirk. Like she was taunting him.

It happened so fast. He didn't plan it. He'd never done anything like it before. He slapped her, hard, across the face. The sound. A rifle crack. Ted wasn't sure which happened first but he thought it was Claire screaming.

"Ted!"

Franny's mouth, falling open, the pain of it, tears popping out, rolling down her cheeks. Her expression like a child, the surprise of it. The how-could-you of it. The instant regret on Ted's part.

And then the explosion from Franny.

"Fuck you!"

And she was gone.

Ted sipped his coffee. Franny looked at her notes. She checked her phone.

"Why did you decide to get into news? Your father worked on railroads."

Your father. Not *my grandfather.*

"I needed a major in college. Seemed like a good idea."

"No . . . influences or mentors?"

How could she not know this?

"My uncle worked in radio. A station in Providence. Read wire service reports, weather, sports scores. We'd hear him. He'd come over for Sunday dinner sometimes and I thought it was like Frank Sinatra visiting."

A half smile from Ted at the memory of it.

"He brought me into the studio once. I thought it was pretty cool. *This is Laurence Grayson for WPRI radio news.*"

Ted sipped his coffee and looked out the window. "I remember it very clearly because it was summer and I was home and my mother had the radio on . . . He was the one who announced . . . the first I heard of it, I mean . . . that President Nixon had resigned. It was an amazing thing. A relative of mine, this man who'd been to our house, who I knew, was saying these words that tens of thousands of people were hearing and would change their lives. It seemed important. August 9, 1974. A Thursday."

Her head was cocked to one side, her mouth open a bit. She looked six.

"You went to the University of Rhode Island," Franny said.

"Yes."

"You played football."

"Yes."

"Quarterback."

"Yes."

"Second-team All-American."

Ted snorted what he thought was a self-deprecating laugh at the recitation of the Wikipedia facts from his daughter, at the second-team All-American line. Franny assumed that he was laughing *at* her.

"What's funny?" she demanded.

Ted put his hands up, a gesture of peace but to Franny false and melodramatic.

"Hey. I was laughing at the thought of me as a second-team All-American. From Rhode Island. It wasn't that impressive."

Franny was looking at Ted's eyes, the caramel brown, the shape, his long eyelashes. They were the same. They had the same eyes. This bothered her.

Her phone buzzed and she reached for it immediately.

"The *Post* got hold of internal numbers on Bryce Ringling," she said to her screen.

Ted said nothing.

"They're . . . good," she said, still reading.

"Oh."

"They beat yours."

Ted nodded.

She watched him get up out of the chair and wince.

"What's wrong?"

"Nothing. Just old."

She watched him walk to the kitchen and take the pot from the Breville coffee maker and walk back and fill her cup, then fill his cup, then walk back to the kitchen. He didn't look at her, in the way you don't need to look at a family member, someone you know so well, have been around so often, physical proximity a given. He was wearing a powder-blue dress shirt and he had hair on the back of his hands and a tiny scar near his eye from when his sister threw a shoehorn at him. He smelled of bay rum. It was the safest smell she knew.

Ted stood by the window.

"Do you mind?" he asked, his back to her. "It's easier on my back if I stand."

She craned her head around, looked at his back. "No."

She was about to check her notes but her phone buzzed. Something about the noise, the relentlessness, bothered Ted. He knew it was about him and he knew it was bad. He turned and watched her hold her phone, inches from her face. It was a kind of mother's milk, this thing. The answer to all of life's questions. It was life, itself.

"The Columbia interview is trending."

He turned and stared out the window at Columbus Circle. The vendors, the hot dog carts and pretzel carts and cheap T-shirt vendors, the tourists on bicycles and the weird guys on Rollerblades and the buildings along Central Park South. The Essex House sign. There was a man walking a dog. No one paid any attention to the man. Ted wanted to be that man.

The double-pane windows kept most of the street noise out. Thick carpet. The tick of a ship's clock on the wall, a present from Claire. The coffee machine in the kitchen occasionally hissed steam, like it was exhaling.

Her phone pinged over and over. Each ping was a paper cut.

"Playing squash?" he asked the window.

Her initial reaction was to lie. She wasn't sure why. She felt she should be playing squash, living a cleaner life. But she wasn't and she felt guilty about that. But her guilt annoyed her. Why can't she not play squash? He had been so proud of her when she was younger, the promise she'd shown, the day she beat Claire when she was only fourteen.

"No."

She was looking straight ahead, at a painting Claire had bought years ago in Provincetown, at one of the art galleries on Commercial Street. A lone cottage on a steep dune, a winding road going off in the distance. It looked wonderful to Franny, a place to escape to, a place she wished she could step into.

"Why not?" Ted asked.

"I don't know," she answered too quickly. "Life. Work. Stuff." None of that was true. There was plenty of time. She smoked too much, drank too much, stayed up too late. She did things she didn't really want to do and wasn't sure why. Things that, as she was doing them, she questioned, looking at herself from a distance. The "Why not?" had a cascading effect on her. Why not, indeed? Why not play more squash, go to bed earlier, live healthier, leave *scheisse*, go to Vox, go somewhere better, start her own place, return to the blog she'd started and stopped? Why not meet nicer men? Why not stop hooking up? Why not treat herself better?

"I don't know," she said.

They said nothing, backs to each other. They stared and didn't hear the clock ticking.

"Can you walk me through the evening of the broadcast?" Franny said.

He suddenly felt very tired. He was done with this. It was a bad idea and he felt foolish. Let her write what she wanted.

"Which one? I've done four thousand, one hundred ninety-seven. I added it up the other night. Not to mention special reports."

She heard the shift in tone in his voice. She knew his voice and his smell and the softness of his shirts and his face but she didn't know him at all. Life and friendship and family are composed of terribly small things, ridiculous conversations. Calls to your mother about a chicken you made, the sea salt you used, how one deals with an ingrown toenail, the trip to the dentist, the old friend from high school you saw, the argument you got into with a brother or father or sibling over where to have Thanksgiving dinner. Small things, day after day, year after year. A visit to a cousin's game, birthday, graduation. You stay close. You make it matter.

But what if you don't? What if you let it slip away? Well, then you sit, back-to-back, interviewing your father.

"I had a bad night. It happens once in a while after nearly twenty years on live TV."

"Did something precipitate the outburst?"

Well, yeah, as a matter of fact, it did. Your mother told me two days before that she wanted a divorce and was in love with someone else. And it was my birthday and no one in history has ever enjoyed turning fifty-nine, with the possible exception of the terminal cancer patient who was supposed to be dead at forty-five. The questions, coming from her—from anyone, revisiting that evening—but from her, after all this time, the history . . . he felt the anger building.

Also, you couldn't find three seconds to type *happy birthday* in a text?

The thing was—and he couldn't really get his head around this—he didn't fully trust her.

"It was my birthday," he said, unaware that he was going to say it.

She'd remembered. Of course, she'd remembered. She'd just chosen to ignore it.

"Oh. Happy birthday."

"Thanks."

He'd listened to a radio program recently, late at night. Online. About religion and philosophy. A writer and poet who used to be a Catholic priest. He said he used to have to give last rites and that was a wonderful gift sometimes because you could feel the people who'd lived full lives. But the saddest were those who, he said, had a look on their face as if to say, *That was it?*

Ted thought of his mother for some reason and the image of the sink in the house he lived in growing up, a chip of porcelain the size of a nickel in the right corner, of walking in after football practice to her peeling potatoes. He'd watch her, tell her about his day. She was so proud of her broad-shouldered, popular boy. So handsome. She peeled and scratched her nose with her wrist, the clinking, rasping sound of the peeler on the potato, the earth smell. He would give all the money and all the fame and everything he had to stand in that kitchen in that moment talking with his mother.

"What's your story about?" he asked. He asked it in the same tone he used with young reporters who had taken three minutes to explain a story idea they wanted to do.

Franny looked up. "You, obviously."

"Yes, but what about me? That I called this woman a bad name?"

"It wasn't a bad name. You called her a whore. You screamed at her."

He hated the word, hated hearing it out loud. Vulgar, guttural, shameful.

"I'm aware of that," he barked back. "But that story's been told, don't you think? A few hundred times."

"Yes, but . . ."

"So then what are you writing about?"

She felt herself getting angry. Felt herself getting ready to react. She tried mightily to rein it in.

"I don't love the tone of your voice," she said. "I don't work for you."

"I'm aware of that. I just want to understand what we're doing. Is this a profile piece? Because there are a fair number of those out there already. What's your angle? What's the story?"

She snorted, annoyed. "My angle?"

"Yeah, because . . ."

"My angle," she said in a voice a little louder than her normal register, "my *idea*, my *story*, is about the end of network news as personified by Ted Grayson. It's about pulling back the curtain on a tired, archaic offering that dies a little every day. One that if Edward R. Murrow watched he'd throw up in his mouth. And mostly, it's about the face of the offering. And how he is one giant *lie. That's* what I'm writing about. Okay?"

She was breathing heavily. Her hands were shaking. She thought she might cry.

He wasn't surprised. He knew from the moment she emailed him. How could he not? Yet why did he also welcome it? Why did he want it?

"Sounds like a helluva story," he said.

She might have asked a few more questions. Ted wasn't sure. These exchanges with her left him depleted, unable to focus. They lingered, an emotional hangover. It had been so long since they had done this but it was so familiar.

She asked to use the bathroom. When she came back she gathered her things and he walked her to the door, held it open.

"Okay then," she said.

She made no move to embrace her father. It wounded him. He

was surprised how much. He wasn't angry. Just sad. Empty and sad. He wanted her to go.

"You know what they want you to write, yes?" he asked.

She nodded.

"You should write what you need to write."

She stared at him. Then turned and left.

No one said anything about a tumor.

As the days passed, as the story continued to grow, new groups jumping on to say how outraged they were—the National Organization for Women, the Komen foundation, the Girl Scouts of the USA, the LGBT community—Ted began to wrap his head around the thought that he would be fired. That he would need a plan for life after. He had assumed that he was simply too valuable, too important to be replaced. He was stunned to learn how fast it could happen, how fast everything could be taken from him.

Polly had called to check in. She left messages. She sent a gift box from Zabar's containing chicken soup, smoked salmon, and rugelach.

He finally picked up.

"I talked to Simon," she said.

"And?"

"Bryce Ringling's numbers are good, Ted."

"What does that mean?"

"I don't know. They want to meet us Monday. Tamara's office. Me, you, Simon."

There was silence on the line for a time, neither quite sure where to go.

Ted said, "Polly, are we going to get through this?"

"I don't know, Ted. I don't know anything at this point."

They had urged him to stay in his apartment. The PR people. It was going to get worse. Stay home, they said. Stay hidden.

The press, maybe eight of them, had gathered in front of his building, waiting for him. A reporter from TMZ slipped a note in Ted's Chinese food delivery saying that they would "pay you $50,000 for an exclusive interview/tell-all."

So he sat in the apartment alone. He couldn't bear to watch the news programs. And yet he couldn't stop watching them. At first it was a dream-like quality, the reaction, the words coming out of colleagues' mouths. People he knew well saying things on national broadcasts about his character and temperament, looking into his childhood, showing photos (where did they find these?) of Ted and Claire, years ago, on vacation, with Franny, talking about him in the most intimate ways while enormous photos scrolled slowly behind the panel of talking heads. One network had brought in an expert on xenophobic profanity. On the etymology of the word "whore." Middle English. Old English. Dutch. Latin. For "dear." If only he had used the word "dear." Russian dear. Dear Russian.

On CNN, the chief marketing officer of a major bank that had, the previous year, been accused of fabricating more than two million fake loans on existing customers' accounts (they settled) spoke about ethics and morality and how the bank didn't want to be associated with this type of behavior.

After Walter Cronkite questioned America's involvement in

Vietnam, Lyndon Johnson said that if he'd lost Cronkite, he'd lost Middle America. If Ted had lost the banks, he'd lost the network.

"Adhesive capsulitis, Ted," Dr. Foot said. "Common in elderly women. I'd like to start with a cortisone shot directly to the affected area. It will hurt. Then I'd suggest PT. Physical therapy." Foot said these words as if they were a new app from Facebook. "Then, in about two weeks, I'm going to give you another cortisone shot, this one far deeper and far more painful. A lot of people pass out from that one. I'm kidding. About half do. Of course, none of this may work at all. Worse comes to worse, it should heal itself in about two years."

This wasn't unusual, of course. It was the time of life when mornings brought new and unwelcome surprises from his own body. Aches in his lower back. Knee pain upon first standing up from bed. Sharp pains in the chest. Shooting pain in the right temple to the point where he had to close his right eye and hold his head. Urination was interesting. Why did it take so long to develop a steady stream, where once it was as simple as introducing his little anchorman to the stall, a powerful stream of urine spilling forth? He slept poorly, for a few hours at a stretch, waking at 3:45 almost to the minute. The occasional night sweats. He routinely forgot to zip up his fly. Of late, Ted had screaming pain in his shoulder and back. And, of course, his testicle. With long, empty days to pass, his anchorman purgatory, he thought a visit to his doctor might be in order.

Ted had known Foot for decades. They'd met through Claire, who was friendly with the doctor's wife. Foot was in his early seventies, gray crew cut, tweed blazer that he'd probably had at Andover. Ruddy complexion. His wife, Margot, was a DuPont. He saw patients as a hobby. Snuck up to Winged Foot when he could. He'd taken Ted out a few times. Ted could hit the ball a mile, but he three-putted if he was lucky. Foot would laugh his good-natured laugh. "You have no feel for the game, Ted. You're like a man wearing a ski glove holding a firm breast."

His offices were in the East Seventies, between Fifth and Madison, in the ground floor of a granite mansion that he and his wife owned. He'd done little to it in forty years. It looked like the inside of a men's club. Dark woods and old leather, his diplomas on the wall, ten-year-old copies of *National Geographic* in the waiting area.

Foot asked Ted to remove his shirt and felt his upper body, asked him to move his arms, palpated his stomach, kidneys.

"Put your shirt on. Physicals are a waste of time and money, Ted. I'm not going to learn anything playing with your testicles. Cough all you want, I'll still never see pancreatic cancer. How's Claire?"

"She's leaving me." The words—the phrasing of them—surprised Ted. He'd meant to say *We're getting a divorce.*

"I'm sorry to hear that."

Ted stared out the window, suddenly embarrassed. "She met someone."

The image came fast, surprising. Claire at twenty-five, tanned in the summer. In Cambridge. Claire on the beach on Cape Cod. She had a white sleeveless dress she used to wear. Simple, conservative. Her hair down, no makeup, the day's sun on her flushed face. The memory caused a sinking feeling in his stomach, a sadness at the loss of something.

Foot opened a drawer in his desk and took out a pack of Dunhill cigarettes. He removed one, lit it, and moved to the window, which he opened a few inches. He inhaled deeply. "It's a miracle any marriage lasts. It's an outdated technology. Like bloodletting."

"How's Margot?" Ted asked.

Foot took a drag, exhaling from the corner of his mouth before he said, "Ted, I don't have any idea. I assume she's fine. We live in the same house, share the same bed most nights, though she's often in the Hamptons with her annoying sister. Too much money is a curse. People don't understand this. A person needs to work. My wife knows my name and could recognize me in a police lineup. After that, who's to say? But it works for us. Bit worried about your testicle."

And here Foot chuckled. "Christ, if that isn't a great opening line for a novel then I don't know what is. Do you read fiction, Ted?"

"Not as a rule, no."

"Me neither. No one does. A bit of biography here and there. Mostly I watch TV shows. The golden age of television, isn't it?"

"That's what they say."

"I'd like to have someone take a close look at that ball of yours."

"Said the bishop."

"Humor," Foot said, smiling. "Very good. How's Franny."

Ted stood and reached for the pack of Dunhills. "May I?" he asked the doctor.

"Help yourself."

Ted took one, lit it from the old Zippo Foot had on his desk, and sat back down.

"They say they're bad for you, cigarettes," Ted said.

"You've got to live a little, Ted."

They smoked.

"She calls herself Frances now," Ted said.

"Kids. My daughter lives in Beijing. I have no idea what she does. She FaceTime's me once a month." Foot took a deep drag. "What's Franny now, twenty-five?"

"Twenty-eight," Ted said, inhaling. The smoke felt good. Powerful. A light buzz in his brain. He enjoyed the smell of the tobacco, the hot taste in his mouth. He couldn't remember the last time he'd had a cigarette.

"Imagine that." Foot was smiling, a benevolent grin, the long ash on his cigarette looking like it would fall any moment. "Married? Kids?"

Ted shook his head.

"She's young. You close?"

Ted smiled. "Well. She kind of hates me."

Foot smiled and nodded. "That's hard."

"Yeah."

"Lot on your plate," Foot said, opening the window more, and waved the smoke out. "I was sorry to hear about all of this . . . stuff on the news with you."

"It's fine."

Foot nodded. "Is it?"

"It'll be fine. When it's over."

"Seems a pardonable crime to me," Foot said with a kind smile.

"You'd think."

"So you're feeling okay, though? Because I can see where this whole thing could take a toll. And, of course, this business with Claire."

"I'm fine. For the most part."

"Interesting. But how are *you* feeling?" Foot chose to enunciate a different word this time. A kindly smile, a man you could confide in.

Ted found himself smiling back, though he was in no mood to smile. He was enjoying the smell of the tobacco. "I'm okay. I think, considering, you know."

"Sure, sure. But on a scale of . . . I don't know . . . one to ten . . ."

Foot paused and took a deep drag, threw the butt out the window. He exhaled an impressive plume of smoke out of the side of his mouth. "Ten being euphoria. One being . . . one being a weekend with my mother-in-law. God rest her soul."

"Five. I'd say a five."

"Wow. Five. That's pretty good. True, though?"

"Maybe not a five," Ted said.

Foot smiled. "Fair enough. But I guess what I'm wondering is how you're feeling." Foot pointed at Ted and laughed, as if they were both high.

Ted was laughing now, in a way that felt a bit out of control.

"Well . . . I'd say, if I'm honest . . ."

"Why not?" Foot joined in, still laughing.

"I'd say a one," Ted said. "Maybe less than one. Can I go with less than one? I'm joking."

"Are you?" Foot was still smiling. So was Ted.

"Not really."

"Would you say you're having suicidal thoughts or tendencies?"

"Thoughts? How do you mean?"

"Mmm. Great question." Foot lit another cigarette. "I guess I'm wondering if you think about dying."

"Maybe a bit."

"Who doesn't? Especially when I hear this rap music. I'm joking, of course. Do you ever think about dying, say, by your own hand?"

"Suicide?" Ted asked.

"Sure, let's call it what it is."

"Well, yeah. Yes. But doesn't everyone from time to time?"

"Interesting. They don't but that's okay. No judgments. Do you have a plan?"

"Not really," Ted said, taking a final drag of the cigarette, stubbing it out in a small ashtray on the desk. "I mean, it's a loose thought more than a plan, a fleeting fantasy. Loose, though."

"I make plans all the time. I planned on getting a haircut yesterday. Did I? Nope." Foot laughed. "May I ask what the plan is?"

"Well, hypothetically . . ."

"Sure, sure," Foot said, still smiling.

The idea seemed to come to Ted as if a forgotten memory, suddenly there, so clear. "I'm going to jump off the roof of my building. In my underwear."

"Okay."

"But first I'm going to defecate in the elevator."

"Of the building?"

"Yes."

"Interesting. And why is that?"

"Co-op board." Ted shrugged, as if these two words spoke volumes.

"Good for you. Co-op boards . . . forget it."

Foot tossed the second cigarette out the window and sniffled loudly.

"Okay. So, a little concerned here. There are all these . . . *rules* and regulations if someone tells you what you just told me. It's a lot of paperwork, frankly, and a headache for both of us. Do you think you're really going to do it?"

"Depends how much I have to drink tonight."

"Ha! I'm right there."

Ted laughed but it came out too loud.

"Bit of a curveball here, Ted, but would you say you're sexually active?"

"Well . . . the divorce . . . and the incident . . . I'm not the most popular catch these days."

"Still. You're Ted Grayson."

"True."

"So . . ."

"I'm not . . ."

"It's called a little blue pill."

"It's . . . I'm not . . . I'm not interested."

"Not sure I understand."

"I have no interest. It doesn't cross my mind."

"Like, for a whole day?"

"Days. Many days. Months. Longer."

"This happens."

"Does it?"

"Not often. But I've heard about it."

"You have?"

"Not really. I want you to see someone."

"Are they going to put their finger up my ass?"

"You mean my uncle Morty?"

"Ha." Ted faked a laugh.

"I'm joking. I don't have an uncle Morty. What good times we have, Ted." Foot laughed. "How long has this been going on?"

"What?"

"The lack of drive, shall we say?"

"I'm not sure."

"Since the incident?"

"Yes. Maybe a little before as well."

"Could this divorce business have precipitated it?"

"Yes. Definitely."

"My God, she's an attractive woman, Claire."

Foot stared off at his wall of diplomas and Ted had the sense that Foot was thinking about Claire.

"But also before the divorce?" Foot said after a few seconds.

"I think that's right."

"But maybe before that, too."

"Possibly, yes. Maybe a bit."

"A few months before, would you say?"

"Yes, I think that's fair, a few months. Or maybe years."

"Hmm. Ted, do you think you've been depressed your entire adult life?"

"I think that's also fair to say."

"Do you like pound cake, Ted?"

"How do you mean?"

"Pound cake. It's nice."

"What, like, as a cure for depression?"

"There are worse things," Foot said.

"Okay. I'd like you to see someone."

"So I'm depressed? That's it?"

"I think that's part of it. But I want to do a complete workup. The headaches worry me, though the stress in your life is enough to grow a tumor the size of a grapefruit."

"You think I could have a tumor?"

"No one said anything about a tumor."

"Didn't you just . . ."

"I'm sure everything is fine."

"Really?"

"No. It rarely is."

Foot began coughing and couldn't stop.

Ted walked across Central Park.

He made his way to the 1 train and got on a northbound train by mistake, only realizing at 110th Street and Cathedral Parkway. It had been a while since he'd taken the subway. He wore a baseball cap and had a three-day growth. Baggy clothes. To the casual observer on the 1 train southbound, he looked a bit like that guy on TV, only older and dirtier.

Ted came up out of the subway at Houston Street. He stood at Varick Street and had no idea where to go. He'd eaten half a banana at breakfast. He walked east. He saw a church at the corner of Houston and Sullivan and decided to enter on the Sullivan Street side. The doors were open and a priest was finishing Mass. Ted removed his hat and sat in the last pew.

The smell of incense, the place cold, a dozen, maybe fifteen parishioners. Mostly very old women and a few men, scattered about, heads bowed. He envied their good lives, their reverent lives, their giving lives, their spotless home lives, their Pine-Sol—smelling lives. Their Irish-soda-bread-made-each-Saturday-morning lives. Their chicken-and-potatoes-and-carrots-for-dinner lives and *Jeopardy!* at 7:30 and a crossword and to bed, up with the first light, the early Mass. *Bless me, Father, for I have sinned.*

Give us this day our daily bread, and forgive us our trespasses, as we forgive those who trespass against us . . .

Ted listened, the words coming back from high school. Something about them, the rhythm and cadence, felt grounding. He folded his hands, and let his head fall forward. "Forgive me," he whispered. "Please." He sat for a time, after the Mass had ended. Go in peace to love and serve the Lord. What if you didn't know how?

He walked outside, needing a bathroom. He walked down the stairs and entered a basement room in the church. Folding metal chairs were arranged in a circle, men and women of varying ages sitting and sipping from paper cups of coffee. The person who was talking stopped when Ted entered and everyone turned to the latecomer.

"Are you a friend of Bill's?" one of them asked.

"Who?" Ted asked.

"Are you here for the meeting?" the man asked kindly.

"Oh," Ted said, embarrassed. "No. I . . . I just needed a . . . a bathroom."

The man smiled and pointed. Ted hustled away. He could tell some of them recognized him.

In the bathroom, which smelled heavily of disinfectant, Ted had a hard time starting a stream of urine, even though there was pain in his overfull bladder. He felt foolish for being here. Like some alcoholic homeless man. Don't judge them, Ted, Ted's other voice said. For God's sake, these are good people just trying to make their way. They didn't choose to scream at a sweet young woman, to call her a vile name, you selfish prick.

The shame washed over him again, as it did more and more. He winced and moaned audibly. His head hurt. His right testicle throbbed in pain. He'd leaned his head against the cold tile and had inadvertently changed his aim so that now he was peeing on the tiled floor, the splash hitting his five-hundred-dollar suede chukka boots. He was urinating on himself. This struck him as a new low. "I'm *peeing* on myself!" he said aloud.

A voice from inside a stall said, "Yeah, well, I'm trying to take a dump here so maybe shut the fuck up, okay, pal?"

The voice startled Ted and he managed to finish urinating, at least in part, in the actual urinal. He washed his hands aggressively and exited.

Now he hustled toward the door, steering clear of the meeting. He walked with his head down, a boy without a date at prom making his way to the punch table.

"Excuse me." A woman's voice. Loud. Strong.

Ted knew it was directed at him but pretended it wasn't. He quickened his step.

"Excuse me." Louder. It startled Ted. Fuck. He knew what was coming.

"You're Ted Grayson," she said.

Ted stopped, turned. They were staring at him now. He was a man so used to people staring at him, most everywhere he went. That's wrong. You never really got used to it, Ted thought. It was unnatural for people to stare at you. You thought sometimes you knew them, the way they smiled at you, the way they wanted so much to make a connection with you. They felt they knew you. They'd spent so much time with you, in their home, alone, sick, naked, at dinner in a restaurant. You had told them things. But they didn't know you, of course. And yet they thought it was okay to stare. To talk with you. Interrupt your dinner in a restaurant. Stop you on the street. In the airport. Now he stood facing the AA meeting. He wanted to flee. He wanted to scream. When she judged him he would explode. He would begin throwing folding chairs, upend the coffee table, hurl the donuts.

DO YOU TAKE CREAM WITH YOUR CRAZY? the *Post* headline would surely read.

ANCHORS ANONYMOUS!

"Yes!" Ted said, though it came out too loud, too angry. "What of it?"

Here it comes, Ted thought.

"I just wanted to say," the woman said, "hang in there."

Ted waited for the punch line. The mean line. It never came.

She smiled. "It gets better."

They were all smiling. Kind smiles from strangers who knew real pain. Ted felt his throat constrict, felt the tingle in his eyes. He tried to say something but nothing came out. He nodded, turned, and left.

Hey.

It had turned cooler and Franny had a chill after she left Ted's building. She bought a coffee from a cart on the corner. Her mother had texted and wanted to know how it had gone.

Fine. TTYL.

She stood by the cart, holding the coffee, taking small sips, trying to warm up. Crowds moved around her. The traffic down Broadway, up Central Park West, along Fifty-Ninth Street. Everyone in a hurry. Meetings to attend, children to pick up, job interviews, auditions, an affair to keep, classes to attend. There goes a woman writing a memoir. There goes someone who's thinking about suicide. There go four tourists speaking Dutch.

She needed to write the story. Henke had emailed the night before to check on her.

A woman who looked to be about Franny's age walked by, holding a four-year-old's hand. In the other hand, she held a pair of ice skates. They must have been heading to Wollman Rink. Franny wanted to follow them. She wanted to go skating. And then go home. Not to her apartment. Not to the sparse one-bedroom that cost $3,400 a month. But home.

She wanted to call someone. She didn't know who, though. She tossed the coffee in a trash can and took the C train downtown, back to the office, where she helped out on a story about the fifty times celebrities had worn underwear as clothing.

She had her Bose wireless headphones on, staring out the window, listening to a Tycho song called "Coastal Brake." Henke came up behind her, tapped her shoulder too hard, startled her, and ruined her moment of bliss.

"Where's the story?"

His grating German accent and shiny face, too round and plump, hair too short on the sides and too long on top, the style now, too much pomade, too much cologne and expensive clothes that didn't fit him quite right. The way he looked at her. The thing a man could do with his eyes, his expression. Franny stared back, dead cold.

The *scheisse* holiday party. Four months ago. The Bowery Hotel. Henke was drunk. He bragged he'd taken Ecstasy and he was touching everyone and he was making a beeline for Franny, who was talking with friends, and he pulled her by the arm, smiling, and said, "I need to confer with the great Frances Ford." And he walked her to the end of the bar and smiled and said, "Let me fuck you." At first, Franny wasn't sure what was happening because of the shock of it, the did-he-just-say-that surprise, and also he was smiling so maybe he was joking. But he wasn't joking. He was grinning and so confident, the confidence of the very rich, and she was disgusted by him and also by herself for working at this place, tired at being disgusted with herself because that was what men like Henke did to women, made them feel bad for *his* behavior, made them question how they dressed, as if the problem involved cleavage and not personal responsibility. Have I egged him on? Have I given him the wrong message? Why was he staring so openly at my breasts? Why did he wink at me? Who winks? Why do men think they can do this?

She needed to leave. To be clean again. She was going to Vermont for Christmas break. To Stowe. She had to change everything. She had to get out of here. Except in the moment, as she stood there, Henke leaning in, she was afraid. The panic-fear from as long as she could remember. She blamed herself, hated herself, didn't trust herself. She wanted to scream but she also didn't want to make a scene. She was frozen. It was like a dream where she couldn't run. In her dreams, she couldn't run. She had to crawl. Over bridges made of rotting wood, high above black water. She was afraid and felt weak and bad but she had to climb out of it. But she knew how. She'd been doing it her whole life.

Franny stared back at him and said, "Your breath smells like meat and cheese and vomit. Also why don't you go *fuck* yourself. Merry Christmas."

"What story?" Franny said to him now, standing, pulling her headphones off, gathering her things, putting her MacBook Air into her bag, putting her coat on. "The story about Britney Spears's custody battle? The story about underboob selfies from celebrities? The celebrity wife-swap story? We do a lot of stories here at shit. I mean *scheisse*. Isn't that what it means in your lovely-sounding language?"

"What crawled up your ass?"

She could feel it coming on, shaky and electric, and she hated it. She'd always hated it. Since she was a child. The trapdoor fall, the energy drop. It felt out of control and terrifying. The moods. The therapists since she was eleven and the overheard conversations her parents had about her, the arguments and shouting about her, the fights and the bullying in school that she never told her parents about. What had ever become of Joey Staley, Franny wondered, the meanest girl in Bedford? She played a game at recess. *Who do you like better? Franny or Lila?* she'd ask to a recess crowd. *Lila!* they'd shout.

"I want it tomorrow," he said.

"Tomorrow, *please*," Franny said.

"What?" Henke said, clueless, Teutonic tit.

"Don't bark at me like you're ordering a coffee."

He stared, all bluster, secretly intimidated by her.

"Tomorrow," he said, then turned and walked away, "*bitte, mein Fräulein.*"

She tried to do a SoulCycle class but it was full. She didn't really want to do a SoulCycle class.

She stood on the corner of Ninth Avenue and Sixteenth Street, the young and fortunate streaming out of Google and the tech companies, the ad agencies and talent firms, the editing houses and music studios, New York fast walk. Where were they going? she wondered. To Equinox, to yoga, to tai chi, to Rolfing, to a spa treatment, to sushi, to the newest and hippest overpriced bars and restaurants on the Lower East Side, to Contra, to Dirty French, to Stanton Social, in buildings once home to Judaica shops and butchers and tailors, whose upper floors contained overcrowded apartments, cold-water flats, one toilet at the end of the hall, long gone, long forgotten.

Let us go then, you and I, | When the evening is spread out against the sky | Like a patient etherized upon a table. Let us go through certain Uber-crowded streets, the constant tweets, our headphones made by Beats. In the room the men and women come and go talking of Google and Apple and Facebook.

A guy named Matt had texted earlier.

Hey.

That was it. Just . . . *hey.*

They'd met on Tinder, gone out a few times, hooked up a few times. He was in finance. Or insurance. She wasn't sure. He was cute. He was sweet and fake and needy and vacuous and knew the right things to say, a soap actor who could memorize lines, a guy who would marry a pretty woman and be unhappy in ten years, divorced in fifteen. He wasn't a man. He wasn't a grown-up. He never would be. He was a guy who would always think about "great tits."

Hey.

In previous generations, young men stood below your balcony, looked up with wonder, spoke poetry.

But soft, what light through yonder window breaks?
It is the east and Juliet is the sun!

Or *hey.*

Hey spoke volumes, a language unto itself, a worldview. *Hey* told you everything about a guy. *Hey* said he didn't really respect you. *Hey* said he wanted to dispense with thousands of years of courtship and mating rituals, of decorum and chivalry. It said, instead, that he wanted to meet you at your apartment—or his place, if you thought you might be in Midtown later—with boozy breath, begin making out before the door was closed, hands fumbling for clothing and breasts, for ass, moving awkwardly to the bed.

And it begins.

Him, sucking a nipple too hard, you pretending it felt good.

You holding his semi-erect penis, thinking "penis" is just a stupid-sounding word.

Him, *squeeze my balls* (Shakespeare!).

You, *slow.*

Him, stopping, looking at you, the look men gave, the wide-eyed lust at your body, the lines and curves, the flair of hips and contour of thighs, hair splayed out on a pillow.

You, a desperate sadness that the look was only lust, no love, never love, *why am I doing this?*

Him, reaching for the condom, the moment changing, like a doctor's office now, the smell of latex, the foil wrapper tossed to the floor, his eagerness and hopes for a non-fading erection.

You, eyes closed, finding a place as he enters you, that moment unlike any other physical sensation, like surprise, like a gasp of air, the best moment.

Him, single-minded, laser focus, a series of calisthenics soon to follow: hands under ass, hump; flip, ride him; half turn, half screw; facedown, from behind. On your back again, him close, telling you to touch yourself.

You, why not, you're here. Eyes closed tight now. How strange the images that drift across your mind in that moment of deepest lust, hungry desire. Vivid, ethereal, physical, sensatory, until your head, thrown back, the small sound escaping.

Him, gone. The sound alone enough.

You, watching his contorted face.

Him, pulling back, rolling off, falling on his back.

You, the moment gone, the lust gone, the fleeting, false connection long gone in the seconds since it ended. Strangers now. What are his parents' names? Where did he go to grade school? How did he get that small scar on his chin? Who was this person you just had sex with?

She texted back, *Hey*.

Because *Hey*, in response to his *Hey*, was *I'm just as powerful as you. I can have casual sex just like a guy. I can care just as little as a guy. Hey*, in response, was victory. Freedom. So why, to Franny, did it feel like surrender?

They met at his place, so she could leave, come home, and pretend it never happened.

When she got home she showered and got into her pajamas. She didn't feel like cooking and ordered in Thai. She sat down, unsure where to start. She poured a glass of wine and opened her laptop and reflexively checked CNN and HuffPo and WaPo and nypost.com and Vox and TMZ. There was a message from her mother that she needed to return but didn't want to right now.

She put on music. She sipped her wine. She decided not to write it. She'd email Henke and tell him. She wasn't the right person. No.

That was wrong. She didn't want to. She didn't know where to start. Too much history. She paced. Fuck it. She wasn't going to do this.

She wrote.

He hit her once. She was home from college. She was late for dinner. She'd lost track of time, got stoned with some friends. It was a beautiful early spring evening and they were in a cemetery in Bedford dating back to the Revolutionary War and they were lying on the grass and staring at the sky and it was so peaceful. She might have dozed for a bit and somehow it was late and she rushed home. And he hit her. She tried to explain. He slapped her across the face and her mother screamed.

He became a stranger to her, walking past her, not saying a thing. True, she was the same way. True, she knew they feared her at times. But still. Couldn't he try? They forced her to go to boarding school. Fine. Technically her father was against the idea. But he let her go. And that winter. The storm. The time in the hospital. Where was he then? When she'd overdosed. Maybe don't mention overdose. It's not necessary to the story. It's her story and she gets to tell it the way she wants, revealing what she wants. The point is she was hospitalized with an illness and he didn't show. Who does that?

She wrote until almost 2:00 a.m. She wrote and rewrote; sometimes it flowed and sometimes she sat and stared out the window. She wrote in bursts, whole paragraphs, whole pages. It poured out of her like a good therapy session. Her sense of being wronged in full flow. Why hadn't he . . . why hadn't he . . . why hadn't they . . .

She was sure she knew the whole story.

■　　■　　■

It was late when she finished, hints of lights in the eastern sky. She felt very tired and sat for a time looking at the file on her screen. "Ted Grayson." The words that had defined her life, defined who she was. She went to the window and stared out. The city was quiet, a few birds beginning their morning song. It felt cleansing to have written it. To have told it all. Almost all. She was tempted to call him. To read it to him. Could they ever start again? She asked herself this sometimes, a deep, fearful hope. But she couldn't see it happening.

The real question, the question right now, the one that she had stored away since Henke had asked her to do it, was whether she could actually hit send.

She emailed the piece to herself, a habit. Then she dragged the piece to the trash, heard the sound of it landing there. She sat and stared at the icon of the old trash can. *Go ahead, delete it. I dare you.* Then she dragged it out of the trash, saved it to the *scheisse* cloud. Henke would be waiting for it. She knew. But she couldn't send it. She couldn't print it. She texted him. "Can't run story. Talk tomorrow." She took an Ambien, got into bed, and did something she hadn't done in many years. She turned off her phone.

Sag Harbor, one last time.

Claire had spoken with her lawyer earlier and confirmed the meeting with Ted's team to finalize papers and ownership. But she couldn't quite manage to call him. Instead, she had done errands; bought plants, ordered new bathroom tile, gone food shopping at the A&P in town, called Franny and left a message. Franny had texted back seconds later. *TTYL*. She had also made an attempt to pack up Ted's things, an exercise she found to be less satisfying than she'd initially imagined. Shirts she had washed and folded hundreds of times. Khakis and sweaters and old baseball caps and belts and ties. A Dopp kit full of toiletries. She abandoned the effort halfway through in favor of some vigorous digging in the garden, the smell of the dirt rejuvenating, followed by a late-afternoon bath.

Nancy was coming over that evening and they were going to make a Bolognese sauce and open a Barolo. After the bath, she'd dressed in yoga pants and, initially, an old shirt of Ted's, until she realized that it was an old shirt of Ted's, changing to a T-shirt and cashmere sweater. She'd laid the food out, all the ingredients she'd need for the sauce and the salad. She always did this. She liked the way it looked, a still life. She turned on music, picked Van Morrison's "Into the Mystic." College days. Boston and Cambridge days. She opened the wine, poured herself a glass.

It was their ritual in the evenings. A long time ago. A shower, pajamas, music, wine. The giddy excitement of the hard part of the day done, the possibility of the evening, of talking and listening to music, drinking the wine and eating the food, watching half a movie. This was what marriage became for most people, time with a best friend. It may be dark and cold outside but here we are, in this warm, safe place. There is garlic to peel and a dressing to make and a salmon to poach. We are not alone. There is a person to talk with. A person who is endlessly interesting and interested in you, a shared history, someone to talk with about the price of pears at the new supermarket, about the small leak from the eave on the back of the house, about your day. *Who'd you talk with, hon? Wait, what? Phil has skin cancer? Martha and Roger are splitting up? Gary's dad passed away?* These things that happen to other people. You talked about it and lived with it for a moment or two and then thanked the good Lord it wasn't you, returned to your life, to the music, to the warm kitchen, to the sauce and a sip of the wine and the feeling as your husband came up behind you, wrapped his arms around your hips, his strong body against you, how it felt like home. He could sense the smile on your face as his face fell into your neck, how you could feel how much he needed you, as he inhaled your smell, his eyes closed now, a smell he knew. It was a moment and you were there, together, holding on, the music playing. Your music. Your moment. Your life together. Until it was gone.

Claire sipped her wine, alone in the kitchen. The song had ended. She tapped the iPad and played it from the beginning. She should call Ted and ask him to take his belongings from their two homes. Take it all. The clothes, the photos, bikes, and exercise machines used nine times and abandoned. She rubbed her forehead. The good feeling was ebbing. She'd call him tomorrow.

The knock at the back door startled her. She turned and saw Nancy smiling as she opened the door, talking, carrying a bottle of wine. Claire couldn't make out what she was saying. She wasn't really listening. She was listening to Van Morrison. She didn't want the song to end.

Ted inched along the dense traffic on the Long Island Expressway on a Wednesday evening. He sat behind the wheel of an eight-year-old Volvo wagon. The helicopter was in his contract. He should have sensed something wrong when they said it wasn't available to him. The network had two: a Bell 430 and a Sikorsky S-76. He preferred the Sikorsky, as its top speed was 180 miles per hour, whereas the Bell's was only 160. Though even thinking this caused Ted to feel like a monumental blowhard.

Every one of the drivers around him—the overworked nurses coming home from a twelve-hour shift, the construction workers, the bankers and lawyers, the dentist getting a hand job from his assistant before dropping her off a block from her house in Ronkonkoma (Ted's demographic, in other words)—knew who Ted was, had seen his face a million times, had probably read about his shame in newspapers and online, heard it on *Entertainment Tonight*, on the late night talk shows. He felt that they could see him, in the dark, as the car made its way east.

. . .

Claire had initially wanted to simply split everything, fifty-fifty. She didn't care about the money. She wanted a clean start. Yes, she loved the Bedford house and hoped to keep that.

Claire's lawyers, however, felt differently about what Claire was owed.

"Did you give up a lucrative career in advertising to raise your daughter?"

"Well, yes, but I'm not sure I'd call my career lucrative."

"Were you rising? Do you think if you had stayed with it you could have achieved a high position?"

"I think so. I was good at it."

"Over, say, a thirty-year career, how much could you have made?"

"Oh, I have no idea."

"We do. We spoke with a top recruiter in New York advertising and she assured us that someone in your field could have made close to five hundred thousand dollars a year, not including bonuses. Now, if you were earning this salary for just half of those thirty years, that's $7.5 million that you forfeited to raise Ted Grayson's daughter, tend to his home, and emotionally support him."

The numbers surprised Claire. She was not someone who thought in those terms.

"The next thirty years of your life, Claire, will be years where you won't earn an income. How will you live?" She thought of Dodge but her brow furrowed because she didn't want to be taken care of. She didn't want to be kept.

Her attorney continued, "It is our experience and our opinion that you deserve far more than half. You earned this. I understand this language is uncomfortable for you and your sensibility. But it's my job to think this way."

And so, after giving it some thought and talking with Nancy ("Take it all," was her advice), Claire instructed her attorneys to ask for the following, with the assumption that Ted's attorney would come back with their own demands and that they would land somewhere in the middle:

The Bedford house (including all artwork, furniture, rugs, and draperies);

The adjoining ten acres of the Bedford house (which were Ted's idea to buy and which had more than doubled in value);

The Sag Harbor house;

Ted's vintage and pristine twenty-seven-foot Boston Whaler that Ted repainted himself every spring, alone, at the Sag Harbor house, to get away from Claire and Franny;

The new Audi;

The two-year-old Volvo wagon that they kept in the driveway for God-only-knows what reason; occasionally the maid used it, sometimes Franny when she came home. Mostly it sat, clean and gassed up, in the garage, depreciating in value;

The 1968 Mercedes coupe, garaged at the Sag Harbor house, that Claire bought Ted as a fiftieth-birthday gift;

Annuities, life insurance policies, various stocks, 401(k);

And a lump-sum payment of $20 million in cash.

What Ted got to keep was the Upper West Side apartment, though he would forfeit all of its belongings (except for his own clothes), including artwork, furniture, rugs, lamps, window treatments.

Despite vigorous pleas from Polly, Ted didn't want to negotiate. "Let her have it all," he'd said.

What would he do with the Bedford house, anyway? Or Sag Harbor? The plan had always been to put it in Franny's name, anyway.

That woman gave you her life, Ted's mother would have said about Claire. Surely, she deserved the money.

Claire had called. She had called and asked him to move all of his belongings out of both houses. He wasn't ready to do this in the Bedford house yet, to remove what he owned, to ship it to a storage unit in White Plains or some industrial part of town. It was too much. It seemed unreal. He really only had clothes and some boxes of old papers in Sag Harbor. He'd start there.

It was dark when he finally arrived, the house cold. It had a smell that always pleased Ted. Old wood, perhaps. He couldn't quite place it. He turned on lights, the heat, though it was a drafty place and it always took a while. He was hungry. He thought about going out to dinner, sitting at the bar of the American Hotel in the village, having an overpriced meal and a few glasses of wine. But he would know people. People would recognize him. He hoped never to be recognized again.

He found a ski hat in the front closet, pulled it low on his head, and walked to the market, where he bought half a dozen eggs, a quart of milk, coffee, butter, and a can of Campbell's Pork & Beans, along with a bottle of locally grown red wine.

A damp cold on the walk back, wood smoke in the air, still months before the crowds.

At home, he found dry wood in the mudroom and got a fire going. The main body of the house had been built in 1812. The rooms were small, the ceilings low. They'd taken down a wall to open the kitchen to the living room. He took down a saucepan and opened the beans, placed them on the burner on low heat. He took down a bowl and cracked three eggs, whisked them with a fork. He melted butter in another pan and opened the wine.

He poured the eggs in the pan and used a wooden spatula to move them around. Claire had taught him this. Move them around constantly or they will burn. The beans began to bubble and he turned the heat down to simmer. He turned to see the fire in the fireplace. It had caught well and was throwing heat. The kitchen was warm now, too. He would miss this place.

He sipped his wine and felt the first moments of happiness, until he remembered who he was and what had happened. Like the recent death of a close friend, it interrupted everything.

Eggs done, he moved them to a small plate and ladled out the beans next to them. A bit of salt and pepper. He brought the plate to the living room, by the fire, topping off his wine. He had never eaten food so good.

Ted opened his eyes and realized he must have dozed off briefly after eating. The fire had died down and the room was cold. He got up and put a few more logs in the fireplace, coaxed the fire back to life. He went in search of a sweater.

In the bedroom closet, he saw the boxes. He opened one and saw his clothes. In another his books. Claire had packed the things already. He rifled through one and found an old Patagonia fleece of his, pulled it on. He opened the lid to each box, saw more clothes and books; clothes he had long ago stopped wearing or forgotten about; polo shirts barely worn, cashmere sweaters, Ralph Lauren khaki pants, half a dozen pairs of shoes and a sweatshirt with the words "Sag Harbor" on it and baseball caps and belts and socks and dress shirts from Brooks Brothers and Paul Stuart. Thousands and thousands of dollars of clothing. Clothes he never remembered wearing or buying. What a waste. What an embarrassment of riches. Ted wanted none of it. He'd burn it. No. He'd have Claire give it away to the Salvation Army. More boxes and more clothes but in some there were papers. Old utility bills and bank statements and Fidelity Investments statements. Useless paper that spoke to a life he no longer remembered.

And there, among it all, a box marked *Franny*. Claire's lovely cursive. Inside, a mess of photos and drawings from preschool, crude little stick figures, crazy large heads and three eyes and giant smiles. A big yellow sun in the corner. Mixed among them were vacation photos—Cape Cod and London and the Grand Canyon. Photos of Franny playing squash. Class photos and graduations. Ticket stubs from Rye Playland and Radio City Christmas Spectaculars and a Brearley kindergarten class photo.

Ted lifted the box and brought it into the living room. He put it on the stone in front of the fireplace, sat down to get close, to get warm. He poured himself another glass of wine, took out more photos from the box.

Claire, trying to hold back a smile, at the base of the Eiffel Tower, wearing a pale-yellow dress, tanned, her face so young, her hair long.

Claire with her arms around Ted's mother and father, beaming, her belly full and round. This would have been Walt. His parents looking old but smiling. Claire's head leaning toward his dad's shoulder.

The Bedford house, Claire in the garden, when it was a tangle of weeds, dirt patches, the elderly couple whose children sold it to them having let the too-big place fall into disrepair.

And Franny. Franny and Claire. Franny on the beach and Franny by a Christmas tree and Franny and Claire in the snow, Claire pulling her on a sled, Franny pouting from the cold.

Here was Lucky, their first dog, a springer spaniel, sitting by Franny's crib.

And there was Ted, in a rocking chair Claire's parents had given them, Franny maybe three years old, footie pajamas, head leaning on his chest, Ted reading to her from a book.

A slim, tattered paperback. *Harold and the Purple Crayon.* Ted leafed through it. He knew it but hadn't seen it in so long. It had to be fifty years old. Harold is maybe two, and he takes his purple crayon on a walk, drawing as he goes. A road, then a tree, then apples, then a dinosaur to protect the tree. But the dinosaur is too scary so Harold's hand shakes, which makes the crayon draw waves, which Harold falls in. He draws a boat. And on and on. Until he draws a mountain to climb to find his room, his bed. Only he falls. He falls from the mountain.

He was falling, in thin air.

On those nights he was home in time to put her to bed, this was the final book, the one she needed to know it was time to go to sleep. She leaned in against him during these times, her breathing slowed, and by the end, her eyelids heavy, her large eyes glassy, she was ready. Ted would turn his head a bit and watch her, the long eyelashes floating up and down, deep in her own world now, aware Ted was there but also alone, until finally, her eyes would close and not open again, a perfect little round face at peace. His love for her at these moments was so profound as to be almost sad.

He put the book to his nose, sniffed it, the pages. A piece of notebook paper, folded, aged, slipped out. Ted opened it. Claire's handwriting. A date in the upper corner.

January 12, 1992. Franny and Ted, at bedtime.

Ted: "When I think of you my heart gets this big."

Franny: "When I think of you I turn my heart to happy."

Had you come upon Ted in that moment, walked into the room and found him sitting among the papers, on the floor, by the fire, you would have wondered if he had frozen, Pompeii-like, permanently thunderstruck by the sheet of paper, the words, the memories, milky at first and then a mental high-pressure system moving through his fifty-nine-year-old mind, clearing the years and bringing him back to that nothing evening when he put Franny to bed.

How do we become the people we become?

January 1992 meant she was four. She'd been an early talker. Dressed herself. Potty trained early. Her need for them was desperate, all-encompassing. And yet there were times when her love was so outward and giving, so intense. She would take Ted's face in both of her small hands, keep his head focused on her.

■   ■   ■

He put a parka on and a fleece beanie and walked out into the night, down by the harbor, largely empty save a few docked fishing boats. At this time of year you noticed the air, the quality of it, clean and salty, the kind that made you want to take a deep breath. So many stars away from the city.

There was a print he'd bought for Claire on the street in SoHo, years ago. A simple pen-and-ink drawing of a coffee cup. He knew Claire would love it. The look on her face when she opened it, when she tried not to smile, smiling all the more. A thing she did. His pride at her reaction. Such a small thing. This was the history of a marriage, too. She had hugged him. He remembered it, the feeling of it. To have her love. She hung it in the kitchen, on the wall near the table, the only picture on the wall, set off by the creamy oils of Benjamin Moore "eggshell" white (number 287).

Here were the images that floated through his mind as he walked, as the water lapped against the wood pilings of the pier, against the hulls of the boats, as the wind shifted, increased, caused a chill in him. The image of Claire removing the drawing from the wall and replacing it with something else. Removing all traces of him. Maybe a gift from Dodge would go there, instead. Something large and "happy." Something he'd bought and flown to her in his plane. Not that that mattered. Ted's gift, his now worthless little coffee cup drawing, would, in all likelihood, get boxed up and put in the basement, where it would be forgotten about, until years later, when Claire was forced to move from the too-large home and into a smaller apartment in town or close to Franny and her children. Ted would be long dead, having frozen to death on a park bench and not been found for days. Franny would have to go through the house. Perhaps she'd come across the print. A vague memory of it. Or not. Perhaps, instead, she'd look at it and think, *What is this crap?* So she'd put it, along with items like it, in a box and toss it into the back of her SUV or station wagon and drive it to Goodwill, where it would be bought by two young women starting a coffee shop in Brooklyn. They'd buy it for five dollars. Their coffee shop would fail within a year and the print would find its way into the trash, no memory of the gift it once was, of the expression on Claire's face that day, of the home it hung in, of what had gone on there over the years, of their little family, long since over and gone, like it had never happened.

He stopped briefly and looked to the sky, the stars and their light, already a thing of the past. The future is already happening.

He returned home, chilled, and took a hot shower.

The bedroom was cold and he slipped under the thick duvet. He leafed through the book. *Harold and the Purple Crayon.* He put it on the nightstand.

He would call her in the morning. Franny. He would call her. It wouldn't be easy. It would take time to mend. But for God's sake, he was her father. That had to count for something. There was time. Surely there was time.

The *scheisse* hits the fan.

Henke had returned home after a typical evening for him. He'd dined out with friends. They'd gone to the Soho House for drinks, then on to the Spotted Pig. What had started out as six morphed into fourteen. Friends. Friends of friends. Most owned or ran websites or data firms. All were wealthy, many were foreign born, and no one was over thirty-five. They ordered wine with abandon, unconcerned with the price. The women in the group were young, mid-twenties, and uniformly beautiful. Drugs were consumed in the bathrooms and, later, sexual acts consummated. They raged like it was New Year's Eve.

By 4:45 a.m. they parted, noisily, unconcerned about sleeping neighbors who had to get up to work, about toddlers asleep. They were the center of the world.

He had come home and taken a long shower, made an espresso, and rolled a joint, the two drugs seeming to contradict each other. He wandered his loft-space nude, a fan of his own body, the large windows open to the building across from his. The smoke smelled good, the marijuana creating a calming effect, elongating time for him.

Franny's story hadn't arrived. Throughout the night he'd been waiting for it. He was eager to post it. Now he stood at the kitchen counter and browsed the company's server, one of only three people with the password to do this, looking at stories and photos and videos that employees had uploaded and thought private. Henke didn't care. And he had made sure his lawyers had spelled out, deep within the pages of any employee contract, that Henke had complete autonomy over the *scheisse* cloud.

So there it was, in Frances Grayson's folders. He read it. Against her wishes, against any semblance of decency and morality. He read it fast, excited by its deeply personal nature, by the shame and embarrassment he knew it would cause both. Other people's shame excited him. He was of the opinion that most people felt this way but just refused to admit it. That we liked it when others fell, that it made us feel superior. He read it again, more carefully this time, and knew what it was, what it would be.

How strange people were, Henke thought, as he took another hit from a joint. How sentimental and foolish. Maybe it was an American thing. Their naïve, wide-eyed optimism. Their narratives of good and bad, right and wrong, of justice. They were genius screenwriters of their own false history, one that caused so much pain to others, so much war and death, so many lies. That's how Henke saw it. And yet they were such a trusting people, believers in a basic goodness. Try history, Henke thought. Try the history of the world. Of Europe from 1932 to 1945. Of Russia from 1917 to now, really. Of Africa since the dawn of time. Of America, itself. Slavery, segregation, mass incarceration. Of race and poverty and vast wealth in the hands of a few. No more fake narratives. Everything out on the table. Show it all. It doesn't matter who you hurt because the ultimate good is light. They were the ones who would change the world.

And if we were going to lay it out on the table, he hated Frances Grayson.

It was so easy. A gift, really. He found a picture of Ted from the *New York Post*, one where he was trying to hide his contorted face. He dragged the photo to a *scheisse* template page, entering the password allowing the creation of a post. He cut and pasted Franny's story and took a deep drag of the joint before typing these words in all caps.

THE TRUTH ABOUT MY FATHER, TED GRAYSON. BY FRANCES FORD GRAYSON.

The cursor blinked, daring Henke to click it. Or so it seemed in his addled state. And click he did. It was 6:21 a.m. It was alive.

He turned out the lights and walked to his bed. This, he thought as he lay down, was journalism now. He felt very good.

Claire stared at her phone. It was early and she was making coffee and since she'd turned the ringer on it had pinged again and again and again. She scanned it the first time, then sat down and read it.

Her palms were sweating now. Her stomach in knots. Maybe it was the hour, so early, a half sleep. Maybe it was the vitriol of the piece itself, the anger, the personal nature of it, Claire and Ted still, always, Franny's parents and Claire somehow complicit in this story.

Claire downed an espresso and had set up another when her cell rang. Franny.

"Oh God, Franny."

"Mom." The old Franny. Pure panic. "I didn't . . ." She couldn't finish.

Ted slept until almost 7:30. Late for him. He opened his eyes and felt refreshed. He lay in bed and listened to the sound of birds outside the open window, the wind through the pines in the backyard. Sun streamed in at an angle, illuminating the old floorboards. The room was cold. He was looking forward to a cup of hot coffee.

He looked at his phone. He would remember this. That is what one does in the new world. Before you have gotten out of bed. Before you have gone to the toilet for a morning pee. You look at your phone. Except for some reason he decided not to. What would he find there but a new posting about his shame. A new demand that he be fired. The day had so much promise. He would call her. Coffee first.

He dressed quickly, threw on a jacket, and walked into the village. The day was sunny and cool, high clouds moving fast. His head was clear. He seemed to see things in sharper relief. He stopped into a café and bought a coffee, a lemon poppy seed muffin, and the *Times*.

He returned home, sat in the kitchen, sipped his coffee as he leafed through the *Times*, starting with the obituaries and moving on to sports. He liked the box scores. Baseball season had started. How were the Red Sox doing?

He stood to heat up his coffee and saw his phone. Reflexively, he turned it on. Texts, emails, missed calls. From Polly. From Tamara.

From Claire. Producers from morning shows. *We can work with you on this. Call me. Call me. Call me.*

And, of course, a link to the story. He read it. Skimmed it, really. His eyes couldn't quite land on the words. He started again, forced himself to slow down. And what surprised him was this. He didn't know he still had the capacity to be so badly hurt.

Emergency state of mind. He packed up and left. He needed to move, to run. He didn't make the bed. Didn't wash the dishes in the sink. He got in the car and left. He had to escape, to get away from the words.

The phone rang and pinged. He drove and listened to the messages.

Polly. "Ted. This is a problem."

Simon. "Ted. What the fuck? She was supposed to show it to us."

Tamara. "Ted. Hoping we could have a chat soonest. Call me."

A producer from the *Today* show. "Ted. We'd love to have you on tomorrow. We feel the world needs to hear your side of the . . ."

A producer from *Good Morning America*. "Ted. We'd love to have you on tomorrow."

An agent from William Morris Endeavor in Los Angeles. "Ted. I think we can sell this as a series to Netflix."

He was about to turn the phone off when Claire called.

"Claire," he said. Flat. Dead.

"Ted," she said.

Her voice was urgent, pained. He could picture her. Standing at the kitchen sink, looking out at the backyard, at the garden. The wisteria and pachysandra, the hydrangea and the Japanese maples, and his favorite, the boxwoods, so elegant, so English garden. He knew the names. He pretended he didn't. But he knew. It had mattered to her, so he learned them. He thought it was their joke. He thought she knew.

"Did she call?" Claire asked.

"No."

"She was going to call."

And say what? he wondered.

"Ted, I'm so sorry," she said. She felt it had happened to her, too. To the both of them. She was apologizing for the failure of their marriage, for their failure, perhaps, as parents. Ted drove largely unaware he was driving. He drove and listened to his own heavy breathing.

"I didn't clear out my stuff," he said.

"What?" she asked.

"From the house. I forgot. I just . . . left. This morning. I'm sorry."

Claire's face contorted. The pain of it for him. He sounded odd.

"Don't worry about it," she said.

Neither knew what to say now.

"Claire?"

"Yes."

He couldn't quite get it out. He decided against asking it.

"Was I that bad?" he asked.

She was standing at the sink. She was looking out the window at the garden. At the pack-a-lunch-sandwich. That's what he called the pachysandra. He'd never learn. She had a lump in her throat. She closed her eyes. She looked up. She said nothing.

•   ▪   •

Franny sat on the edge of her bed and stared at her phone. She had eleven voicemail messages, twenty-three texts, and thirty-one emails. The story, on the *scheisse* website. It made no sense. It wasn't possible. She texted Henke.

WTF!!!

She stared at her phone, waiting for his reply. It came quickly.

Isn't it wonderful?!

He missed the exit from Route 27. He missed the exit to connect to the Long Island Expressway, the highway back to the city. So he drove down 27, half watching the road, half in a daze. He felt he should get to the network. When things happened like this in his life that's where he went. But he had nowhere to be.

He slowed the car, as he was driving too fast. He wanted to stop, to pull over to the side of the road for a bit. He saw the sign a few miles outside of the town of Shirley, just past Center Moriches. A billboard with a woman's face. She was wearing goggles, her eyes wide with joy, her mouth open, gleaming teeth. She looked so happy and alive. *He's happy.*

JUMP-START YOUR LIFE! the headline read. LONG ISLAND SKYDIV-ING CENTER. EXIT 58N. DON'T BE AFRAID TO FLY!

The day was so beautiful. The sky so blue. The photographers would be waiting for him at the apartment. The phone wasn't going to stop ringing. The stories were going to keep coming. It wasn't going to end.

He got off at exit 58N and pulled the car to the side of the road. He sat for a while and listened to the engine cooling, ticking. Thermal expansion. Static clicking. Murray had written a piece about car engines. He saw a sign. Same one as on the highway. Parachuting. The idea came to him so clearly. Here was the answer. Yes. Maybe it was a good day to jump-start his life.

You needed a reservation to jump out of a plane. He didn't just sit around waiting for people to drop in. That's what Raymond had said to Ted when he walked into what looked like an old garage. It had the pleasant smell of old wood and motor oil. It reminded Ted of so many garages in Pawtucket. An American flag hung on one wall. Above a cluttered desk, on which sat a rotary-dial phone, photos of previous jumpers. Dozens of them, along with letters and printed emails saying what a great time they'd had. Near them, an aged photo of a young, fit man in an army uniform, a young Raymond, Ted guessed.

"Have a seat," Raymond said, his back to Ted. Raymond was rooting around in the filing cabinets, taking out forms like he was mad at them.

"Wasn't even supposed to come in today," he muttered to himself. "Forgot a present I bought for my wife's birthday. Big dinner at the house later."

He slammed a filing cabinet drawer closed.

"Have to charge you a supplement," Raymond said, Ted finding the word choice curious. "Got to call my pilot. Lives in Greenport. Going to take him a bit to get here."

"No problem," Ted had said.

"Ever jumped before?" Raymond asked.

"No."

"Any special occasion? Birthday? Anniversary?"

"No. I just saw your sign."

Raymond turned and looked at Ted.

"Have we met? You look familiar."

"I just have one of those faces."

It was only after Ted had filled out the extensive paperwork, signed the waivers, and handed over his license that Raymond realized who Ted was.

"Sonuvabitch!" he said, smiling. "I sure as hell knew you looked familiar. I've watched you a million times. Real nice to meet you."

They shook hands. "Christ. Wait till I tell my wife. She's been watching you for an age."

Ted forced a smile.

"You doing a story or something?" Raymond asked, still shaking Ted's hand.

"No. Just . . . you know . . . saw the sign."

"How do you like that? Ted Grayson at my place."

They practiced on the ground, falling, rolling. Raymond set up two sawhorses and put a sheet of plywood over them. They practiced jumping from this.

"You hit the ground hard. A lot harder than you think. The jumping isn't the dangerous part. Any dodo can fall out of a plane. Can you land without breaking a bone?"

He told Ted about his time in the army, his experience at jump school, the jumps he'd made, how much he loved the military, how it taught him how to be a man. Should be compulsory, Raymond said.

"These kids today. Christ, I don't want to sound like an old man, but they're like babies, Ted. Hell, if these so-called millenniums or whatever the hell they're called stormed the beach at Normandy they'd have complained about the sand and where were the artisanal muffins."

The pilot arrived, a grumpy fortyish man with a dense beard named Alvin. As he readied the plane, Raymond led Ted back into the garage and gave him a flight suit, Ted needing a toilet before putting it on, a body-shaking fear suddenly coming over him. Raymond fitted Ted with a helmet, explained how each had a GoPro on top, how Raymond would send Ted a video.

"Hell, you'll have it by the time you're back in Manhattan. With music and everything. I edit the goddamned thing myself, Ted. On an Apple Mac. How do you like that?"

The three of them boarded the small plane, a 1982 Cessna T303 Crusader, according to Raymond. Miracle it still flew, he said, cackling, as Alvin pulled the stick back and launched them up over the airstrip. The smell inside the plane of metal and motor oil and old leather. They banked left, out over the ocean, the empty beaches of eastern Long Island, climbing, higher, the noise of the engine drowning out Raymond's incessant talking, a distant boat below, Ted remembering Franny's words from the story.

It's not self-pity. That's not what drives a person to do this. It's pain. Too much pain. The absence of any hope that this feeling will change.

An unfamiliar calm came over him. Everything seemed to slow down. The sound seemed to go away, the engine noise and wind muted. He felt drowsy. He wanted to give in to it.

In the book, Harold only draws one-half of the mountain. He gets to the top and *there isn't any other side of the mountain. He was falling, in thin air.* He smiled at the memory. He smiled at the view of the water below. At the blue, blue sky. At the sight of Raymond chewing a Slim Jim.

Raymond opened the door and looked at Ted. Ted shimmied over, the edge of the plane, the wind furious. He looked over at Raymond. A last look. He smiled. Raymond grinning and motioning with his head to go. And to Ted's mind it was a kind of affirmation. See, even Raymond agrees. But he couldn't quite move his body. He suddenly felt quite leaden. It was just . . . and that's when Raymond pushed him out of the plane.

He fell. And he had no intention of opening his chute.

The camera panned down, Raymond's point of view following Ted. At 5:16:12, like a scene in a movie, our hero surely dead, no way to save him. One one-thousand, two one-thousand. Not three seconds after Ted failed to pull his own chute, Raymond, a cartoon character, this squat, broad-shouldered man who looked like he could pick Ted up, throw him over his shoulder, and run a mile, became a human bullet, a rocket, reaching Ted, grabbing hold, pulling Ted toward him with one hand, and finding Ted's rip cord with the other. Who are the people who can do that?

Raymond's head fell back as he pulled Ted's chute and Ted rocketed up, away from Raymond at a hundred million miles per hour. Or so it seemed. Raymond falling like a shot, a radar blip, a goddamned supernova. And Ted thought ... just for a second but Ted thought, Oh Jesus Christ Raymond's chute isn't opening. But it did, so fast, silver-white explosion, old-Kodak-time-lapse film sped up of a flower opening, plumes of white billowing out of his back, ripping him up near Ted.

And here Ted looked over at Raymond. Ted looked almost directly into the camera, a thing he had done his whole life, the camera not three inches above Raymond's eye line, and began to sob.

Ted remembered almost nothing of the drive back to the city. Apparently, he managed to park his car in the garage and make his way to his apartment, where he stood, without pants, looking out the window, high above the city.

This was a bad idea and Franny knew it. But she couldn't stop.

She entered the office and felt the eyes on her. Or was that her imagination? She walked to her desk but the screen was gone. Her books in a box on the floor, and a woman who looked to be about twenty-two sitting at her desk.

The woman removed her headphones and smiled. "Can I help you?"

"Who the fuck are you?"

The young woman's face contorted in disgust. Franny didn't wait for a response. She marched to Henke's office. He was with Toland.

Franny entered and shouted, "How fucking *dare* you!"

Her hands shook. They were perspiring and they shook. Inside she felt thin and breakable. Henke and Toland looked up at her, German cool, *Who is this crazy* Fräulein? Toland left and closed the door.

Henke smiled a condescending smile and said, "Would you care to sit?"

"No."

Henke sat, took his time, very pleased with himself.

"I'm sorry, Frances. How dare I what, exactly?"

"Run the goddamned piece! Steal my goddamned—"

His voice was thunderous. "Because I don't work for you!" he screamed, his face a contorted image of rage. "How dare I!? You pompous child. Because I *felt* like it. Because I can. Because what you write I *own*. Read your contract. If it's on my cloud it's mine!"

She had no comeback. Except rage. "Fuck you," she said.

He snorted and nodded slowly. "Fuck me. Really. That's the best you have? And you call yourself a writer? Perhaps that's the real reason you're here and not someplace with real writers."

She had no comeback because he was right. Her throat began to tighten. Her eyes tingled. The old fear and anxiety welled. Her whole life, this feeling.

"Do you want to know the real reason I ran it? Do you?"

She waited.

"Because," he shouted, "you never would have accepted the assignment if you didn't want me to put it up. What daughter does that?"

It was as if he'd slapped her.

"You're fired, by the way," he said. "Now get out."

The car service made its way through Midtown traffic. The driver had the radio tuned to 1010-WINS. *You give us twenty minutes, we'll give you the world.* Ted would have preferred quiet and was about to ask the driver to turn the radio off but decided against it. The driver would surely tell a reporter that Ted had rudely asked him to turn the radio down. That's how it would be reported. No. It would be worse, using only a hint of truth. *He screamed at the driver to turn the radio down.* No. *He threatened to have the man fired if he didn't turn the radio down.* No. *He was a madman, this guy. He pulled a machete and threatened to cut my penis off.* It would be on TMZ. Gawker. On *scheisse.* CNN. It would be everywhere, even though it wasn't true. It would *seem* true. Wasn't that enough?

His palms tingled. The knots in his stomach wouldn't subside. He was fidgety and decided to get out and walk. He was about to ask the driver to stop. He started to say it. It was four o'clock. He would remember that forever. The beep for the top of the hour. "WINS news time at the tone . . . *beeeep* . . . four p.m. Disgraced anchorman Ted Grayson has been forced out by his network. Sources say a leaked memo confirms the firing, effective immediately. Grayson was caught on tape screaming at a hairstylist, a Polish immigrant, calling the young woman a Russian whore. A network spokesperson declined to comment. Apple computers announced its first-quarter earnings today, topping expectations largely due to its new . . ."

The driver looked in the rearview mirror at Ted. The car was moving slowly. Ted opened the door. The driver hit the brakes, said, "What the hell?"

"Sorry," Ted said, closing the door.

He was walking fast and breathing faster and for a moment he wasn't sure he was heading in the right direction. It was the feeling of a story breaking, of a thing happening that only a few knew about, that he would report on. He wanted to sit in that chair. He wanted to tell the story himself and hand it over to a reporter standing by in the field. Then back to Ted in the studio to sum up. Then dinner out and a stiff drink to soothe the adrenaline rush. Then home to bed, only to wake and find all of this never, ever happened.

He wanted to call someone but couldn't think of anyone. Claire. He wanted to call Claire.

The traffic was dense and car horns blared and somewhere close by a fire truck siren wailed relentlessly and Ted was finding it hard to concentrate, the bad flow starting, the edge of out of control. He cut across Forty-Ninth and started jogging for no reason, then slowed when he reached the corner of Forty-Ninth and Sixth because he had to wait for the light to change. He looked at his shoes and noticed his breath, short bursts coming fast, wiped at his brow and felt the beads of sweat at his hairline. It will be fine, he lied to himself. There's been a mistake. This isn't real. He looked up, turned, and saw, two blocks down Sixth Avenue, the liquid crystal display banner on the Fox News headquarters, these words scrolling by: "Woman-hating anchor Ted Grayson canned by network . . ."

Ted looked down to see two women in their late fifties staring at him, wide-eyed, mouths agape.

"Ohmigod!" one of them squealed. "Are you him?" Her friend was giggling, reaching for her phone.

Ted looked back to the Fox News crawl but his name wasn't there anymore. Had he dreamed it? Now the crawl said something about a new climate change report.

"You're him, aren't you?" the woman said again.

"Jesus?" Ted said to the women. "Am I Jesus? Am I a prophet about to be crucified? Yes. Yes I am."

The light had changed. So had the women's faces. It can't be him, they thought. No, no. It's just a crazy person.

Simon and Polly were waiting for Ted outside of Tamara's office. When Ted had walked through the lobby he'd felt people staring at him. Not like most days. Not like, "Hey, there's Ted." It felt different. It felt whispered and dangerous. An assistant showed them in.

Tamara, Max, and two men who introduced themselves as the network's lawyers. All standing. Not good, Ted thought. It's over. They're standing. It's real and I'm about to be fired.

They sat around a table.

"Firstly, thank you for coming in, Ted," Tamara said. "I know this is a very difficult time. Can I offer anyone water, coffee, something stronger?"

No one said a thing. Tamara smoothed her skirt without looking at it.

"Right. Ted. After careful thought, we believe it would be in the best interest of the network if you resign."

"I heard on the radio."

Tamara's poker face faltered here. "Yes . . . well . . . I'm sorry for that. Bit of a miscommunication with our crack PR team. We're amending so it will be reported as a resignation."

"Good luck with that," he said.

He wanted to scream. He wanted to beg forgiveness. He wanted another chance. He wanted to be made clean. He wanted to rip the drapes off her windows and throw one of the lawyers to the ground, punching him repeatedly in the face, a hockey fight, blood everywhere. But that was deep, deep down, in places he'd learned to hide from the world. Unless that world was your wife and daughter, who had a front-row seat to your anger and distance and emotional wasteland.

Ted said nothing. Emoted nothing. To the point where even Tamara was unsettled. Secretly she'd hoped for an explosion, a meltdown, a good story to share at the dinner party she was attending that evening. You'll never guess what happened at the office today.

"Why?" he said finally.

And here it was Tamara who blinked, whose face gave away confusion and annoyance.

"*Why?* Are you *joking?*"

"No. I'm the furthest thing from joking. After almost twenty years of consistently superb ratings, hundreds of millions of dollars in advertising revenue generated, dozens of Emmy awards, I'd like to know on what grounds you're firing me."

She wasn't ready for a fight. She assumed he'd go quietly, the wounded animal in the woods left to die.

"Because," she said, "there is currently an iPhone-captured video of you on YouTube trending at"—and here Tamara tapped at her MacBook Air, fingers dancing over the keyboard—"8,743,981 views. And your daughter's story isn't helping much."

"I'm fully aware of that. But I'll ask again, why are you firing me?"

Tamara turned to Max, an expression that suggested she was smelling something particularly repugnant.

One of the lawyers started to jump in.

"Ted, no one is firing you. We're asking you to resign . . ."

"Excuse me," Tamara said, the anger in her voice palpable. "What part of this aren't you understanding, Ted?"

Ted stayed cool, though he did lean his broad frame over the table. "I made a mistake. I apologized. I'll do that again if you want. I'll have the girl on the air. I'll do a series on men who don't understand anger or the power of outdated words. But I don't understand how a single mistake outweighs a twenty-year career. I lost my temper. I had a bad day. I didn't kill anyone. How?!"

And here Tamara sat back, anger gone, because she felt genuinely sorry for Ted. He had no idea how the world had changed. He thought it could go away. He didn't understand that the internet was the first creature in the history of the world that could live forever. It never died.

Tamara folded her arms across her chest, looked down at the table in front of her. She sighed and looked out the window.

"You're right," she finally said. "You didn't kill anyone. And you have served this network with honor and distinction for twenty years. And for that we owe you an enormous debt of gratitude. And I wish you could have continued to sit in that chair for a few more years, go out on your own terms, a special final evening where we review your finest moments, create a banner with its own typeface and theme song, run a full-page ad in the *Times*. But what's happened, what you did, while not murder, was, in the year 2016, a kind of murder. You killed yourself. You killed your brand. You might as well have killed someone. Ted, we might have a better chance of putting you back on the air if you had committed vehicular manslaughter. If, in other words, it had been an accident, something that the angry masses could understand. But you ... you screamed at an innocent young girl, a hardworking immigrant, someone's daughter, and you called her a Russian whore. The internet ... the world today ... and the world is nothing if not the internet, Ted ... it never, ever forgets. Or forgives. There is no mercy anymore, Ted. Because we can see it again and again and again, as it happened. Not a story in a newspaper but that actual event. And it makes us angry. And we want you to pay. Not the we in this room. We want you in that chair, wooing viewers, bringing in pharma marketing dollars. We want steady as she goes. But they ... the foaming-at-the-mouth anonymous commentators ... they want you to pay. Deep down they're excited because it's not them. They know it could be any one of us. They know. But it's you today. And you have to die."

Tamara found that she was leaning forward on the table, that the eyes of those around her were wide. She sat back, breathed deeply, smoothed her skirt again.

"The world changed, Ted. *Every*thing changed. Letters to the editor? Picketers? Boycotts on the sidewalk? Coups d'état? Please. Do you know what the most powerful force in the land is? It's not Congress, those useless, spineless wankers. It's not the soulless hedge fund boys in Greenwich or the pond scum on Wall Street or the C-suite who will do anything for a profit. It's the comments section on any story, any tweet, any video. It's comments, Ted. Comments rule the world. Do you think I control this company? Or the board? Because we don't. Not really. There is a new power. This company, though it would never admit it, is controlled by anonymous posters. Grimy, possibly nude, portly men sitting in dark rooms, posting comments late at night after a long evening of vigorous masturbation to exceedingly filthy online pornography. They comment and comment and incite other comments and foment the anger. Do you know how angry these people are? They have a petition with . . . wait for it . . . almost four million signatures. Do you know what kind of comments we're getting? I don't know, either, because it was so astronomical that our website crashed. Nuance is dead. In its place, we have judgment. Instant judgment. That's the world we're living in. There's no truth. There's no fact. There's only what you can get to trend. And it's only getting worse."

Tamara took a folder with Ted's resignation, noncompete, nondisclosure, and radically reduced pension due to a breach of a morality clause, and slid them to Polly.

"Please review, sign, and return these within twenty-four hours. At twenty-four hours and one second, they are null and void and you get nothing. Is that understood by your counsel?"

Polly nodded.

"Odd question, I know," Tamara began, "but might I ask if you recently went skydiving, by any chance?"

Ted looked up at her, startled. "I . . . yes. Why?"

"Oh. No reason. Except someone named "ArmymanRayRay" has posted a video that appears to show you either having an accident or trying to kill yourself. Quite a popular post."

Ted closed his eyes for a few seconds. More shame. There was no privacy anymore.

"I . . . yes . . . I just . . . lost control."

"So it would seem."

They practiced a two-minute drill. In college. On the football team. They practiced being down, late in the game, eighty yards from the end zone. A last gasp, no time-outs left. He always felt like there was a chance.

"I have one request," Ted said.

"What is it?" Tamara asked.

"I'd like one final broadcast." He surprised himself with this. Hadn't seen it coming. Feared she'd say no. But he could almost see her calculating the ratings bump if they announced it beforehand. *Ted Grayson. The Final Report Before His Death.*

"Scripted," she said finally.

"Yes," he said. "But I want sixty seconds at the end."

Tamara hesitated. Ted saw it on her face.

He said, "Almost twenty years. I just want sixty seconds to say goodbye."

Tamara sighed. She felt unsettled. She stood and walked to the window.

"Anyone familiar with the short story 'The Lottery'?" she asked, her back to the room. No response, which annoyed her.

"About a town that once a year has everyone draw a slip of paper. The loser is stoned to death by the town. The girl, Tessie, I think is her name. The one who draws the bad slip of paper, do you know what she says at the end. 'It's so unfair.' And it is. But that's who we are now. No one is willing to stand up. Should I? Maybe. But I'm afraid to get stoned to death."

She turned and faced Ted.

"You have your sixty seconds. And I'm sorry, Ted. I hope you believe that. I'm actually sorry for all of us."

Claire had just finished playing squash when she got the call. A regular game with her friend Julie.

"I assume you've seen the wonderful news?" her lawyer asked.

"No," Claire said. "What?"

"Your husband has just been fired. And there's a video of him jumping out of a plane. Might be trying to kill himself. Hard to tell. I just sent it to you. The timing couldn't be better for us. Goes to character. And with Franny's story, it's gold. I'd like to suggest we up our ask. I think we can take him for everything."

Her lawyer's tone repulsed her.

"I'm going to have to call you another time," Claire said, hanging up without waiting for a response.

The calls were coming in to *scheisse*, asking for Franny, asking for interviews. *People, Us Weekly*, the morning shows, the afternoon shows, and several urgent calls from a producer on *Dr. Phil*. But Henke wanted more. He needed more. It was no longer enough to run a story. You had to keep it alive. Update it. Find new ways to retell it.

Claire urged Franny to come to Bedford and stay for a while, until it blew over. But Franny said no, that she wouldn't be bullied.

A few colleagues from *scheisse* had texted her.

So sorry.

Shit storm.

But a few others had been less kind, tweeting;

Sort of feel bad for her. But she's also kind of a bitch sometimes.

It surprised her how much these hurt, how much it felt like grade school again. They were saying her name on TV. On cable news. On late-night talk shows. They were making fun of her and people in the audience were laughing.

Life is timing. It's timing and moods and chance. It's one-too-many cruelties experienced. One-too-many unkind words heard. It's the unfairness of not being loved. It's spring coming too late to western Massachusetts and the raw, damp cold making a person long for warmth, for human touch.

Lauren Loeb sat in the office of the director of the Greenfield, Massachusetts Social Services, listening to absurd and frankly cruel charges against her. Sexual harassment of female coworkers, stalking, calling them in the night. She herself would not use these words to describe the events that had transpired. Yes, there had been contact. But it was welcomed by both parties. Phone calls. Sure. She didn't know they'd been made that late. And why can't a person wait for a colleague in front of their home even though that person might not want that to happen?

She was being fired. For trying to be nice to others!

She cleaned out her things. Found a box and piled in her books and stuffed animals, her posters with sayings on them about being positive, her Northfield Mount Hermon diploma. She was under pressure. She was planning the reunion. She felt foolish. People were watching her. How could she have misjudged these people. Was it so wrong to want to be loved?

Lauren opened a bottle of wine when she got home. She felt shaky and she drank the wine and felt an anger rise. She thought it might feel nice to throw a plate at the wall so she did that. And she was right, it did feel good. So she threw another. And another. And another. Until there was a banging on the door and her landlord asked what in holy hell was going on.

"I was moving some dishes and they fell," Lauren said, smiling, keeping the door largely closed to the sight of her apartment.

That seemed strange to the landlord, but Lauren had always been a lovely girl, easygoing if a bit weird. Come to think of it, she did look like she might have been crying.

"Okay . . . well . . . be careful. And maybe keep the noise down, please."

She didn't feel like cleaning up the broken dishes. She didn't feel like doing anything. She sat on the couch, holding her wine, thinking that it might be time to start again. Leave western Mass. She checked her phone. Scanned the news. Checked her alerts.

Imagine Lauren Loeb's surprise to see Franny Grayson's story about her famous father. That awful misogynist. Except. Wait. She read it again, to make sure. Franny Grayson was writing that her father wasn't there, that he never even bothered to come when his daughter was in the hospital with a sudden illness. No. That's not true. Lauren was there. That terrible night. In the hospital. And it wasn't an illness. Unless you call a drug overdose an illness. Lauren poured more wine. She was tempted to throw another plate. Franny Grayson was a liar. And Lauren Loeb was going to tell the world.

Paradise lost.

Kuh, Feinman, & Steuben, LLP, occupied the top three floors of the Bank of America Tower, just off Bryant Park. The building was LEED Certified Platinum. Solar panels powered all of the building's heating. Rainwater captured from the roof was used to cool the internal systems. Automatic blinds gauged the sun's position in the sky throughout the day, rising and lowering to conserve the energy.

In a small conference room on the thirty-second floor, overlooking Sixth Avenue and Forty-Second Street, Ted stood and stared out the window. The windows must have been very thick, perhaps double-paned or treated somehow, because Ted couldn't hear any noise from the street below. He looked down at his shoes. The carpet was unusually thick, a deep blue with gold trim around the outer edge. He wondered how much it cost.

Polly sat at one end of a long polished table and texted. They waited. Polly occasionally sniffled. It had always annoyed him. The door opened and even with his back to the door, even without turning, he knew it wasn't an assistant bringing coffee or water. He knew it wasn't just the lawyers. He knew in a purely animal sense, a deep primal sense, that it was his family. He couldn't bring himself to turn around. He no longer had the energy.

The lawyers followed. Everyone sat. It began.

My father's cold emptiness as a human being.

He is a disappointment to my mother and me.

A model for everything I don't want in a man.

My mother's weakness at not leaving him.

In a phone call after the Westport fund-raiser, Claire had told Franny about the scene Ted had made with Dodge. It was a slip, something she'd not wanted to mention but found herself telling her. Franny used it in the story.

And this. During Ted's apology, he spoke of his wife, his only child, a daughter, the women in his life. At no point, according to Franny's story, did he tell the truth, that his wife had asked for a divorce and that he and his daughter were largely estranged.

Claire and Franny sat at the other end of the table from Ted and Polly, on the opposite side. Franny had to be there because the Sag Harbor house was being put in her name. She'd slept little in the past few days, given the fallout from the story. Initially there was a measure of support from women who saw further proof of Ted's misogyny. But a steady drumbeat of anger at Franny began to build. *Who does that to their father?* people asked. *Spoiled brat*, they said.

And then Lauren's tweets.

Franny Grayson is a liar!!! I was her roommate at NMH and was THERE that winter break. I was THERE in the hospital room when TED GRAYSON visited.

It was sent and resent, aired and replayed, commented on and parsed, ridiculed. It was featured in *scheisse*. It was inflamed by *scheisse*.

And this from Lauren.

She OD'd!!! Did drugs all the time! Where's that mentioned in her little story?!!

The weight of the thing. The shame of it. Things said in print and online that can never be taken back or taken down.

The lawyers were talking and Franny's head was down and her phone was off because the texts and emails kept coming, from friends and network and cable TV producers wanting to interview her. She toggled between anger and depression, fear and rage. She wanted to sue Henke. She wanted it to have never happened. She couldn't bring herself to look at her father.

Claire could and did look at her soon-to-be-ex-husband. She knew him and she knew he was not listening as the lawyers spoke their gibberish. "Relinquish all ownership and claims in perpetuity . . ."

She watched as he stared at a healthy *Ficus benjamina* plant, though she was sure he wouldn't remember the name.

The song the summer they met. She listened to it over and over back then. On a turntable. She'd long forgotten the name of the album but the song was called "No One Is to Blame." Side A, track three. She would play it after a shower in the morning as she dressed for work. She'd play it after a run in the evening, before going to meet him. She would place the needle down, listen to the scratch of the vinyl, and every time she heard it, she thought of him. Howard Jones. Claire hadn't realized that she was still staring at Ted.

He must have felt her because he turned and looked at her while the lawyers were still talking. Her eyes were wide, caught in her memory of the song, unguarded, a face he had looked at a hundred million times. He looked at her now, at her face, so lovely and open, those kind eyes that still had the power to stop him, and in looking at her, his own expression changed. The smallest smile, made broader by trying to hide it. And perhaps something in him fell away, revealing his true self. He couldn't help it. That face. That girl on the bench by the Charles River that first evening talking about her life and her future as the fireflies danced. Claire saw it and began blinking, felt the corners of her mouth rise, found that it was suddenly hard to swallow. The lawyers finalized their divorce and spoke of numbers and properties and codicils while they, across the table from each other, saw each other for a moment, for just a moment, as they once had. *My God*, she thought, as if looking at an old photo, *there he is. There's Ted. My Ted.*

March 2005. Claire was on the Hawaiian island of Kauai, known for its snorkeling, beaches, and volcanoes. She was there with Nancy, whose divorce had just come through and who had decided to stop crying and drinking a bottle of white wine every evening, and instead try to feel alive again. They were staying at an exclusive resort called Paradise Lost. Due to the divorce settlement and Nancy's lawyer, Nancy said she would pay for two first-class tickets, a five-star hotel, and pretty much anything else Claire wanted for the next few days. Thus, a six-hour flight from JFK to LAX. A three-hour layover. Then another six hours to Honolulu. Then a puddle-jumper to Kauai. They had been there for three days when the call came.

On the other end of the line was a woman from Northfield
Mount Hermon. A woman named Amy who was one of the few people on campus, as it was winter break and there had been a blizzard
in western Massachusetts recently, which Claire already knew, as
Claire the good mother always checked the weather where her
daughter was.

Franny. Overdose.

Those were the words Claire heard before her mind started doing multiple things as she half listened to Amy, who, to Claire's
mind, wasn't adding to the words "Franny" and "overdose," except
to add, *infirmary, unconscious but stable, road conditions, lucky doctors
stayed here, snow.*

Claire heard the words but she was also calculating the time. If
it was 5:32 in the afternoon in Hawaii, that would make it 11:32 at
night on the East Coast. Could she get a flight this evening to Los
Angeles and then a red-eye . . . no . . . wait . . . with the time difference it was 8:32 in Los Angeles and by the time she got there . . . five
hours from Honolulu and she had to get to Honolulu . . . fuck, why
did she come here . . . Jesus fuck . . . she'd sleep at LAX and get the
first flight out to Boston and then rent a car . . . three hours' difference between Los Angeles and Boston so a 6:00 a.m. flight from
LAX, five hours, had her landing at Logan at 2:00 p.m. tomorrow
and a two-hour drive. Twenty-four hours. Wait. Was that right? She
hated math. What about the time difference? And assuming there
was a 6:00 a.m. flight out of LAX that she could get on. She sat at a
table and opened her laptop. There was a 7:00 a.m. on JetBlue but it
was sold out. Shit. There was a 9:45 on American. But it didn't get in
until almost 6:00 p.m. Which meant getting there at 8:00. If the
roads were clear.

Claire did a thing with her tongue, bounced it back and forth, edge to edge, in her mouth. Nancy watched her do it now, holding the panic back.

"When can you get here?" the woman on the phone was saying.

The body under severe stress. What happens to it. What is released. Pure adrenaline. Her heart rate increased. Run. Run. She had to go. She had to move. But she was trapped on this goddamned island off a larger island in the middle of the ocean. She couldn't get to her child. Try that on sometime.

It was 5:30 a.m. in London and Ted and a small crew had just gotten off an overnight flight from New York. In a few hours they would board another plane to Sarajevo, then drive several more hours to the outskirts of Kosovo.

He was drinking a bad cup of coffee in a Heathrow café when he heard the same words from Claire through his little Nokia phone. "Franny" and "overdose." He heard "stable." But he also heard Claire's tone. It was a tone he'd not heard in a long time. He was looking at his watch. He was doing the math. He was bad at so much in life that was important. Empathy and kindness. He didn't know why. He didn't really care to know why. He was a grown man and he wasn't going to change, didn't believe people really changed. He thought it better to accept others for who they were instead of trying to change them. This, perhaps, the crucial worldview difference between Claire and Ted.

But there were a few things Ted Grayson was very good at and one of them was the ability, under pressure, to maintain calm. Because of course it wasn't calm. He felt what any normal human being felt. He just put it in a small box, off to the side. Because if he thought about it, if he really thought about his daughter, alone, overdosed, well . . .

"Claire." And for a moment he thought the line had gone dead. "Claire?"

"I'm here."

"Honey. Listen to me. I'm on my way."

It was the "honey."

"Ted," she said, an involuntary intake of air, a gasp, his name coming out in barely a whisper. A whole world in a name. A lifetime and a family and this girl who desperately needed them.

"I know," he said.

Two and a half hours later he was on a flight to Boston. The winter storm made landing there impossible so they were rerouted to Providence. Most of the car rental companies were closed but he tracked down a rent-a-wreck place; the guy behind the counter, greasy shirt, Lucky Strike hanging from his lips, a tubercular cough, just shook his head as Ted filled out the paperwork.

The drive should have taken two hours. It took five and a half.

When she first came into the infirmary she had been vomiting. Later, in a semiconscious rage, she tried to leave the infirmary, swinging at the doctors and two nurses. They sedated her and she had been unconscious for several hours.

"How long has she been using drugs, Mr. Grayson?" the doctor asked Ted.

"I don't know."

The doctor stared at Ted, not the first time he'd heard a parent say these words, feel this emptiness as they looked down on their child in a hospital bed.

"Her mother will be here this evening," Ted said.

The doctor seemed to understand. He nodded.

"I'll check in later. I enjoy your newscast, by the way."

He sat in the room throughout the afternoon and evening, staring at her. Should he put a hand to her forehead, like they do in movies? Should he hold her hand? Should he give a touching speech. That would be the movie version. Real life is harder. Real life was his worry that she would wake and explode upon seeing him there.

There was a cafeteria and he bought himself a coffee and a stale muffin and brought it back to the room. She was pale. Her lips were dry and cracked. Her hair matted. She spoke in her drug-haze sleep. Mostly unintelligible sounds, head moving one side to another.

A nurse came in and wiped her head with a damp cloth, put a salve on her lips, gently wiped back her hair, a care and intimacy that Ted found moving.

"It happens everywhere now."

She looked up at Ted.

"The drugs," she added. "We see it all the time."

They'd done a five-part series about it. About the Massachusetts city of New Bedford. They'd spoken to families whose teenage children had died from heroin overdoses. It was just a story, though, to Ted. Overdose segue to war segue to corporate corruption segue to political scandal segue to global warming segue segue segue. It never ended. How was he supposed to do his job if he didn't have some veneer, if he wasn't able to distance himself from the horror of it?

Ted turned to see someone at the door.

"Hi, Mr. Grayson. I'm Lauren. Franny's roommate."

Claire arrived, breathing hard. She sat on the edge of the bed, felt Franny's forehead, her cheeks. It was as if she had to make sure she was real, that she was here.

Only then did she turn to Ted, her coat still on.

"She's going to be fine. A detox, which won't be pleasant. But she's lucky."

Claire nodded.

"I want to bring her home. I don't want her here anymore."

"Whatever you think."

"You look tired," she said.

He managed a half smile.

"Do you have to get back?" she asked.

To Claire, it was an invitation to stay. Please stay. Please make the right decision.

To Ted, it was a suggestion to leave. What good am I doing here anyway. She hates me.

"I should," he said. "We're reporting from Kosovo all week. Unless you want me to stay."

Of course I want you to stay, she thought. But I want you to want to stay.

■   ■   ■

The lawyers left them alone in the thirty-second-floor conference room. Polly had gone. Just the three of them.

Claire now owned their home, possessions, automobiles, art, and retirement savings. And $14 million in cash. Franny now co-owned the Sag Harbor home and had $3 million, via a payout Ted was owed from the network.

Ted had $275,000 and a MetroCard worth $27. But he didn't care. The video, Franny's story, the firing. Claire's lawyers had everything they needed to demolish him. He put up no defense, told Polly not to say a word. He sat there and took it all. In an old New England, puritanical way, it felt good. A penance. He had been stripped of everything.

He stood at the windows with his hands in his pockets, jingling change. He was his father, he thought, almost smiling. Except not a fraction of the man.

He turned and saw them both looking at him. He suddenly felt very awkward.

"Okay, then." He forced a smile.

"Dad." Franny's voice. Higher than normal. Urgent. "I'm sorry."

"Never apologize for reporting the truth, Frances."

She wanted to say more. She wanted to explain what happened. She was rubbing her tongue against the back of her lower teeth. She wanted him to prove how much he loved her. She wanted to make him prove it. Because she never believed it. Because she needed it so much it terrified her. Because it couldn't be real. So push him away. Make him prove it. And then he stopped trying. And that was the worst thing in the world.

Frances. Please don't call me Frances, she thought.

Ted walked around the table and put a hand on Claire's shoulder, light as a bird landing. It caused Claire's head to fall forward.

"I'm the one who's sorry."

Tracking her down was easy, of course. Through her Facebook page. Her Twitter account. LinkedIn.

My name is Henke Tessmer, he'd written. I run a website in New York City. *Scheisse.* Perhaps you have heard of it? I would love to talk to you about your old roommate. Might you have time to talk on the phone?

Henke called her. And listened. She talked. Without interruption. Henke knew what he had in her, this troubled, lonely soul who only wanted to be listened to. Henke listened and typed, recorded the call, would use it on the site over images Lauren was more than happy to send of her time at NMH.

"We were friends once. I think. I mean . . . we were. That story was just so . . . mean . . . about her father. Her mother is sooo beautiful. I met her once. And her father. During the snowstorm, the time Franny OD'ed."

"Sorry, what's that you said?"

"Oh yeah. You don't know that story? Do you want to hear more? I feel like I've been talking a lot. Have I?"

"No," Henke said. "Not at all. Tell me more Lauren."

This is Cassini, over and out.

Ted was watching himself die. How many people get that chance? He was watching it, right there on his MacBook Pro, in a wildly expensive apartment high above Central Park West. It was late now and he'd put a good dent in a bottle of Ketel One and, for some reason, he was not wearing pants.

He'd watched the video several times, which may have accounted for the fact that he was crying. Ted found this partially amusing, the pathetic image of himself, and laughed between sobs in a way that would have made an onlooker think, *That fellow is unwell.*

Maybe it was the music that was affecting him. Raymond had used Elton John's "Rocket Man." He'd met him, for Chrissakes. Ted had. Interviewed Elton. Sir Elton. He'd met everyone. Robert De Niro. Idi Amin. Prince Charles. The Dalai Lama. Bono. The Pope. The Pope bummed a smoke off him. Beat that.

High above Columbus Circle, cocooned in warmth and wealth, pantless, Ted watched himself, a milk glass of vodka, tears streaming down his face once again. Who among us wouldn't react that way, watching what was almost our own death?

■   ■   ■

It was almost 3:00 a.m. The worst time for Ted. Deeply tired but unable to sleep, lying on the couch in the dark, lying in his bed. But sleep wouldn't come.

So he clicked through YouTube. He was looking for his life, for the moments that were gone but that, for him, in his memory, were still alive. Once hopeful things. Bobby Orr and Carl Yastrzemski and the moon landing. My God, what a thing. Neil Armstrong and Edwin "Buzz" Aldrin walking on the moon. The iPhone? The iPad? The Pentium processor? Fuck you. Try putting a man on the moon. He said this out loud. His own voice surprised him.

Ted sat on the floor of the living room, his back against the couch, the lights off, his laptop on the coffee table. He pulled on a sweater. He had a chill that wouldn't quite leave him.

He watched a clip of Walter Cronkite reporting that man had landed on the moon. It was a clip he had seen before so many times. Vague memories as a boy. His father and mother and little sister. The part where Cronkite took his glasses off, tried to suppress his joy but simply couldn't, the mind-bending idea that human beings had somehow figured out how to travel to the moon. He watched it again and Cronkite's expression, the childlike innocence of it, the purity, brought a lump to Ted's throat. The nation was watching him. Watching his dignity and grace, his humanity.

Here's a question. Have you ever listened to Vince Guaraldi's version of "Moon River" when your drunk has worn off and you've watched the sky begin to change, from dark to blue-black light, softly turning gray, another day in the world, a kind of pause button in New York, the streets almost silent, no people, just a play of light and time and all those plans that came to nothing, that no one cared about now? And the panicked need to run back to a place in time, a moment, a person, long gone. Have you ever done that? Ted wouldn't recommend it.

He stood now at the tall windows, looking out. And the memory came so sharp and so fast. She was almost five and she sat on Ted's lap on the porch of the cottage, looking out at Barnstable Harbor. Late August, dusk. Ted had given her a bath and washed her hair. He'd put her pajamas on and later he'd showered and shaved and put on a clean shirt, Claire looking over at him as she stood at the stove boiling steamers, handing him a drink, Ted carrying his bundle of girl out onto the porch. They sat on a wooden deck chair, the cloth sun-faded, and now a gentle breeze, the colors in the sky as the sun set, the sound of water against the beach, against the smooth stones, over and over and over. She was tired from a day of swimming, a day in the sun.

"Dad," she whispered, her head against his chest, damp hair against the side of his face. "Is wind the softest thing?"

Now, watching the colors of the sky change over Manhattan, he smiled as he stood with his forehead against the cool glass of the window, the heart-stopping beauty of the light in the eastern sky. The memory of her. That it could still give him such joy. He had that. Maybe that was what hope felt like.

Ted arrived early, the newsroom empty. He stopped at Dunkin' Donuts for a coffee and decided to buy a dozen donuts. Something about walking down the hall now carrying a dozen donuts made him feel foolish. He walked past the writers' room and found Murray already at his desk, reading the newspaper. Ted watched him, Murray unaware for a few seconds that Ted was at the door.

Murray looked up. "Jesus. Ted. You scared me."

"Sorry."

"You're in early."

Murray regretted saying it, but Ted smiled.

"Always get in early on your last day," Ted said. "You know who said that?"

"No. Who?"

"No one, ever."

Murray snorted. Ted put the box of donuts down on Murray's desk.

"Donuts," Ted said.

"Oh. Wow. Thanks."

"What's in the news?" Ted asked, motioning toward the paper with his head.

"Oh. Well. The usual heartwarming fare. War in Syria. Staggering degradation of the polar ice shelf. Tax cuts for the rich."

"Sounds reasonable."

"My personal favorite, though. A new study says that paper towels may cause cancer."

"Perfect."

Ted stood by the door. "I'd like to close with Cassini."

Murray nodded. "I've been working on something. Send it to you in a bit?"

"Thanks."

Ted turned to go.

"Ted," Murray said, too urgently.

Ted turned back.

"I'm sorry. About all this." Murray had stood.

Ted managed a small smile. "Me, too. But thank you."

He left but from down the hallway Murray heard, "The donuts aren't just for you."

Murray had his headphones on. He was listening to Brian Eno's "Thursday Afternoon," a sixty-one-minute song. He had found footage of Ted's first broadcast. He was so young, Murray thought. He was a kid. Murray wasn't sure whether he remembered the broadcast or if the video was giving him the false sense that he remembered it.

He then listened to their first report on the launch of Cassini. But he stopped it halfway through, found himself with a lump in his throat. He clicked over to NASA's live feed, a blip of light 746 million miles from Earth. He watched as it flew, at 186,000 miles per hour, exactly as planned, around Saturn, certain death. It overwhelmed him. Made him profoundly sad. This thing, out there in space. A life's work. Dying. Murray had nothing else. This was it. This was what he looked forward to each morning. He wanted desperately to feel sorry for himself, but he didn't have time. He needed to write. He ate a third donut.

Grace and Jagdish finished their stories, went out for coffee, bringing one back for Murray. It was almost 5:00 and they needed to lock the show.

Murray hit print. Grace heard it, stood, and walked to the printer.

"May I?" she asked.

Murray nodded. Grace read. She looked up at Murray, who refused to look back at her. She kept reading. She read part of it out loud.

"What have we seen in the past twenty years? Who has been born? Who has died? What books have been written? Movies made? Technology created? Wars fought? What have we learned? What has moved us forward? What has set us back? What has opened our eyes? Given us joy and wonder and hope? Cassini mattered."

She paused, briefly, and, picking up a pencil from her desk, made a small mark on the page.

"It showed us a time and a place. A world we hadn't seen. We are better for it."

She looked up at Jagdish. Looked at Murray.

"It's perfect," she said.

She walked to his desk and put the copy down. Murray saw the mark she'd made on the page.

"You typed 'he' mattered," she said. "I think you meant 'it.'"

"Oh. Yes. Of course. Typo."

Grace leaned down and hugged him.

"Thirty seconds," Sean said.

Ted looked around the set. Sean, Lou, Simon, Murray, Grace, Jagdish. They'd gathered, out of eye line, to witness this. Ted saw them now. He'd seen them most every working day for nearly twenty years. And tomorrow, after the drinks this evening, after the promises to keep in touch, he would likely never see them again.

He cleared his throat. "Thank you," he said, quietly. He looked up at them. "You guys. Thank you. For . . ."

They applauded. And it moved him in a way that surprised him.

"Sorry. Quiet, please." Sean. "In five, four, three . . ."

"This is my last broadcast as anchor of the nightly news. It has been a privilege being a small part of your evening five nights a week. I hope this broadcast and the remarkable women and men who make it happen each evening have helped you, in some small way, see the world more clearly. If not, if network news has failed you, then I have failed you as its managing editor. A few months after I first sat in this chair, something extraordinary happened at Cape Canaveral, Florida. A twenty-two-foot-high space probe called Cassini-Huygens rocketed into orbit for a twenty-year journey. It orbited Saturn, the second-largest planet in our solar system, for thirteen years. It had course coordinates, a detailed plan of work, a script by which to go. But, of course, that's not how life works. We can plan but we cannot see what lies ahead. In my almost twenty years here, we have gone by a script each evening. But who among us could have imagined in 1997 the world we would see. Cassini traveled 4.9 billion miles since its launch. In that same time, we, as a nation, as a world, as individuals, have traveled a great distance, too. We live, today, in a world radically different than just twenty years ago. We have seen extraordinary advances in technology, communication, medicine, transportation. There is, contrary to so much of what we see and hear, remarkable hope. But something fundamental has shifted in America. The advances of technology are extraordinary. But we are living in a new, digital wild west. A world yet to be fully formed. A world lacking rules. So what now? We have a choice. In how we use technology to advance humanity. Kindness. Generosity. It is easy to become a skeptic sitting in this chair night after night. To become callous to the beauty and possibility of the world. My job, the media's job, isn't to share the news. It's to share the worst. To horrify you. Imagine it was different, though. Imagine if the job was to inspire? Educate? Instead of show you the worst of who we are? If I have a regret—and I have many—it's that we didn't do that more. Demand that from the news. Demand that from media— social and otherwise. I am a kid from Woonsocket, Rhode Island, who never thought he would grow up to sit in this chair. It has been my honor and my privilege. Thank you for the opportunity. This is Ted Grayson. Thank you. And goodbye."

How do you say "I'm sorry" in Polish?

The Realtor had asked Ted to leave the apartment. It was the first showing and they already had calls, along with two cash offers, from the listing on the Sotheby's real estate website. The Realtor was actually a team. That's how it was described to Ted, who would had preferred putting a listing in *The New York Times*, but that world had died. Now it was a video put on a website and a team of remarkably good-looking people marketing Ted's apartment. "We'll make no mention, of course, that it's your place."

In the days that followed the final broadcast, something seemed to shift for Ted. Not a resignation to this new reality but a lightness. Not joy by any measure. But an acceptance that his life, as he had known it for twenty years, was over. He stopped carrying his cell phone with him, stopped looking at his laptop. He knew only that he needed to leave. A plan began to form.

He walked. He had little need for sleep. He planned, took notes, searched online. A small doze here and there but the notion of eight hours of sleep seemed an epic waste. And now, of course, the apartment was largely empty. Claire had movers take the artwork, the fine rugs.

He walked. The air was cool, crisp, but the trees showed signs of life and flower boxes held pansies and daffodils. He wore a ski hat pulled down over his head, his beard unshaven for over a week. He bore little resemblance to that man on television. He wore headphones, a gift from Claire years before. He listened to music he'd come across on YouTube. Trappist monks chanting Latin hymns. He'd found it soothing.

He walked without destination. Side streets, his pace matched by the slow chanting, by the ancient dead language. People around him walked quickly, with purpose, even if they weren't in a hurry. They were New Yorkers on a weekday and even if they were on the way to the corner store for half-and-half they walked as if they were late for a job interview. Perhaps it was the monks and their Latin. Perhaps it was his lack of sleep and the buzz of too much coffee. But he felt as if he saw people and the world more clearly. The stress on the woman's face at the corner, holding one child's hand and strolling another, who was mid-meltdown. Two women, eighty if they were a day, making their way down Fifth Avenue, turning into the park, heads down the whole way, knowing the route by heart. Ted imagined stale bread in their bags, an afternoon feeding birds and talking of . . . what? Ted envied them. Envied what he thought their life might be.

Along the side streets off the park now. Somehow, he had walked up to the Nineties and was in front of the Spence school and the lower grades were letting out, the girls in their uniforms and oversized cartoon-character backpacks. The monks chanted and the girls filed out, large-eyed, looking for their caretaker, which, if it was a mother, elicited a sprint and a neck hug, little soldiers returning home after years at the front. Ted imagined what happened next. Home for a snack and a rest. Then to swim lessons or piano lessons or a playdate. Later dinner, bath, bed. That's what Claire used to say to Franny. Dinner-bath-bed, as if one word. Franny wanting always to know what was happening. *Tell me the day*, she would ask each night, before Claire or Ted left the room.

And still the monks sang. How different life is with a music track.

Into Central Park now. It appeared to Ted like a private country club. Like something in Bedford, only it was open to all and French tourists wandered by and couples sat on the lawn and young families kicked a ball. Bicyclists and runners. A tall Sikh man in a turban sat on a milk crate next to his "Nuts for nuts" cart, the sweet smell. Sun broke through dark clouds and the wind made it cool, but the winter was over and the tulips were up, daffodils, too, and the grass was an Ireland green and people needed to be outside, to walk or sit on the benches and look at the trees and the sky and breathe it in.

What did they do, these people, so many of them, that they were outside on a Thursday afternoon? Older women being helped by nurses' aides and mothers strolling babies and Japanese tourists looking at maps. Here was an off-duty nurse and there was a young couple holding hands and there was an old man asleep on a bench, his chin on his chest, a book on his lap, a woman next to him, reading, holding his hand.

Near the Olmsted walkway two men, maybe twenty-five years old, had a good crowd gathered and were preparing to jump over eight people in a line. On a hill, a man was teaching a woman how to cast a fly rod. The yellow line snapping in the wind. In the playground the children squealed. A horse pulling a carriage went by, leaving the clean scent of manure. In the distance, someone must have been cutting the lawn. The smell almost brought tears to Ted's eyes.

Ted bought a hot dog and found the taste sublime. Perhaps it was because he'd not eaten all day. Sodium. When he thought of hot dogs he often thought of sodium. A story they had done a while back. Hot dogs are high in sodium. Ted had looked at a chart that Jagdish shared. The periodic table of the elements. Every high school student had seen it. But Ted looked carefully. Bismuth. Seaborgium. Hafnium. These were elements. There were 118 elements in the periodic table. Ted found this out recently, on a late-night Ketel One fest, searching the internet. These names, names he had never heard before. And here Ted was seen as a wise man by eight million people. How was it possible that he had never heard of most of the elements that make up the planet?

He reached the West Side and the monks sang as Ted walked down into the subway at Seventy-Second Street. He rode the local downtown, standing room only, the faces so somber. The construction workers asleep on their way home, the groups of high school kids, the boys too loud and the girls laughing and hitting each other, sharing an earbud, listening to the same song. Crowds poured out at Fourteenth Street and Ted took a seat. He watched a mother and son, a boy of perhaps eight, Down syndrome. The boy sniffed at his hands and made kissing sounds at his mother. Ted assumed she was the boy's mother. The mother smiled at the boy but mostly stared out the window. Legs double-wrapped around her calf, black baggy pants, white waffle long-sleeved T-shirt. She stared at a spot on the floor. He stuck his tongue out, plump lower lip extended. She looked

over at him, stared at him as he looked out the window. He turned
and he looked at her with such a look of love that Ted had to look
away, the moment so real, so raw, so private.

Why not put this on the news, he thought. Film this and put it
on the news with the monks chanting. Would that not tell his audience more about what went on in the world that day than any ten
reporters on assignment in Kabul/Jakarta/the Pentagon/The Hague
telling stories that were carefully scripted by governments or corporations or breaking news that told of nothing and offered not one
scintilla of news? Maybe this was the new news. Micro stories about
nothing, about everything.

Henke got the email late. The photographer he'd brought in to cover
her. The shot was perfect. Franny's underwear. You could see Franny's underwear. The photograph showed her getting out of a car, an
Uber. The photographer clearly having waited for her to move one
leg to the sidewalk. It didn't help that Franny had been drunk. But
the photographer knew that, too. Because the photographer had a
stable of bartenders he paid tips to. He'd gotten a call from one of
them, heard that Franny Grayson had been in with a few friends,
had downed four glasses of wine in ninety minutes, and had left in
an Uber. The photographer knew where she lived, of course. He had
that from Henke. It was too easy.

So was the headline.

FRANNY GRAYSON. EXPOSED.

He linked the photo with the interview with Lauren. He found a
stock photo of cocaine on a mirror and used it next to the picture of

Franny stumbling out of the Uber, even though the two photos weren't related. True, she hadn't known her father was in the room. But it didn't matter. She'd gotten the story wrong. He could paint her as a liar. And she'd hidden the drug use. All in all this was a good day's work.

Yet a curious thing happened the next morning in the office. Some employees found the photo offensive. Five women and three men signed an email saying they would quit unless the photo was taken down.

He thought hard about the email for almost forty-five seconds. He fired all of them.

Claire watched the footage in Bedford. She didn't watch it the way people in offices watched it. The way young men on a trading floor at investment banks watched it, chuckling as the drunken woman stumbled out of the car, freezing the frame on her legs parting. She didn't watch it the way hipsters at ad agencies and PR firms and design firms did, commenting and laughing. The way they did on university campuses, making a drinking game out of it. She didn't watch it and then comment on YouTube:

Ha ha! Dumb bitch.

Whore's got nice legs.

Rich kid drug addict.

She watched it as a mother who couldn't protect her child. She needed to do something. She picked up the phone to call Dodge. But she dialed Ted.

Ted had seen it, too. His little girl, debased, shown drunk. Her underwear. There for the world to see. Because of him. Because of who he was. It wasn't Franny's fault. His rage built. Beware the man with nothing to lose.

"Ted," Claire said. "Make this stop."

He took the subway, purposefully going one stop past where he wanted to get out so that he could walk back, to see if anyone was following him. He felt like a reporter again. He walked for a time, the clouds bringing on an early dusk. He followed the directions on his phone and found the building. He stood out front and suddenly felt foolish, like an unhinged stalker. One doesn't show up unannounced at a total stranger's home.

He entered the building. The main door gave way to a vestibule with mailboxes and buzzers on one side. It smelled vaguely of cat urine and damp wool, the walls covered with half a dozen coats of peeling paint. Six buzzers, a United Nations of last names. Wizbicki. He pressed the buzzer and winced. No camera. Just a buzzer. He waited. She probably wasn't home. Maybe buzz again. Maybe leave.

Ted had gotten the girl's address from Lou, who pulled strings with human resources.

Through the metal speaker, an accented female voice. "Who is it?"

Every weeknight for twenty years Ted had said the name to eight million Americans. His name. Bigger than life. The most trusted man in America. Now he could barely get it out.

"It's Ted Grayson."

One one-thousand. Two one-thousand. Three one-thousand.

"I don't believe you. You're the paparazzi. I'll call the police. Go away."

It came into his head and was out before he knew it. "You saw my bald spot," he said. "That night. And you used hair spray. Lou ... my producer ... told you to use hair spray."

Silence.

"What do you want?" she asked.

"Just ... to talk. Just for a minute. Please."

Nothing. Ted waited. He thought of pressing the buzzer again but didn't have the courage anymore.

He saw her boots coming down the stairs, through the glass door, arms folded tightly across her chest. She stopped at the landing when she saw him. She had an overcoat on, the kind that looked like it was from a secondhand store. Scarf. Behind her another woman. Her sister. It was the sister who opened the door.

"What do you want?" she said, pure hatred in her voice.

What did he want? He wanted to apologize. Simple. That was a lie, though. I want to be forgiven, he thought. He realized the absurdity of it. The foolishness of standing here, wanting something from her.

"I want to say sorry."

They walked a block or two and then stopped, not saying much, until they found a coffee truck near a construction site. Ted bought them two coffees.

"I just wanted to say how sorry I am. I shouldn't have screamed. Should never have called you what I did. I don't have an excuse. I just ... I was having a bad day, and ..."

What else to tell her? About Franny? Claire? His birthday? His bald spot?

She stared at the sidewalk. "I'm sorry about what happened to you."

"Don't be. I probably deserved it." He smiled.

He handed her an envelope. She worried for a moment that there was money in it.

"What is this?" she asked.

"It's the names and numbers of some people at networks who'll take your call. They can help you get work."

She looked at the envelope, then to Ted.

"They call me, you know."

"Who?" Ted asked.

"The networks. The . . . the cable news and the websites. They ask me to be on TV and talk about you."

"Oh?"

She nodded. She looked so young.

"But . . . you haven't," Ted said.

"No."

"Why not?"

"Because it's not really anyone's business but mine and yours."

She held up the envelope. "Thank you."

"*Przepraszam*," Ted said, and watched her smile.

He'd looked it up online. He'd found a video on YouTube that showed the proper pronunciation.

"Is that . . . *przepraszam*. I hope that's right."

It was right. It was pretty good, in fact. Natalia hadn't been prepared for this and something about the past few weeks, the fatigue, the hope that maybe it could all be over, made her laugh.

"What?" Ted said, embarrassed. "Was it that bad?"

"No," she said. "It was good."

Ted smiled.

"Are you close with your father?"

She seemed surprised. "Yes, of course. Why?"

"Call him. I bet he worries about you."

The tip came in to *scheisse* at 4:43. And with it a dozen iPhone photos and a twenty-four-second video of Ted and Natalia standing on a sidewalk. It showed her looking sad. Or at least not happy. It showed Ted talking and then handing her an envelope. It was far enough away that you couldn't hear what was being said. Not a word. It just looked like Ted was lecturing her. And bribing her. They posted it immediately.

He met Polly for lunch at a coffee shop on the East Side. It was still cold for late April, a raw day. A tuna sandwich sat in front of him. Lightly toasted white bread, tuna, iceberg lettuce, a dill spear, a small pile of ruffled potato chips. What a perfect plate. How many plates like this had sat before him? The meal of children after school. The meal of the elderly. So simple, nutritious, honest. Could a sandwich be honest? In his current state, Ted felt it could. He also felt like he might cry. And that thought made him laugh, which he did now.

"Ted, you're freaking me out a little here," Polly said. "You know that sandwich or something?"

He stared at Polly, smiling at her. Then did something he had never done before. He leaned forward and kissed her on the forehead.

"Ted, I'm eating here," she said, a lump of egg salad at the corner of her mouth.

He told her about the plan.

He'd come across a story online about passage, for very little money, on container ships. The accommodations were spartan and the food wasn't particularly good but it was quiet at sea. He would leave New York for Mumbai. He figured he'd make his way around India, the Bay of Bengal, Myanmar, Thailand, Cambodia, Vietnam. It didn't really matter where to him. He would travel by bus, perhaps make his way to Bhutan and their Gross National Happiness.

"So?" Ted asked her. "What do you think?"

"What do I think? I think it sounds disgusting. I think there will be bugs. I think you've lost your freaking mind. Do you want pie? I'm going to have some pie."

They had pie. Ted listened to Polly talk about her house in the Berkshires. Her garden. How maybe it was time to sell the apartment and go there. She had friends in the area. They had dinner parties.

"New York is over," she said. "Our New York. It's gone."

They were standing on Madison in the Seventies.

Polly said, "You going to be able to navigate in a foreign city without producers and handlers and no corporate credit card?"

"It's unlikely. So this could be the last time you see me alive."

Ted grinned. Polly started to smile but her expression changed quickly.

She had always stood by him, always a friend, this squat, badly coiffed woman who lived alone with a cat.

She reached up and held his face with both hands. "You're a good boy. Be happy."

She blinked back tears. He gave her a squeeze and she held on for a time. They parted and Polly started walking north. Ted watched her.

He shouted, "Call me if the *Today* show is looking for a woman-hating anchor."

She half turned, one arm in the air, and shouted back. "You'll be my first call."

He'd been asked by every network and cable station to do an interview. He declined all of them. Just a few days ago, a producer from CNN had emailed saying that *Anderson Cooper 360°* was doing a show on the state of social media. They were bringing in a number of writers and thinkers on the subject, including Henke Tessmer. Would Ted want to appear on a segment of the program? He had not responded.

He emailed her now. He said that both he and his daughter would be happy to appear. He urged the producer to email Frances.

Franny stared at it for a moment. The idea of telling it, admitting to it, of being forgiven. She said she'd be there.

We're live with Ted and Frances Grayson.

W e're live in ninety seconds."

Ted settled into the chair at the desk and the PA began to put the lavalier mic on him but Ted smiled and took it, put it on himself. He could do it with eyes closed. Raise his seat, sit on his jacket, blow down lightly on the mic, turn to the sound engineer seated off to the set's side, a guy who can't help smiling and giving Ted a thumbs-up.

It's a cocaine rush, the moments before live TV. You can't know it unless you've done it, unless you've sat in that chair, ready to stare down that big lens and all it represents, all that's out there.

A PA walked Franny to set—they'd kept them in separate green rooms—and Ted could tell she wasn't ready for this. She had on a demure dress, navy blue, just below her knee. The PA mic'd her and sat her on the other side of Cooper, who walked to set and took his seat.

"Thirty seconds. Clear the set, please."

Cooper sat between them and turned to Ted, extended his hand.

"Ted."

A hair and makeup woman appeared and did a light touch-up on

Cooper, though God knows he didn't need it. She turned to Ted and lightly touched his hair, smoothing it over with her hands. The woman looked at Ted and it unnerved him.

"Thank you," he said.

Anderson Cooper turned to Franny, reached over, and touched her hand. "It's going to be okay. There are no surprises here. I don't do gotcha. We'll talk. Just . . . talk to me."

Franny nodded.

Cooper looked at notes, though Ted sensed he was composing himself. Anchor's prayer. Calm the breathing. Clear the throat. Energy up.

In five, Anderson . . . four . . . three . . .

"This is *360*, I'm Anderson Cooper. We open tonight with the state of the media, *social* media. Of truth, lies, and videotape. We'll talk with some of the leading figures in media today, including the head of Google's ethics commission, Sloan Kent; Facebook's social policy leader, Ann-Marie Olivery; and Henke Tessmer, CEO of the website *scheisse*. But first up, Frances Grayson, formerly a senior correspondent for sensationalist website scheisse.com. And her father, Ted Grayson, the longtime anchor and managing editor of the evening news, recently resigned. We'll take comments and tweets right after this."

Anderson was talking, giving the context of the story, the video showing Ted calling Natalia a "whore." But Ted's remarkable memory was playing back the little book. The feeling was odd. He no longer heard Anderson Cooper's voice. He saw his mouth move but heard nothing but his own breathing. He turned to Franny and heard his own voice. Heard himself reading the story. *Harold and the Purple Crayon.*

"So Frances," Cooper began, "I said no surprises, but I have to ask, did you lie?"

Except time stops and Franny is four and they lie on the floor of the studio. It's a bed. Ted and Claire's bed. The big bed, Franny called it. That's where she liked to go to sleep. *Frog and Toad* and *The Cat in the Hat* and *Are You My Mother* and *The Polar Express* and *If You Give a Mouse a Cookie.* And *Harold and the Purple Crayon.* Always the last one. It was, for a long time, the book she needed when she was calm and still and ready. The one when she stopped talking, pulled the blankets up, folded her arms behind her head, like an old man on a chaise lounge. That's when you knew sleep was coming. Her eyelids got heavy and Ted slowed his voice, his wonderful voice, her favorite voice, until it wasn't, deep and strong and soothing, a good reader, knew the cadence, the pauses, the word to hit. Quieter now. Eyes almost closed.

"You're Harold, Dad."

Ted's middle name. Franny loved that. Imagining Ted as a small boy. "We would be best friends," Franny would say. "I would take care of you."

Ted looked at Franny and then looked—if you go back you can see it on the tape online, it's there—Ted looked off camera. He looked off camera and stared at a space. The producer wondered what he was looking at and even Anderson looked for a moment, listening to Franny answer.

Couldn't they see what Ted was seeing? he wondered. It was so clear. Ted and Franny, lying in the bed, Ted still in his suit, tie loosened, sleeves rolled up, his big clean-smelling head, his bay rum aftershave, the lingering scent of it after a long day, still there. A scent Franny would forever find comfort in, a deep sense memory. Her father's smell. Her father's voice. She was safe.

What if the entire universe is in your children? What if every answer you've ever been looking for is in your children?

Ted looked at Franny. He'd not seen her, really seen her, in so long. He'd seen his own failing, his own fear, his own anger, his own wish for what he'd wanted her to be. He hadn't stopped to see her, this separate being. But he did now. And he saw the world. The universe. The history of time and space and whatever might or might not be out there. She was it. He had been born to be her father. God bless Walt and his brief, brief life. But she was here now and he was here now and someday he would be dead and she would have children of her own and they might ask, *What was your father like?*

What would she say?

"Did you lie?" Anderson Cooper asked Frances Ford Grayson.

Franny's hands were shaking but she had to say it. She had to tell the truth. But she never got the chance.

It's so easy, Ted thought. It was a gift. He was being given a gift.

"No, she didn't," Ted said, voice strong. "I did."

Ted's eyes were locked on Anderson's. He knew how to do this. He knew how to tell the truth. And it was the truth. The emotional truth. The larger truth. He was there but in body only.

He could feel Franny staring at him. Felt the crew staring at him. But he was used to this. He was comfortable in this. A life being watched. People waiting for him to speak.

"I'm sorry, Ted. What are you saying?" It was Cooper.

"What she wrote was true. I'm not sure this young woman . . . the woman who tweeted . . . who's been saying she saw me there when my daughter was . . . ill . . ."

Cooper steps in. "I believe what this woman . . . Lauren Loeb is her name . . . what she claimed is that Frances overdosed and that you were there."

Ted nodded, the story coming to him so naturally, as if it happened.

"My daughter was ill at the time. There was a winter storm and she was in the infirmary. My wife called me in London, while I was waiting for a flight to Kosovo. I chose that over . . . over my daughter, when she needed me. I'm not proud of it. My wife . . . Claire . . . is . . . an . . . exceptionally kind woman . . . a wonderful mother. I'm sure she told Franny I was on the way. What child wouldn't want to hear that?"

"Why would Ms. Loeb lie?"

"I can't answer that. I do know people like attention, like to try to take people down. I think what my daughter did in that piece took courage. I'm not proud of the kind of father I was. I'm not proud of the kind of husband I was. And it is exceptionally difficult to have that revealed to the world. It's a level of shame that is . . . that has left me ruined professionally and personally. I say that not for pity. But I would ask for privacy. I'm no longer a public person. Nor is my daughter."

Cooper. "Why didn't you come forward sooner?"

"The honest answer? Because I was weak. I was embarrassed. Because I wanted my job back. You know what it's like to live in the bubble. The money, the entrée into worlds others don't get to see. You could pick up the phone now and get an interview with most any major politician, CEO, movie star, athlete in the world. Couldn't you?"

"Well, I'm not sure . . ."

"Of course you could. Because you have that microphone. Because people respect you. Because you are good at what you do. Because you are trustworthy. I was, too. And I didn't want that to go away."

There is a moment, maybe two, when Cooper seems touched by the whole thing, a bit thrown from his game. He pauses. He looks like he wants to push, ask more. But instead he says, "What have the last few weeks been like for you?"

"I wouldn't recommend it," Ted said, looking at Franny, who forced a grin.

"Ted Grayson. Frances Ford. Thank you for being here tonight. Perhaps we do owe you privacy. Our conversation continues with the CEO of *scheisse* media, Henke Tessmer, when we come back. This is *360*."

This was where Claire dropped her fork.

She was at Dodge's, along with another couple, preparing dinner, and the TV was on. She was holding a serving fork and she watched her soon-to-be-ex-husband and her daughter on the television in Dodge's kitchen and the emptiness that she felt was frightening. The feeling of standing at the check-in counter to fly home to see a sick child only to find the flight has been canceled. A fear and panic. She knew only that she had to get to them. She dropped the fork when Ted spoke, when he told the story. It wasn't true. But she believed it. She wanted to believe it. She picked up the fork and looked at Dodge. "I have to be with my family."

She walked out of the kitchen, grabbed her coat by the door, and left.

■   ■   ■

Henke walked to the set, accompanied by a PA. Ted saw him as he passed through the corridor. And maybe he would have kept going. Maybe he would have simply walked on. But Franny froze, just for a second. She stopped walking. An abrupt thing. A thing she used to do when she was scared. Ted looked over and saw it on her face. She looked at Henke and then looked away. Things seemed to move slowly for Ted. He heard his heart beat in his eardrums, this loud beating, as he took in Franny's face, her fear, the change, and the bravery as she starting walking again, as she stared directly at Henke. This tough kid. Tough woman. Who she'd become, through no help from him. But then he turned to see Henke smiling. Not a friendly smile. Taunting.

Why are we here? What's the point? After we are stripped bare, naked before the world, after everything is taken away, all we have is our children. And we have two basic, fundamental jobs as parents. To love them. And to protect them.

Ted gently pushed Franny back, making space. And Henke stopped. He would think about this moment for a long time after, about stopping and saying what he said. If he had just kept his mouth shut. But he didn't. He leaned forward and whispered to Ted. "She didn't want to run it. The story about you. She asked me not to. I did it, anyway. I ordered the photo of her getting out of the cab, too."

He smiled, his bulbous, Teutonic head jutting forward. No self-respecting kid from the streets of Woonsocket would ever be dumb enough to do that. There was the briefest hesitation from Ted. A small shock, really, that a person could be this way. Henke seemed to be the embodiment of everything ugly about social media. Shocking and angry and ugly and mean. I'm sorry for all of us, Tamara had said.

By the same token, fuck him.

The shock faded fast, replaced in full force by anger, by the moment, by his own absence and apathy as a parent, by his own sins as a father and husband. Ted found a quickness and strength he'd not known in years. A muscle memory from his tougher days, in the gym, punching a big bag. He reared back now and hit Henke as hard as he could in the face, smashing his nose. Henke's head snapping back, the sound a comical Hollywood Foley, a fist hitting a head of iceberg lettuce. Except it wasn't lettuce. It was a smug, spoiled German wearing surfer clothes. Henke's legs buckled, a Wile E. Coyote moment, except this was an actual man and he seemed to hang for a moment before dropping to the floor like a string of bratwurst dropped from a great height. He moaned loudly. Remarkably, no one had an iPhone trained on the incident and it went unrecorded. The punch, that is. The evidence of the felony. The moments after, however, were, indeed, recorded.

His hand went to his bloodied nose, his eyes wide in disbelief, the searing pain of it, displaced cartilage, the electric pain of the impact itself. All of it captured as his guttural German spilled forth. He tried to stand, unsuccessfully at first, though eventually he made his way up.

Franny's hands covered her mouth but Ted could see that she was smiling. She stood behind him, leaning her head out. She reached one hand out to hold on to his back, to his sports coat. And in that gesture, he felt whole. He could have died then and there.

"I'll *kill* you," Henke screamed. "I'll fucking kill you. You're nothing! Your fucking daughter is nothing! Do you know who I am?! I'm going to *ruin* you!"

A small crowd had formed, cell phones trained on the event, humans turned to space aliens watching this bizarre scene unfold.

"Ruin me?" Ted asked, oddly calm. "I couldn't get a job cleaning toilets. I have nothing. But you . . . you *are* nothing."

"Fuck you!" Henke screamed, drawing even more of a crowd, turning even redder, more iPhones. There was already a tweet. "Henke Tessmer losing his shit on Ted Grayson."

"What is it you do? What's the point of it? To embarrass people? Harass them? Spread gossip and slander? Ugliness? You're a bottom feeder. You're not a journalist. How dare you call yourself a journalist. We tell stories. We tell the truth. You ran that story when you knew my daughter didn't want to. You disgust me."

Henke wasn't able to form words now. His rage was too complete. He was shaking. He wanted to strike Ted but he was also afraid of him.

"One more thing," Ted said. "If you ever come near my daughter again, I'll kick your teeth down your throat."

Here Ted took a step toward Henke and Henke stepped back, his hands going up to his face. It was an image that would be played millions of times on YouTube over the coming weeks, an image that would become a meme for fear and overreaction, one shown for ungracious athletes, pouting starlets who didn't win an Oscar, grumpy politicians. It would be watched the world over and become a symbol for standing up for what's right. Ted Grayson's *High Noon* moment, they called it.

.   .   .

The Uber driver had no idea who they were. But he got a sense they were someone when he pulled up to the gate and saw the photographers waiting. Franny had a gate fob in her bag and Ted fished it out and told the driver he'd give him two hundred dollars if he could make it through the gate at sixty miles per hour, which he came close to, exhibiting remarkable driving acumen. Ted pulled Franny close to him but did nothing to hide his own face. In fact, he stared out the window, as if daring someone to try to get to his daughter.

Claire was waiting for them and when Franny saw her tears rolled down her cheeks. She sat Franny down on a sofa off the kitchen, the family room. Bismarck looked at the three of them. Ted felt the dog was confused.

Claire put the kettle on, found an old fleece, and draped it over Franny. It was only then she really looked at Ted. She started to speak but stopped. She reached out an arm and touched his shoulder. Something about the gesture. She leaned into him and held him, for just a few seconds.

Ted realized he'd have to call a cab, take the train back. He didn't mind. He'd walk back if he had to.

Franny stood up.

"Dad."

Ted looked at her.

"Why . . . I mean . . ."

She was a little girl. Her face looked so much like little Franny. Her head to one side, her hand rubbing her chin. Ted was suddenly very tired, the force of it all. Of lost time. Of what she was to him.

Dear God, forgive me, he thought. How little she understood about anything real or valuable or lasting. About being a parent.

He looked at Claire, who was staring at him.

"Someday you'll understand," Ted said.

And here Claire turned her back to them, faced the sink, held on to the counter, her head down.

"I should go," Ted said quietly.

Franny started to protest but Claire beat her to it.

"I thought I might roast a chicken," she said to the window.

Dusk turned to dark and it started to rain, a cold rain. The cameras dispersed, as there were almost no lights on in the front of the house, though one of them noticed wood smoke coming from the chimney at the back. And what was there to see here, anyway? Just three tired, wounded people sitting by a fire, watching an old movie. How was that interesting? There was no story here. Nothing worthy of news. Just their life.

TMZ ran a photo of Ted standing above Henke, who lay on the beige carpeted lobby of CNN, face contorted in pain and fear, Ted looking like Ali over Liston. Some writer or editor put the headline, DON'T MESS WITH MY DAUGHTER. At no point during the confrontation did Ted say these words. But the line was repeated dozens and dozens of times on network news, cable news, talk shows.

And a strange thing happened. Others picked it up. Not just the bottom feeders. *The Guardian* in London ran a piece. The *Times* ran a piece about the reaction, which was swift and sustained, the comments almost uniformly supportive of Ted. Calls came in from the *Today* show and *Good Morning America.* He didn't return them, though. He had no interest in being on TV anymore.

In the weeks that followed, the news programs and websites talked of social media, of the conscience of the nation, about the need for rules and reform, of accountability, of veracity. It faded, of course. There were new scandals. There were mistakes made, foolish things uttered. There were people to shame. To ruin.

They would go for walks in the afternoon, Ted and Franny, along the trails of the Pound Ridge reservation. At first, they said little, as if finding their way again. But after a time they found their own rhythm. She talked of graduate school, maybe documentary filmmaking. But often they just walked and listened to each other's silence in the cool spring days.

"Venezuela," he said on one of these walks through the woods.

It took so much to do it because he feared the response. For Chrissakes, Ted, he thought. Try.

She was confused at first, thinking perhaps that he was suggesting she move to South America and not understanding, until she looked at him, saw him looking back, saw him swallow with difficulty, saw that his eyes appeared watery, right before he turned his head and looked forward.

"Venezuela," he said again.

And she recognized that voice, that tone, from a long time ago. A lifetime happened in that moment. A chance for both of them.

"Caracas," she replied. She was looking straight ahead now, a little grin on her face.

Something lifted in him at the sound of the word. It was a key. It unlocked everything.

"Benin," he said, his throat tightening, a smile on his face.

It took her a minute but it was there, a long-hidden trove.

She smiled. "Porto-Novo," she said.

He turned and looked at her. What a thing. To be forgiven. To watch yourself be given life.

"Burkina Faso," he said.

The tweets continued.

That's a good father.

I would have done the same thing.

A real man.

God bless him.

He's so handsome.

#BringBackTedGrayson.

The network noticed. A movement grew. An angry, self-righteous mob. They weren't marching or voting or calling their congressmen. They weren't writing editorials or taking up arms. They were doing something far more powerful. They were commenting. They were clicking. They were posting.

Ted was trending.

Acknowledgments

You write a book only partially alone. You rely on a lot of people for help.

To my editor and dear friend, Sally Kim, for believing in me and making this book better. I feel exceptionally fortunate to have an editor who supports her writers like a mother bear. Assuming that a bear could use a pen.

Thanks to many other wonderful people at G. P. Putnam's Sons. Danielle Dieterich, Gabriella Mongelli, Alexis Welby, Ashley Hewlett, Ashley McClay, Brennin Cummings, Jordan Aaronson, and Bonnie Rice. There are also men who work at Putnam. Ivan Held is one of them and I thank him (not for being a man, but for being a kind, supportive man).

Also at Putnam, Joel Breuklander. I missed several crucial production deadlines and Joel was kind enough not to use his extensive collection of samurai swords on me. I would like to thank him and the entire production team for the most valuable thing a writer needs besides wine. Time.

To Andy Bird, my boss and mate at my day job. Andy routinely walked by my work desk and saw me working on my novel instead of, say, the things he actually pays to work on. "Ya awright?" he said with a smile. At least I think that's what he said. He actually may have fired me. But he's from Newcastle and thus has a Geordie accent so it can be hard to tell. A kinder, more creative soul I have never met.

Several trusted readers gave guidance and support, including my brother, Charlie, and my good friends Debbie Kasher, Rick Knief, and Bill Landay.

A special thanks to my mother-in-law and friend, Linda Funke, for reading and guiding and catching my many mistakes. Thank you, Ninna.

My children, Lulu and Hewitt, for their patience.

My wife, Lissa. Reader, editor, tireless listener. Thank you.